# SURVIVING WORMWOOD
## END TIMES PROPHECY SERIES
### BOOK 3

## TOBY NEIGHBORS

**Surviving Wormwood: End Time Prophecy Series Book 3**

Copyright © 2023 by Toby Neighbors

ISBN: 978-1-952260-57-5 ebook

978-1-952260-60-5 print

Mythic Adventure Publishing, LLC

Idaho, USA

# CHAPTER 1

WELCOME back to the ongoing events in what the world is calling the Great Reset, but of course, if you're reading my book then you know the truth. The world isn't being reset, and the human race isn't evolving. God is in the middle of giving people one last chance to accept his free gift of salvation by believing in his son, Jesus Christ. And while things were dark and deadly this past year, they were about to get even crazier.

I'm still not sure how I got here. Don't get me wrong, I'm insanely grateful, but before the Vanishing, I was just a regular guy trying to make my way through life without attracting too much attention. There's no need to go into all that, but if you haven't read my other books, I'll catch you up.

During the last few months of my service in the United States Air Force, I saw the body of a giant. If that sentence didn't scare you off, then there's hope you'll make it as we move forward, and things get pretty supernatural. Back to my story, after getting discharged from the Air Force I went to work for a guy named Lorenzo Maltza. He became my mentor and friend. And speaking of the supernatural, Lorenzo was an expert. From UFOs to ancient legends, Lorenzo knew it all, and saw past the conspiracy theories to the truth - namely that we are in the middle of a divine war, but we'll get more into that as the book progresses.

Lorenzo taught me so much, but like a lot of people who hear the truth, I was oblivious to my own need. I thought of myself as a good person, but little did I know I was dead because of my sins. It seemed to me that religion was just as corrupt as politics, and despite Lorenzo's excellent teaching, I didn't connect my need with God's free gift of life until millions of people suddenly just vanished. Of course, after that, I knew instantly what had happened. The alien ships that conveniently appeared over the capitals of the world didn't fool me. You may still be on the fence when it comes to the Visitors and their actual intentions, but trust me, they are not what they seem.

Shortly after the Vanishings, I took as much of Lorenzo's videos, from interviews to conference appearances, and began to share them online. I was moving from place to place to avoid the online watchdogs and trolls who didn't like Lorenzo's teaching of the supernatural. After the historic peace accords, which were written about in the Bible nearly three thousand years ago, I found myself in the mountains along the border of Idaho and Montana. There I met the woman who would become my wife. Her name is Mira Jones, but everyone calls her Cat. Through a series of unfortunate events, we left the Northwest and headed south not long after the Chinese-American war settled into a stalemate. It was a difficult trip, but we made it down to Texas and found ourselves in a government-sponsored aide camp where I was recalled to active duty.

I can't say for certain, but I've heard stories about some of the other camps. None of them are happy tales, and ours certainly didn't end well. When the local gangs from Abilene decided to work together, the camp was their first target. My immediate superior, Lester Barski, who everyone calls LB, and a fellow service member, Allie Mendolson, hung with us, and while the rest of the survivors pushed east in hopes of getting help from the government, the four of us, went our own way. Oh, did I forget to mention that people like me have become persona non grata in a country that was once known around the world for the freedom of religion? That's right, I was about five seconds from getting my head chopped off for my faith in front of the entire camp when the bad guys launched their assault. LB got wounded, but we stuck together, and since then he and Allie have both become believers. Unfortunately, Cat's still on the fence, but I hope and pray she'll accept the greatest gift ever, very soon.

One of the benefits of being a believer during the tribulation is knowing where to find out what's really going on. It certainly isn't the internet news sites. The Bible, however, tells us everything that's going to happen in the world during these days. I do try to catch some of the online Bible teachers, but with the recent mandate to kill on-sight anyone who denies the new world religion, they can be hard to find. Pax Davino is just an amalgamation of ancient religious beliefs. Anyone who claims that Jesus is the only way to know God is now public enemy number one, which makes it difficult for people to share the truth online or with anyone they don't completely trust. These are dangerous days, but God has been faithful to me. I don't deserve it, and yet here I am, still typing away, sharing my story with anyone and everyone who takes the time to read it.

So now that we're all caught up, let me tell you about the farmhouse we found, and how it saved our lives, literally.

# CHAPTER 2

IT TOOK us three days of walking to find the old house. From the outside, it looked exactly like that, an old, abandoned house. The paint was long faded, the porch sagged, the windows were covered with grime, and a few were even broken. The roof was metal but dented and dinged from who knows how many North Texas hailstorms.

We reached the property purely by chance, or maybe as the Holy Spirit was leading us. All we really hoped for was to find some shelter that would be safe until the sixth seal judgment was released onto the world. That's right, God's judgments are being played out on a global scale. But don't get me wrong, the judgment of God isn't like a court officiant handing down a sentence. It is our loving Father stepping aside and letting his dearly loved children fail on their own and experience the pain of that failure so that they will turn their eyes back to him.

The first seal judgment was the peace accords in the near

east, brokered by Paul Eon. The Man of Peace, as he is called by many people, is actually what the Bible calls the Man of Lawlessness, or the Little Horn. He came from obscurity and rocketed to worldwide fame by doing what no one had ever been able to do, bring peace to the Near East, but it is only a temporary peace. He will break that peace agreement himself, but that won't happen for another two years.

The second seal judgment was the rider on the red horse, or War. We've witnessed territorial conflicts and full-scale wars between multi-nation alliances. I don't have to tell you how bad it is. Here in the former United States of America, we have been pummeled in a nuclear war with China. The east and west coasts of North America are radioactive waste-lands, and the resulting global cooling caused by the dust and ash has killed millions of people.

The third seal judgment was worldwide famine. If you're reading this then you found a way to survive, but many didn't. The entire world is starving, and people will do anything for a scrap of food, including kill. Believe me, I've seen it.

The fourth horseman was a pale horse, and death rides with him. Cat worked in the infirmary at Camp Abilene. She saw just how bad the new Death Flu is. No hope for those who contract it, and millions have died. Some days it felt like the world was going to be completely wiped out, but some-how, we managed to avoid it so far.

The sixth seal judgment is the persecution of Christians. We've all seen the video feeds. There's more being posted every day. Beheading seems to be the most official means of execution for those found to be Jesus followers. I've seen chop-ping blocks, guillotines, and people cut down in the streets with machetes. One video even showed the executioner using a double-barrel shotgun on the back of the neck. It was horribly gruesome, and how a religion that calls itself Pax Davino can sanction outright murder is completely beyond my ability to understand. People are dying all around us, and instead of helping, the new global government is sanctioning more death.

So, the farmhouse wasn't merely shelter for us, it was a place to hide. I have Lorenzo's Bible in my pack. I lost the laptop with all his lectures and interviews, but just that one item is enough to get my head lopped off. Of course, I would never deny my faith. I'm all in, one hundred percent. The Bible says that all we need to do is believe that Jesus is the Son of God. That's all it takes, just believe in him. And I do. I won't ever back away from that. Not after all he's brought me through.

But the sixth seal judgment is coming. The Bible describes it as a worldwide earthquake, the likes of which the world has never seen before. But we'll get to that in time. First up, let me tell you what we found at the farmhouse.

The house itself was nothing special. I can't say how old it was, but pretty old. Allie guessed it was from the nineteen twenties. It had two bedrooms upstairs and a single bathroom. It had been ransacked early on, by the looks of things. The rain had stained the walls around the broken windows. The door was barely holding onto just one hinge. There was dirt and leaves that had blown in. The kitchen was wrecked, too. Some of the cabinet doors were ripped off. There was no food left, but to our surprise, there was power and water. Between the house and the barn was a windmill. It was constantly turning from the prairie winds, powering a bank of batteries that powered the lights and more importantly, the well pump.

We didn't need lights. We were hiding out after all, but we were happy to have showers and a working toilet. The real treasure however was hidden in plain sight. Among the house's many design elements was a built-in bookcase. It was filled with pictures in frames, souvenirs, and decorative plants. But right in the middle, on a little stand, was a book by Dr. David Jeremiah called *After the Rapture: An End Times Guide to Survival.*

You can imagine my shock. Whoever had lived in that old farmhouse knew what was coming and guessed that people like us would find the house. They left that little book on display. The looters had missed it completely. But I found it, and my hand shook as I picked it up.

"Find something?" LB asked from across the room.

"Yeah," I managed to say.

"Too bad it isn't food," Allie said. "I'm down to about four rations, and they're all vegetable soup. I hate that stuff."

"All least we can sleep on real beds again," Cat said.

"I thought you were a survivalist or something," LB pointed out.

"A primitive skills subsistence hunter," Cat corrected him.

"But you lived out in the wilderness, right? How come you like having a bed so much?"

"I just do," Cat said, giving me a wink.

I probably turned red, but in the dim light filtering in through the dirty, broken windows, no one noticed. My trembling hands thumbed through the pages of the book I had found. A slip of paper fluttered out.

"What's that?" Cat asked.

"I don't know," I told her as I bent down and picked up the paper.

It was lined, and the writing on it was a little hard to read. I could tell an older person had written it. The words were in cursive and said, "We have been praying for you." The sentiment was followed by a series of numbers: 9078123645.

"What's it say?" Cat asked.

"We've been praying for you," I read. "Nine, oh, seven, eight, one, two, three, six, four, five."

"What do the numbers mean?" LB asked.

"I have no idea," I said.

"Probably a lottery number," he replied with a chuckle. "Won't do us any good now."

He couldn't have been more wrong.

# CHAPTER 3

I PUT the note back in the book but held onto them as we explored the house. The discovery of the water in the bathroom was such a surprise that I honestly forgot about it. After getting cleaned up, we used a hot plate to heat some water. The old stove in the kitchen was gas, which had been shut down. But as I said, the house still had electricity. We ate rehydrated vegetable soup, which was both flavorless and disgusting at the same time. But with warm food in our stomachs and actual beds to lay down on, we all got some much-needed rest.

It wasn't until the next day that we went out to explore the barn. Like the house, it looked ancient. The interior was dark and musty. There were large blocks of hay, but it was mildewed. There was an old tractor and some tools. I had seen nothing of real value and was about to leave when I spotted a red light inside a little alcove where a couple of old saddles and some tack were kept. I hadn't seen any horses. They had probably escaped the farm and ran south, if the elderly couple in the photographs inside the farmhouse had even kept horses as they got older. Again, I didn't think there was anything I needed inside the tack room until I saw the red light.

"LB," I called to my former boss. "Come take a look at this."

"What you got?" LB asked in his jovial, baritone voice.

"I can't say for sure," I replied stepping into the tack room. It was dark inside, but I felt a pull string brush the side of my face as I approached the small, red light. I reached up and pulled the string. A very dim bulb came on. It lit the room in a dull light. There were two saddles, bridles, bits, lead ropes, and lassos on the walls. But to my surprise, there was also a metal door. The red light was from a digital keypad. The strong door seemed oddly out of place.

"What the hell?" LB said as he stepped into the tack room. "This place is full of surprises."

"Could be storm shelter," I said.

"With a lock like that?" LB asked. "Nah, it's more than a shelter, bro. But I don't think we're going to find out. Ain't no way to jimmy that door."

Cat and Allie were surprised by the door too. Cat even punched in a few numbers on the keypad. The lock flashed red and didn't open.

"What could they have down there?" Allie asked.

"Could be anything," I told her. "Or nothing at all."

"They were smart to put it out here, though," LB said. "The looters didn't find it. And if they did, they couldn't get in."

By that point, I was starting to think that maybe, just

maybe, the book for those of us left behind, *After the Rapture*, held a clue.

"Hold on," I said. "I think maybe they left us the combination."

I sprinted back to the farmhouse, where I grabbed the book and pulled out the slip of paper. It had to be the combination, I thought. What else could the numbers be for? I started back out the back door of the old farmhouse but stopped cold. Between me and the barn was what I took for a big dog. It stared at me with yellow, almost soulful eyes.

"Hey there, boy," I said, holding out my hand.

The dog flew into a rage. It barked as it charged toward me. Not a playful yap, but a furious, growling barrage of ravenous barks that clearly indicated the dog wanted to rip my head off. I just managed to get back inside the old house, when the dog slammed into the screen door and nearly ripped it from the hinges. I closed the wooden door and looked back through the window. White foam was flying from the dog's mouth, and it continued growling and barking at me, its claws digging into the soft wood of the door.

Looking up, I saw Cat, LB, and Allie appear at the door of the barn. We were all armed. It was the one benefit we had taken from Camp Abilene. LB and Allie both had M-16s, military surplus rifles. Cat and I had pistols. I hadn't even thought about shooting the dog. I could see an old collar around the K-9's neck, nearly hidden in the matted fur. The dog had been someone's pet, but it was wild and like most animals, had become a vicious predator.

LB motioned for me to move out of the way, as Allie raised her rifle and took aim. My stomach lurched. Don't get me wrong, I'm not a dog person. I never had a pet growing up. My foster parents didn't like animals. But I hated to think of killing the innocent animal. It was just doing what its instincts told it to do.

I moved back into the old kitchen, angling away from the door toward a window. As soon as LB saw that I was out of the way, Allie made the shot. Her rifle made a pop sound. It's nothing like the movies. There was no echoing report, just a loud pop, followed by silence. The dog was no longer trying to get inside.

My friends met me just outside the back door. The dog was big, some sort of Labradoodle maybe. White foam bubbled from its mouth.

"That was close, brother," LB said. "That mutt's got rabies."

"We should move it," Cat said. "The body will draw more predators. It's too bad we can't eat it."

"Seriously?" I asked.

"People eat dogs," Cat said. "Native American tribes ate dogs. They still do in other cultures."

"She's right," LB said. "I seen 'em when I was overseas."

"I wouldn't eat a dog," Allie said.

"It's better than the dehydrated rations we've been living on," Cat said. "I wouldn't mind doing some hunting, but it's too open out here. The animals see you coming."

"And who knows what is clean anymore," LB said. "We gotta be careful what we eat."

"The other animals won't be so picky," Cat said. "They'll eat this dog and get rabies too. We have to do something with the body."

"I saw shovels in the barn," Allie said.

"And we better keep watch from now on," LB added. "A single bite would pass on the disease. That's a hell of a way to die."

I'll admit I was shaken by the incident. The dog looked so normal at first glance, like a lost pet. But the disease it was dying from turned it into a killing machine that wouldn't have been satisfied until it had ripped my throat out. There were times when the pressure of living in the aftermath of war, disease, and famine when people were just as deadly as the dog had been, that it felt like trying to survive was hopeless.

I've been tempted to hurt myself before, and not because I was depressed, or struggling with mental illness. No, the temptation I felt was the direct connection with demonic forces. It isn't like what you see in the movies. It's more like being the new kid in a foster care facility. I know all about that. After my parents were killed, I was left with no family and sent into the system. Fortunately, the accident got a lot of attention, and I was only in the facility for boys a short time before being adopted, but even a few weeks in a place like that leaves a mark on a person's psyche.

Demonic temptation is very similar. I was bullied, coerced, and threatened in the boy's home. When the adults weren't around, I was just the new kid, exposed to constant verbal abuse. Sometimes there were threats, other times they just made fun of every flaw I had. Nights were the worst. We slept in bunks in a large, open room. The bigger kids whispered through the night, tormenting the smaller, weaker children. The demonic temptation I experienced was similar. A constant barrage of hate, ridicule, and threats, that build with each passing day. The suggestions to hurt myself, or to hurt others were often very intense.

At times, surrounded on every side by hardship and fear, I wanted to just give up. Heaven waited on the other side of death and often seemed like the escape I longed for. I felt that temptation while digging a hole to bury the dead dog in. I could put my pistol to my head and just end it all. The tormenting thoughts were there, just like they had been in the past, but there was also another thought that sustained me. I had a purpose. That was something I never had before. Growing up, I was taught that no one has a purpose, that we're all just an accident. Life on planet Earth was an anomaly, the result of some proteins bumping around in the primordial soup. My goal in life back then was just to get by. I kept my expectations low and focused on getting by day to day. All that changed when I met Lorenzo. He had a purpose and a reason for everything he believed in. Maybe it was ironic, but the guy specialized in the supernatural, and yet he had a deep understanding of things other people said couldn't be explained.

But just knowing him hadn't given me purpose. Even losing him in the Rapture didn't give me purpose. But the moment I believed in Jesus, everything changed for me. There was no dramatic encounter with God. I didn't have a vision, or even hear a voice telling me what to do. It was like the fog that made everything in my life uncertain, suddenly lifted, and I was filled with a burning desire to get the word out about what was really happening on planet Earth. Lorenzo's library of interviews and lectures had been my way of doing that. And I wasn't quite sure how to carry on having lost those resources. The death of the dog somehow made the feelings of helplessness and impending doom all the more real to me.

"You okay?" Cat asked softly, as LB dragged the dog into the hole we had dug at the side of the old barn.

"I guess," I replied. "It's just..."

"Yeah?" She prompted.

"You know," I said.

"Come on, Hank. You have to tell me what's going on in that mind of yours."

"That should do it," LB said. "Poor thing. At least it's out of its misery."

We started shoveling the dirt back over the dead animal. I was thankful for the task just to have a moment to get my thoughts in order. Cat was looking at me, making it clear that she wasn't finished with the conversation.

"Sometimes I feel like we're just prolonging the inevitable," I said. "I know God's at work, and I have to trust him. But it isn't easy for me. Trusting anyone is hard."

"People can let you down," Cat said.

"Yeah, but God ain't people," LB said. "I been reading that old Bible you carry around, Hank. I don't know how I missed it all these years."

"We all did," Hank reminded him.

"Yeah, but damn... the proof is right there. What other book makes predictions and they come true? My auntie took us to church when we stayed with her, but I never heard about any of that stuff in church. No one ever talked about it like it was proof that God is real. It was more like a self-help guide or something."

"At least you went to church," I said. "You know some stuff."

"You never know what's coming around the next bend in the trail," Cat said.

She meant it as a reassuring sentiment, but I felt a pang of guilt. LB and Allie had both listened to the message of God's love and accepted it. Cat, on the other hand, was still skeptical. And her lack of faith was another kind of pressure. I couldn't let anything happen to her until she fully believed that Jesus was the Son of God.

"I know," I replied, forcing myself to sound less stressed than I really felt. "We'll get through it together."

That's not exactly how I felt, but I couldn't push Cat or anyone else to believe. All I could do was hope for one more chance to share the truth with her. It's all any of us can do, and I suppose it's enough. God's in control, not me. So, I put my fears and frustrations aside and followed the others into the barn.

It always seems like God shows up in the darkest of places. And he did that day in a way none of us expected.

# CHAPTER 4

IN THE AIR FORCE, I was a logistics specialist. That means I cataloged stuff. I was an organizational expert and bean counter. But in all my years with the Air Force, I never had any space as organized as the shelter beneath the barn.

We went into the tack room after burying the dog. I pulled out the note and punched in the numbers printed on the small page. The access code was nine digits long. No one was going to guess it. I punched them in, and to everyone's delight the red light turned green, and we heard the locking mechanism open.

"Don't lose that number," LB said, with a shake of his head. "These people weren't playing around."

"What do you think is down there?" Cat asked as we pulled the door open to reveal a set of metal steps leading down.

"It has to be something worth protecting," I said. "Let's find out."

The shelter, as we came to call it, was divided into four spaces. The first was lined with shelves, each one loaded with dried goods, from canisters of flour, jars of yeast, and bags of rice, to stackable buckets of survival food. There were also mason jars full of vegetables of all kinds. Hundreds of jars, each one labeled and neatly arranged on the metal shelves.

"Man, these people were prepared!" LB exclaimed.

"But they didn't need any of it," Allie said. "All the planning and the expense... for nothing."

"It's not for nothing," I said, my stomach growling as I perused the shelves. "It's for us."

"I suppose," Allie said.

"They left us the combination," I pointed out. "They knew we could use this food, and they made sure we could get it."

But it wasn't just dried foods that would stay good on the shelves for years at a time. There was also a large chest freezer. It hummed slightly, and the light on the handle flickered green. LB threw open the lid and we discovered a treasure trove of food that none of us had even dreamed of. Ground beef, steaks, roasts, whole chickens, chicken breasts and thighs, pork shoulders, pork chops, sausages, bacon, and deboned hams. And not just meat either, there were frozen pizzas, chicken wings, ice cream, and burritos. Alongside the purchased frozen goods were stacks of disposable casserole dishes, each one with aluminum foil lids marked with the homemade goodies inside: mac & cheese, enchiladas, lasagna, breakfast casserole, cheesy rice with chicken and broccoli, eggplant parmesan, and even chocolate cake. I won't lie, we all cried at the sight of so much food. It felt to me at that moment like God was giving me a boost. He was saying, "It's okay, Hank. You're doing okay. Don't give up."

The discovery of the food was a relief, but it wasn't the only thing in the shelter. The next section was full of medical supplies. Not just first aid stuff, but practically an entire pharmacy. There was ibuprofen, baby aspirin, allergy pills, cough syrup, and cold medicine. Not just a few bottles either, but dozens of them, all neatly arranged and labeled. There was a cooler too, a mini-fridge-sized unit with a glass door. Inside were some basic antibiotics, and two boxes of insulin. There was alcohol too, a few bottles of whiskey and vodka, along with all the usual first aid supplies, including a pair of adjustable crutches.

"These folks thought of everything," Allie said.

"I can't believe it," Cat said.

"They were people of faith," I pointed out.

"You think God told 'em to collect all this stuff?" LB asked.

"I don't know," I admitted. "But they were believers, and they knew if they didn't need it before the Rapture, that we would need it now."

"Or maybe they were just people who believed in being prepared," Cat said. "There were plenty of doomsday preppers in the world before the Vanishing."

The next section of the shelter proved her wrong. It was a library. Shelves of books, all with wrinkles in their spines to show they had been read. There was a sign on the top shelf that said, "*Start here*" and pointed to the first book. It was a small volume on Bible Prophecy. There were dozens of books on that subject, followed by commentaries and Bible dictionaries. There were also cassette tapes and an old-style boom box with a rack of batteries. They were sermons on the end times, a treasure trove of information. There were other books in the library too. Medical books, volumes on hunting, fishing, and processing animals, repair guides for the off-grid electrical system, full-color books on wild edibles, and even some novels.

In the library section of the shelter, there were several reading chairs and lamps. There was a sofa too, with reading lamps on each side and stacks of neatly folded blankets on the cushions. It was clear that a person could relax in the shelter for days and be very comfortable.

"They thought of everything," LB said, as he led the way to the final section of the shelter.

It was by far the largest. A workspace for all types of jobs. There was a workbench on one side, with all kinds of hand tools hung on a peg board and outlined. On the other side of the room was a sewing station with several sewing machines, one was an antique with a manual pedal that required no electricity. There were bolts of fabric, and bins with needles, thread, buttons, and zippers. Near the workbench there were shelves with all types of materials, from nails to spools of wire. There were racks of batteries, duct tape, flashlights, and jugs of chemical cleaning solutions. But the biggest surprise was hanging from the ceiling. In the middle of the room, a device was mounted that looked like it was from an old submarine.

"What is that?" Cat asked.

"I think I know," Allie said.

She reached up and pulled the strange contraption down. Two handles, one on each side, folded down and there was an eye cup sticking out. Allie flipped down the handles and then looked into the eyepiece.

"Genius," she said.

"What is it?" Cat asked.

"It's a periscope," Allie replied.

"Like on a submarine?" I asked.

"Exactly. It must go straight up to the roof," Allie said. "You can see the farmhouse, the road, all around the property."

We took turns looking through the device. It was amazing how much a person could see from the simple contraption. But that wasn't the biggest treasure in the workshop. On the bench was a layout of the farm. In the fields behind the barn, there were two large sheds used for storing hay. But on the map, one was labeled fuel cache, the other was labeled '69 *Bronco*. Beside the map was a car battery, and a replacement distributor cap still in the packaging from the auto parts store.

"What do you think this is?" I asked Allie, who had been a mechanic in the army before becoming a mom.

"Looks like maybe this shelter isn't the only thing they had hidden out here," she said. "If that Bronco is a vehicle, which these items suggest, we may have found our transportation."

She wasn't wrong. After spending a solid hour in the shelter, and grabbing some food to cook, LB, Allie, and I left Cat in the farmhouse while we set out across the overgrown pastures to find the hay sheds. The fuel cache was the closest. It was a simple, low-roofed, three-sided shed. There were bales of hay in front, but on closer inspection, we found a path between the stacks of hay. Inside the shed were two large fuel barrels on metal stands. Coiled beneath them was a hose, and a simple hand pump. The barrels were made of plastic. It wasn't exactly see-through, but shining a flashlight on them revealed that both were nearly full.

"Wow," Allie said. "There's enough fuel here to last a single vehicle a long time."

"Let's go see if there's a vehicle," LB said.

"Even if there's not," Allie continued. "We could get one and bring it back. Most cars just need fuel."

"I don't know about you, but I don't relish hiking into town to search for a vehicle with a fuel can," I said. "You might as well paint a target on your back."

"Let's hope that isn't necessary," LB said.

The second shed was farther out. It wasn't in sight of the barn, like the first shed. But it was bigger and seemed much older. There were no sides on the second shed, just rotting wooden beams along the sides and back. The top was slanted and covered with rusted metal sheets.

"This thing's been here a long time," I pointed out.

The sides of the shed were lined with hay that had turned black from the mold and mildew. The front, like the other shed, seemed to be a jumble of old bales, but as we got closer, we found it was possible to wind our way through them. Inside the shed was a vehicle with a drop cloth covering it.

"What have we here?" LB said with a chuckle.

They pulled off the cover and found an old Ford Bronco, and when I say old, I mean older than I was, about three times as old as I was. There was no roof on the vehicle and no doors. Just two open bench seats and a small cargo section in the back. Using the flashlights from the shelter, LB and I lit the vehicle up while Allie popped the hood.

"This is amazing," she said. "I'll need to spend some time on it, but I think it's got everything it needs to run."

"Minus one battery and distributor cap?" LB asked.

"Exactly," she said. "I can't be certain, but the wiring, belts, and plugs all look new. It's a small block V8, they're easy to maintain unless it's thrown a rod."

She pulled out the oil dipstick and checked the level. She even rubbed the oil between her fingers and smelled it.

"That's new oil," she said. "Maybe not brand new, but I doubt the engine's been run since the oil was changed. Give me a day to check it all out, but I'd say we have a working vehicle, gentlemen."

"That's fantastic," LB said.

"Can't ask for much more," I added. "Everything we need is right here."

"So, we're staying around?" Allie asked.

"For a while," I replied. "There's no reason not."

"Sounds good to me," LB said. "Let's go eat."

When we got back to the farmhouse, we could smell the food. Frozen chicken wings were heating in the electric wall oven. A pot of rice seasoned with spices was already set out, and another was boiling green beans on the same hot plate we had used to heat water the night before.

"Who's hungry?" Cat asked.

We were all hungry. There were plates in the cabinets. We filled our plates and had a feast. It was one of the best nights since the tribulation had begun. But with six years left until Jesus was prophesied to return, the good times couldn't last. Still, we enjoyed them while we could, and made plans for what we knew was coming next.

# CHAPTER 5

THE NEXT DAY, Allie got the Bronco running.

"It's got a killer suspension system," she explained to us that evening.

We were sitting around a fire pit behind the barn that LB and I had dug earlier that day. After dark, we kindled a fire and cooked some of the steaks from the freezer. It felt good to do something so normal. We sat in old lawn chairs and gazed up at the stars as we talked.

"Whoever restored it did an excellent job," she continued. "Once we got the battery installed and replaced the distributor cap, the engine fired right up."

"That's a small miracle," LB said.

"I didn't notice it yesterday, but it's got new tires too," Allie said. "Big, off-road tires that won't have trouble going just about anywhere."

"Are we planning on going somewhere?" Cat asked.

"Not for a while," I said.

"Can't we just hunker down here," LB asked, "and ride out this tribulation thing?"

"Who knows," I said. "All I can say for certain is what's coming."

"And what's that?" Allie asked.

"An earthquake. A worldwide, never been seen before, devastating quake."

"Which is why you brought us out here in the middle of nowhere," LB said.

"Yeah, I mean, we certainly don't need to be in city or on the coast," I explained. "I honestly can't say any more than what the Bible says about it."

"Which is?" Cat asked.

I had the passage in Revelation six memorized. "When I saw the Lamb open the sixth seal, I looked and saw a great earthquake. The sun turned as dark as sackcloth, and the moon became red as blood. The stars in the sky fell to earth, just like figs shaken loose by a windstorm. Then the sky was rolled up like a scroll, and all mountains and islands were moved from their places."

For a moment we were all silent. I didn't mind. It wasn't a happy prediction, but I knew it was coming, and while I couldn't say just when it would occur, there was no doubt in my mind that it would be soon.

"Damn, Hank, you don't pull any punches, do you?" LB said.

"I'm just passing along the information," I said. "Do with it what you will."

I knew that he and Allie had both taken Bibles from the library in the shelter, but I didn't know what they were studying exactly. None of us were Bible scholars, but there were good books in the shelter to help us understand what we were reading. I had spent a large part of the day reading. I wanted to know how bad things were going to get. Unfortunately, no one could say for certain what causes the earthquake, or what would happen to a little farm in the Texas panhandle.

"I'm not a fan of earthquakes," Cat said.

"At least out here there's not likely to be anything that would fall on us," Allie said.

"My thoughts exactly," I said.

"What if the ground splits open underneath us," LB said.

"We have no guarantee of safety," I told them. "These are dangerous times. The Bible says that if these days weren't shortened, no one would survive."

"So, we just take our chances?" Cat asked.

"We're doing what we can to enhance our odds," I said. "That's why we're here."

"And this is a damn fine place to be," LB said. "Good friends, good food, and about as safe as anywhere I've been since the Vanishing."

"Us too," I admitted. "I'm grateful to be with you all."

"Me too," Allie said. "I won't be whole till I hold my children again, and know they are alright. But for the first time since they vanished, I feel a spark of hope."

Cat remained quiet. She wasn't the talkative type to begin with and didn't really like being in groups. Camp Abilene had been difficult for her but working with the ill had been satisfying at first. After the Death Flu broke out, she had felt like a sanitation worker, dealing with the dead the way a janitor takes out the trash. And even though there were just four people in our group, I got the feeling that she still felt crowded at times. It didn't help that she couldn't get out and walk the farm on her own, even if she agreed with the reasons for it. On top of all that, LB and Allie had accepted what I was convinced of, that we were living in the final seven years of judgment before the return of Jesus. Cat still had doubts.

"You think the shelter will survive this earthquake?" LB asked.

"Maybe... maybe not," I said.

"So maybe we should move some of the dry goods and medical supplies," LB said. "So, they aren't all in one place."

"That's not a bad idea," Allie said.

"We'll need a way to keep them hidden," I pointed out. "Some way to keep them safe if they're outside the shelter."

"Agreed," LB said. "How risky would be to take the Bronco out on a supply run?"

"What for?" Cat asked. "We have everything we need right here."

"Yes, for now," LB said. "But we could use some boxes, or crates of some kind."

"Special operators would hide supplies in strategic locations when going into enemy territory," Allie said. "That way if they ran into trouble, they could fall back and still have access to the vital supplies they needed."

"Now you're talking," LB said.

"You mean we could divide up the food and medicines and hide them so that if we have to run for it, we don't end up leaving with nothing," Cat said.

"Yes, ma'am. That's exactly what I'm saying," LB said.

"We know something bad is coming. We know there are bad actors out there. Sooner or later, we might have to beat feet. In that case, it would sure be nice to know we've got supplies in place that we can get to on the way out of Dodge."

"Makes sense," I agreed.

So that's what we did. The next day, Allie and LB took the Bronco out to see what was around the farm. I had intentionally led us off the beaten path. The road that led to the property was little more than a rutted path through overgrown weeds. The dirt road on the far end of the path was a major step up. That road led to other farms and eventually to a highway. But LB and Allie didn't have to go that far. At one of the other farms, they found a flatbed trailer and bin full of old feed sacks. A few days later, we had all the dry goods and medicine down in the shelter divided into four groups. The mason jars were hidden in the barn and in the farmhouse but were too fragile to go into the feed sacks. Everything else was packed into bundles which were taken and hidden at various locations on the way south.

Cat taught herself to use the sewing machines. She was used to making her own clothing by sewing pieces of tanned animal skin. The sewing machine made things easier. She made each of us go bags which we carried at all times. If calamity were to befall us, we had enough supplies to get by for a few days in our kits, along with what we considered our most prized possessions. I kept Lorenzo's Bible in my go bag, along with a box of ammunition for my pistol, and two of the books I had discovered in the shelter library.

We also divided up the blankets the former owners of the farm had collected. In the workshop, we found a milk crate full of tarps still in their packaging and bundles of paracord which we divided up between our go bags and the caches we hid. It kept us busy, but we still made time to study and keep up with world events. I even made a few videos to help other people, which I planned to upload to the internet, just not at the farm. The last thing I wanted to do was attract attention.

We did have a few close calls while at the farm. The first was a group of travelers, who were mostly men. LB and Allie were away from the farm on a supply run. Cat and I were in the shelter. I made it a habit while studying or working down in the shelter to check the periscope every fifteen minutes. Despite being in the shelter with more creature comforts than we had enjoyed since leaving Lorenzo's home in Spokane, Washington, Cat and I couldn't shake the feeling that danger was close at hand. On one of my regular checks, I spotted the group making their way down the rutted road that led to the farm.

"Cat," I said, trying to keep my voice calm. "We've got company."

"Where?" she asked, immediately drawing her pistol and checking to make sure it was ready to fire.

"Headed toward the house," I said. "Following the road in."

"Should we go up?"

"I don't think so," I told her. "Why don't you lock the shelter door. We'll wait down here and see what they do."

She went up and closed the shelter door. And then we waited. I prayed that LB and Allie wouldn't show up, only to get surprised by the newcomers. There was no doubt that the Bronco alone was worth killing over. And I didn't want my friends to get hurt. Maybe the wanderers were harmless, but I doubted it.

As I watched, they went into the farmhouse. I couldn't see what they were doing, but I could imagine it. They were checking the kitchen for food, which was why we had hidden the canned goods in a closet under the stairs and put a roll of carpet over them. The closet was also filled with cleaning supplies, which we hoped would discourage any looters from searching it too closely.

Cat and I shared one of the bedrooms upstairs. LB and Allie shared the other. I wasn't sure how intimate they were, or if they were just friends, but sharing a bed was better than sleeping on the sofa. We had clothes there and maybe some of the books we were reading. But overall, we keep the bedrooms looking sloppy so as not to draw attention.

The group only spent about ten minutes in the farmhouse. I feared they might come out to inspect the barn next, but instead they left on the same road they had come in on. An hour later when LB and Allie returned, I was glad to hear they had spotted the same group.

"They looked pretty ragged," LB said.

"We hid behind that burnt home a few miles up the road," Allie said. "I don't think they saw us."

It was a reality check. We spent the rest of that day armed and watching for the wanderers to return. That night we ate rehydrated meals that required very little work to prepare. There would be no more campfires, or lavish meals. We ate what we had, mostly from the freezer, and kept watch day and night. Our highest priority was not attracting attention.

A few days later, a troop of Chinese fighters passed

through the farm. Two tanks and well over a hundred men in uniform came through from the east. Fortunately, we were all in the barn that day. The Bronco was hidden in the far hay shed. A pair of scouts were seen first. Cat spotted them going into the farmhouse when she was washing our clothes in a galvanized tub near the barn entrance. I was already down in the shelter, doing some preparations before making a video. LB and Allie were working on a project in the back of the barn.

Cat saw the two scouts and realized instantly the danger. She quietly turned over the wash tub, tossed the wet clothes into a dark corner of the barn, and told the others to get into the shelter.

"Hank," LB said from the top of the stairs.

That one word was enough for me to put down my book and move to the periscope.

The three of them came hurrying into the workshop while I was doing a search.

"I don't see anything," I said.

"There were two men in uniform," Cat said. "They went into the house."

"Could be a couple of deserters," Allie said.

"Ours or them?" LB asked.

"Chinese," Cat said.

"You sure?"

She nodded.

"Good eye, Cat. You did the right thing. There could be more of them."

"There are," I said. "Looks like a full regimen maybe. It's hard to tell at a distance, but I've got at least one tank."

"Oh, hell," LB said.

"What should we do?" Allie said.

"Pray," I replied. "That's all we can do."

The group came through and stopped between the house and the barn. Two tanks and at least three platoons, judging from the way the troops were arranged for marching. They looked absolutely exhausted.

"Long march," LB said.

"A stiff breeze could knock that bunch down," Allie added.

"Not those tanks though," I pointed out.

"Who knows if they've even got any ammo left in those things," Allie continued.

"They wouldn't have the troops carrying jerry cans of fuel if those tanks were out of ammo," I said. "Let's hope they don't search the barn."

The scouts came out of the house and shook their heads. They seemed dejected. The commander was an older man. His hair was grown out and his skin burned from too much time in the sun. Many of the soldiers had bandages and some were limping, but they didn't break formation. It was still early in the day, and the commander gave the order to move out. The soldiers were tired and looked demoralized. They trudged away without even giving the farm a proper search.

"Guess they know everything's been looted round here," LB said. "Ain't even gonna waste their time looking."

"Where do you think they're going?" I asked.

"Headed west," LB said. "Maybe they still got an airstrip somewhere and birds to take them home."

"What a waste," Allie said. "What did their war accomplish anyway?"

"Does war ever accomplish anything?" Cat asked.

"It used to," LB said. "Used to be one group went to war against another and the winner got everything. Land, money, slaves, you name it...to the victor go the spoils. But we're too civilized for that now."

"China went to war to become the world's superpower," I said. "But there's someone much stronger in control now."

"The beast system?" Allie asked.

"The what?" Cat seemed surprised.

She had heard me talking about Bible prophecy and how it described the final world government or empire as a beast that devours everything, but her mind seemed to reject all things supernatural. I for one understood that all too well. I just hoped, that unlike me, she didn't wait until it was too late to accept the truth.

I stepped away from the periscope and let LB take over. Cat was pacing in the workshop, and Allie was tinkering with something, her back to the workbench and wall of tools.

"That's what the Bible calls the final world government," I explained. "It uses the metaphor of a beast, rising out of a sea of chaos."

"Sounds like the times we are living in to me," Allie said.

"But the Regional Government wants peace, not war," Cat said.

"They want whatever government and every politician want," LB said. "More power, more control."

"I'll concede that point," Cat said. "There are plenty of bad actors out there. And I, for one, think the world would be a better place if we all just learned to live and let live. Things were better when people weren't so caught up in trying to outdo everyone else. We need to learn to work together if we're going to have a world worth saving."

Allie looked at me. She was a no-nonsense type of person. I could tell she was thinking I needed to set the record straight with Cat. It's what she would have done, but I knew from personal experience that pushing someone into making a decision wasn't the right way. No one comes to God because they're forced to. They can learn to say and do all the right things, but only a heart that is receptive can accept the free gift of His grace. Otherwise, it's all just an act, and there were plenty of religious pretenders throughout history to teach us that not everyone who claimed to be a Christian really was.

"The Bible says— "

"Can we just not, for one," Cat said irritably. "The Bible isn't the answer for everything."

LB pulled back from the periscope, gave me a sympathetic look, then said, "They're gone."

"We'll that's good news," Allie replied.

"Does it feel wrong to anyone else that we're hiding down here, holding all the food and medicine?" Cat said. "Is that what the Bible tells you to do? I seem to remember something about treating people the way you want to be treated."

"We're just trying to stay alive," I said softly. "There's only four of us, and the Regional Government has mandated anyone who doesn't recant their faith in God should be killed."

"So don't go making a big deal about it," Cat said. "That's what you said when we were in Camp Abilene."

"And look how that turned out," LB said. "We've got to be smart, Cat. We can help people, just as long as they aren't a threat."

"How are we supposed to know if someone is a threat when we hide out down here all the time."

"If people knew what we had, they might kill us to get it," Allie said. "They would at least try to take it from us."

"I think we can learn to work together," Cat said. "Not everyone is out to get us."

She left the workshop and started up the stairs. I looked at LB.

"Let her go, man," he told me. "She just needs some time to cool down. The pressure is getting to her. That's all."

"She'll come around," Allie said sympathetically.

"Like you always say," LB continued. "It has to be her decision."

"I know," I said quietly. "But we're running out of time."

# CHAPTER 6

MORE PROOF CAME through the internet that evening. Starlink was still up and running. The satellites beamed down free wi-fi for all, and while the world had gone dark in most places, the internet seemed unstoppable.

Not that we minded. The power center of the world had shifted from North America to the New Babylon in Iraq. The Near East seemed to be the least affected area on earth. Israel, with its covenant of peace, was thriving. And with the World Bank, now located in Babylon, controlling the digital currency, the Southern Asian region had become the most powerful of the Ten Region Global Government.

But it wasn't all rainbows and butterflies, even in the gleaming metropolis of Babylon, a fact that became crystal clear that night with the news of a coup.

*Here in New Babylon, a sudden shift in power has emerged,* the news reporter said. *After allegations of corruption and mismanagement of the Southern Asian Region were leveled at Abdula Bin Salman, G10 News has learned that he was taken into custody. But the Regional Administrator wasn't alone. The head of the North African and European Regions have been deposed as well. Sources tell us that it was Deputy Administrator Paul Eon who took action. The man who forged peace in Israel has stepped in to end the corruption. I have word now that Administrator Eon is going live in Babylon.*

The news site video feed switched to a camera that showed the polished black obelisk that was part of the Southern Asian Regional Administration Capitol. Behind it was the golden dome of the SARA building. Both were covered in writing that I couldn't read. I wondered if Lorenzo could have deciphered the strange markings.

Above the building was a hovering spaceship. It looked sleek and powerful. The sun was bright in the new world capital, but somehow the spaceship cast no shadow. There were thousands of people in the wide plaza around the towering, black obelisk. On the steps leading up to the SARA building, a podium was set up. The camera zoomed in on the familiar face of Paul Eon, who raised his hand for silence.

"That dude looks like Hitler," LB said.

It wasn't exactly true. He wore a custom suit, had perfectly styled hair, and no mustache. His skin was tan, and he had the chiseled good looks of a movie star rather than a politician. Yet, with one hand raised to silence the crowd, there was something about him that was reminiscent of Adolph Hitler.

"He's pretty," Allie said.

We were in the farmhouse, gathered in what had been the living room. The glow of the computer screen was the only light, but there were times when I feared it was too much. I sat on the sofa with the computer on the coffee table in front of me. Cat leaned against me, her elbow on my thigh. Allie and LB were sitting to my left. We all huddled close, watching and listening.

"He gives me the creeps," I said. "So does his partner."

Behind Paul Eon was the tall, fair-skinned alien who called himself Shemi Hazah. The alien had an almost perfect human appearance, only he was taller, over seven feet. But there was something fake about him too, as if he were wearing a mask to conceal his true face.

Cat shushed me, as the new dictator began to speak.

"It is with a heavy heart that I report to you this morning that a trio of regional administrators were caught in a plot to seize control of the Ten Region Global Government. I won't go into all the sordid details now. Your local news agencies will have a full report on the treacherous plot. Suffice it to say, we discovered their ambitions and have taken action. As you know, the European Region and North African Region have suffered from war and weak leadership. It was not my intention to intervene in their affairs, but in both regions an emergency meeting was called, and both regions have formally requested that I take control of their disorganized and corrupt administrations. I will do so on an interim basis until a reliable and skilled replacement can be found. In my home region, I will take on the role of Senior Administrator. As such, I'll have the ability to share the wealth and resources of the Southern Asian Region throughout the world.

"This is an era of peace and prosperity for all," he went

on, his voice powerful and persuasive. "We have had our growing pains, but the hostilities have been set aside."

"Ha!" LB said. "That's news to me."

"And we are coping with the sudden changes to our world," Paul Eon continued. "With the help of our friends from above, we will rebuild our world."

He paused as the crowd erupted in thunderous applause.

"We will clean up the pollution caused by greed, corruption, and war." He paused again as the crowd went wild below him. "We will secure and steward our natural resources so that future generations have all that they need and more."

The cheering went on for a full minute before Paul Eon raised his hand for silence again. "It does my heart good to see that you and I are of one mind. We must move forward, hand in hand, to create the society we have long dreamed of. And to that end, I'm announcing the move of the regional government capitals. Each one will be built with security and sustainability as the pillars on which the government stands. Pax Davino will join each one with temples built nearby. I want to encourage everyone to begin planning a pilgrimage to your regional capital soon. We'll be announcing new initiatives, including digital identity records, universal health care, and income."

The crowd went wild. The cameras panned back. The people in the plaza were on the verge of a full-blown riot. Clothes were coming off. People were being lifted high into the air. There was dancing and cheering. Soon the crowd was chanting their leader's name: *Paul-E-On! Paul-E-On!*

"They done lost their minds," LB said.

"He's giving them exactly what they want," I pointed out.

"Why do you think he's so bad?" Cat asked. "He's a politician, sure, but he seems focused on all the right things."

I picked up my Bible and flipped to the book of Daniel, chapter seven.

"Listen to this," I said quietly to Cat. I had to hold the Bible down in front of the computer screen to see the words. "After this I saw in the night visions, and behold, a fourth beast, terrifying and dreadful and exceedingly strong. It had great iron teeth; it devoured and broke in pieces and stamped what was left with its feet. It was different from all the beasts that were before it, and it had ten horns. I considered the horns, and behold, there came up among them another horn, a little one, before which three of the first horns were plucked up by the roots. And behold, in this horn were eyes like eyes of a man, and a mouth speaking great things."

"That's pretty vague," Cat said. "And honestly, it could be said about a lot of people."

"I don't know Cat," LB said. "Ten horns... three plucked out."

"Paul Eon just replaced three of the ten regional administrators," Allie said.

"Temporarily," Cat argued.

"Oh, I don't think he'll ever give up that power," I told her. "He just had three of the most powerful men in the world arrested. Now he's telling the others they have to move their capitals."

"And he's setting up Pax Davino holy sites nearby," Allie said. "That's no coincidence."

"Nah, he's in charge now, and the temples will keep the

other administrators in line," LB said. "He's consolidating his power."

"That's a pretty cynical point of view," Cat said.

"It's all in the Bible," Allie said. "I didn't think much of it at first either, but I've been looking at it every day. Dozens of prophesies have already come true, Cat. This is another one."

"Maybe," she said. "I still think it could be talking about anyone."

I sat back as the reporter returned. A graphic with the new capitals of the five kingdoms were shown. The North American Regional Administration was headed south, into Mexico.

"Where is Mérida, Yucatan?" LB asked.

"Beats me," I said.

"It's on the peninsula," Allie said. "Southern Mexico. I went to Cancun for spring break one year."

"That explains a lot," LB said with a grin.

"I guess a lot of the old capitals have been destroyed in the fighting," Cat said.

"Or maybe the new Emperor wants to sink his claws in deep," I said.

"I don't think you should call him that," Cat argued.

"Don't let him fool you," LB said. "He's no man of peace."

"That's the problem with religion," Cat said, getting up.

She was clearly agitated and couldn't sit still. I couldn't tell if she was getting angry, or if she was on the verge of a breakthrough.

"You judge," she continued. "You read your holy book and then you judge everyone who doesn't go along with your rules. But who's to say if your rules are the right rules. I say, live and let live. If Paul Eon wants to do some good in the world, why judge him?"

"I'm not judging him," I said. "But I'm recognizing him for who he is. The man is a liar, Cat. And he's going to do some very, very bad things."

"Oh, good grief," she said, before stomping up the stairs.

"Is it just me, or is she getting more and more tired of hearing the truth?" Allie asked.

"She just needs more time," LB said.

"I guess I'll give it to her," I said. "I'll stand watch tonight. You guys get some rest."

"You sure?" LB asked.

"Yeah," I said. "I won't be able to sleep anyway."

They got up and headed upstairs. I shut the computer and took a moment for my eyes to adjust to the darkness. The interior of the old farmhouse was gloomy, but after a moment or two I could make out the furniture. I stood up and moved to a window. We had covered the broken glass with clear packing tape, so that from a distance it still looked broken, but windows were effectively sealed up. We had rehung the door on the hinges and cleaned out the dirt and leaves that had blown inside. Everything else was left in a disorganized state. We left nothing in the kitchen and didn't try to fix the cabinet doors. Dirty dishes were taken to the barn to be washed, and any trash or leftovers were immediately disposed of. We had learned early on that the farmhouse was the first place looters looked and we wanted it to appear empty and picked over. So far, the ruse had worked, but we couldn't be too careful.

After dark, there were plenty of nocturnal predators in the area, from raccoons to wild dogs. Bobcats had left prints in the dirt around the farmhouse too, and occasionally we heard the animals at night. But I wasn't too concerned about the wildlife around us. The farmhouse could keep them out. It was people we had to watch for. So, I lingered by the front window and gazed out into the night.

The sky was never clear, but the same gray blanket that made the days dull, did sometimes glow with a ghostly light when the moon was full. The area around the farmhouse was an open mix of gravel, dirt, and patchy, overgrown grass that was mixed with hearty weeds. One hundred feet away from the sagging front porch was a line of mesquite trees. They were gnarly old trees, their trunks twisted, the crooked branches entwined. There were no leaves left. Spring had forgotten to show up, the lack of sunlight kept the trees in hibernation.

I could just make out the tops of the trees, but nothing below them. Certainly not the people hidden behind the crooked trunks. We all knew that someone would show up sooner or later. And it wasn't because people knew all the riches we had, but anyone staying in one place for very long had to have supplies. And for people without them, knowing someone else had what they needed was a powerful motivator.

I'm not inclined to think people are mostly good. Being a foster kid, you learn that a lofty view of the world is just a mirage. And of course, the people that were good through the grace of God were all gone after the Vanishing. That left two types of people in the world, the kind like me, who realized their mistake too late, and put their trust in Jesus after the Rapture...and people who continued to reject the truth. Some were deceived. Others were ignorant. But many were willfully and defiantly against God. Nothing and no one would ever change their minds, at least no mortal. The second group were masters at rationalizing their behavior. Nothing was immoral to people who saw no higher authority than themselves. That didn't automatically make them my enemies, but it did make them dangerous.

They sent a group in a wide circle around the property. I wandered back through the house to the kitchen but didn't see the intruders hidden in the shadow of the barn. I was back in the living room when they got to the rear door that led into the kitchen. There was no porch out back, just a set of cinderblock steps leading to the squeaky door. I was lost in my thoughts about Cat. It was impossible not to worry about her. We were much more than friends, although our romance had gone from passionate frenzy to a steady burn. She still found comfort in my arms, but she had her doubts about what I believed, serious doubts. And who could blame her. She knew by that point that believing what I believed could get her killed with no trial, no civil rights, and no recourse. Believers were being killed for having a Bible app on their phones. In the more populated areas, there were reports of people being dragged from their homes on the mere suspicion that they were believers. For someone trying to decide what to believe about God, facing death was a difficult pill to swallow.

Still, despite my concern for Cat, I should have been paying better attention. I might not have seen the intruders anyway, but I'll never know for sure. Fortunately, the squeaky doors and floors turned out to be a pretty good alarm system. I heard the intruders before they ever got inside.

# CHAPTER 7

I'D LIKE to say I wasn't nervous or scared, but I was both. We were careful and carried our guns with us everywhere we went, just like our go bags that Cat had put together. My weapon was a Beretta 9mm service pistol. The military stopped using them in favor of the more powerful 1911 semi-automatic pistol, or the more advanced SIG P226. But at Camp Abilene the security team only had access to surplus weapons, and the Beretta was in good shape. I kept it in a simple belt holster. When the back door squeaked, I drew the weapon and moved as quietly as possible to the stairs leading up to the bedrooms.

The old floors creaked and groaned in certain places. The stairs were all noisy. Getting up to my friends simply wasn't possible without the intruders knowing. And I didn't want to get stuck upstairs with no exit. Still, at the stairwell I could protect my friends and have a good view of both the front door and the entry to the kitchen. I got down on one knee and quietly worked the slide on my Beretta. It held fifteen rounds and with one in the chamber, she was ready to fire. My hands were less inclined and were trembling as I kept the weapon trained on the kitchen doorway.

The intruders opened the door slowly to minimize the squeal of the rusted and worn out hinges, but they couldn't keep their weight off the squeaky spots on the kitchen floor. Still, they moved slowly and with my heart pounding away in my chest it felt like I was waiting forever.

You might be thinking I was quick to rush to judgment against the intruders. Maybe they were just hungry and looking for something to eat? I had no doubts they were hungry and desperate, but people who are innocently looking for something to eat don't sneak into a home through the back door. That's what thieves do, and by the way the intruders were acting, they knew we were in the home.

Before I saw them, I saw their weapons. There were two of them. One had a revolver, the other a hunting rifle of some sort. They were holding their weapons at the ready, just as I was. My heart was pounding and despite the cold night, both inside the farmhouse and out, sweat was running down my back and both sides of my head. I won't lie, I hated fighting. I had shot and killed people since the tribulation began, always in self-defense. But that didn't stop the nightmares or the nagging guilt. Who was I to take a life? Why did I think it was better for me to live than someone else? At least I was prepared for death. My faith was solid, my future beyond this life was secure in my mind as well as my heart. But I didn't want to die. And I was absolutely focused on protecting my friends.

"Don't move," I said quietly.

For a moment the intruders obeyed, then one dropped back into the kitchen while the other dove forward into the living room. It was a gutsy move, but there was no cover in the ransacked farmhouse. The furniture was pushed close together in the center of the room. The intruder hit the floor and swung his pistol in my direction. He even fired first, but he had no idea where I was. His shot sailed harmlessly over my head, mine didn't.

Despite my fear and my trepidation at killing someone, I had firearm training from my days in the Air Force. The intruder was only fifteen feet from where I knelt by the stairs. I squeezed the trigger of the pistol just the way my instructors had taught me, targeting the intruder's chest. The bullet hit the prone man, punching into his side, and sending him flopping over. He tried to scream, but the bullet had punctured his lung. A gurgle escaped his lips, and his revolver tumbled across the floor.

There were shouts outside, and more shouts upstairs. LB and Allie were scrambling out of bed. From the kitchen a gruff voice shouted.

"In the living room! They shot Murph!"

A barrage of gun fire poured through the farmhouse. Windows shattered. Wood splintered. I was already flat on my stomach behind the sofa. The furniture was old and wouldn't offer us much protection, but it was my only option. The gun fire was steady, but not high- powered automatic weapons. It was from pistols and hunting rifles, the bullets ripping through the old home above where I lay. The walls were wooden planks. What insulation there was, puffed out after the bullets like snow falling in fat blobs on the floor.

"Hank!" LB shouted.

"I'm good," I shouted back. "One in the kitchen. The rest are outside."

"Copy that!" LB roared. He was all business. Thirty years in the Marine Corps made him one nasty fighter.

I didn't hear the window go up, but I knew his room looked out over the front yard. The chug of his M-16 in fully automatic mode was music to my ears at that moment. The shooting from outside into the living room stopped abruptly. I scrambled across the floor to the edge of the opening that led to the kitchen. One quick glance showed the other intruder crouching behind a row of cabinets, the barrel of his hunting rifle sticking up over the countertop.

"Throw it down and come out with your hands up," I said.

Maybe it was the tremble in my voice. I was terrified, and there was enough adrenaline in my system at that point to make an elephant jittery. It made my voice sound quivery and instead of obeying, the intruder lurched out from his hiding spot. He was in the process of swinging his rifle toward me. Most of my body was sheltered behind the wall. Only my gun and half my head were showing. Not that it mattered. His sudden movement kicked off my survival instinct. I fired a single shot, hit the rifleman in the chest, and he toppled to the floor.

"Wayne! Wayne! Get out of there!" Someone shouted from the front yard.

But it was too late. Wayne was unconscious on the dirty

kitchen floor, his lifeblood pumping out of the hole in his chest.

"He's down!" I shouted, both to the people outside, and to my friends upstairs.

"You hear that, cowards! Your boy's dead!" LB shouted. "Who else wants to die?"

"Wayne! Murph!" The voice outside shouted.

Neither man moved. After a moment the voice from outside sounded again.

"We're leaving! Don't shoot."

"Get the hell out of here!" LB shouted. "Dirty cowards!"

My hand was shaking hard as I reached for the flashlight I kept in my rear pocket. It was a small handheld, barely wider than my palm. I kept the gun trained on the man in the kitchen and flicked on the flashlight. The blood had pooled beneath the man. It was no longer pumping out, just dripping from the hole in his chest. He had a dirty trucker's cap on his head and a denim jacket that was too small to button. His eyes were closed. and his chest wasn't moving. I had killed another man and despite my reasons, including the circumstances, I felt like I might be sick.

Turning, I checked the other man. He was still alive, his chest rising and falling rapidly. He had less blood beneath him, but I could tell he was in a bad way by the sounds he made. Gurgling noise came from his open mouth, and bloody bubbles were caught on his untrimmed mustache.

I shoved my pistol into the holster and dropped down onto one knee beside the dying man. I pressed one hand against the bullet wound as hard as I could. He was wearing a dirty Nirvana tee-shirt and jeans. His thinning hair was combed back over a bald spot, and he was missing a couple of his front teeth. His eyes were open wide, staring at me. The blood-soaked tee shirt and my palm swished together, making a seal of sorts. It helped the man breathe a little easier somehow, or maybe it was just me.

"I'm sorry," I said. "But it's not too late."

One of his hands gripped my arm.

"Do you know that Jesus loves you?" I asked. "All you have to do is bel— "

Before I could finish, he slashed me with his pocketknife. It cut through my jacket sleeve at the shoulder and might have cut me deep if the blade hadn't been dull. Afterward I examined the knife. It had seen some hard use, cutting and probably digging too. The point was snapped off, the blade only sharp in a couple of spots.

I fell back, jerked my arm free of his grip. The dying man grinned at me. The skin was pale and tight across his forehead. I could see the shape of his skull. He looked like a monster.

"Yo! Hank? He hurt you?" LB called out from the stairway.

"Tried," I said. "But I'm fine."

"A real nasty piece of work," LB said coming up to stand beside me. "Can't save him."

"Had to try," I said.

LB put a hand on my shoulder, and it felt good. His reassuring, calm presence was exactly what I needed at that moment.

"You did good, Hank, real good."

"Thanks," I said.

"Allie's keeping an eye on things upstairs. Cat's pretty shook up, but we're all okay. Why didn't you wake me sooner?"

"Didn't see them until these goons were at the back door," I said.

"Stupid bastards," LB said. "I hit a few out in the trees. They won't be back."

"It's such a waste," I said.

"We would have shared all we have if only they had come and asked. Instead, they came sneaking in at night, with guns, ready to kill us in our beds so they could take everything we have. Don't feel sorry for 'em Hank. You live by the sword, you die by the sword. You know who said that?"

"Who?" I asked.

"Jesus."

# CHAPTER 8

THERE WAS blood on the ground at the tree line. The four of us went together to look and see what had become of the intruders. We waited until dawn. LB watched the front of the farmhouse from the window in his room. I watched the rear from mine. No one slept and by sun-up we were all tired.

"I think it's best if we start sleeping in the shelter," Allie said as we followed the blood trail back to the road.

"I don't like the idea of being underground when the quake hits," LB said.

"And I don't think I'll sleep a wink in that farmhouse ever again," she replied.

"Me either," Cat said. "Maybe it's best if we just move on."

"And go where?" I asked.

"South," she replied. "That was always the plan, right?"

"It was a possibility," I said. "Surviving is the plan."

"Look at that," LB said, pointing at the weedy, overgrown road. Laying across one of the ruts was a body.

"It could be a trap," I said.

"Yeah, could be," he replied. "You and Cat spread out on that side of the road. Allie and I will take this one."

There were trees along the sides of the road, but not many, and none that were bunched together. The fields beyond were overgrown, but the stubby grass and weeds weren't as tall as my knees. If people were laying down in it, they would have to be all the way down to stay hidden. Looking up would give them away. Cat and I spread wide, searching everywhere. Our trail through the tall weeds was visible behind us, and I saw no signs that anyone else had been moving on my side of the road.

"It's clear on this side," I shouted.

"Yeah, looks clear over here too," LB shouted.

We met back at the body. It was a girl, maybe twenty-two or twenty-three years old. Her clothes were bloody, but her shoes and coat were missing.

"They stripped her of anything they thought was valuable," Allie said. "She's just a kid."

"This is a nasty bunch we're dealing with," LB said.

"What are the odds they come back?" Cat asked.

"A hundred percent," LB said. "No doubt about that."

"Really?" Cat asked.

"No doubt about it," LB said. "They want what we've got. They probably don't even know what it is, but they know we're willing to fight for it. So, they'll come back."

It was a sobering thought, and while the shelter was a safe place to hunker down and ride out a storm, I was beginning to think that Cat was right. As we walked back to the farm, I talked to LB.

"What are you thinking?" I asked him.

"I'm thinking we're between a rock and hard place," he replied.

When we got back to the farm though, the decision was practically made for us. We hadn't realized it in the night, but when we tried to open the door to the shelter, the lock didn't respond.

"Power's out," LB said.

"The batteries were in the house," Allie said as the realization of what had happened rushed over us all.

I felt a sense of fear as we returned to the farmhouse. The bodies of the two men I had killed were still there. I would have been happy never setting foot in that place again. But we moved past the bodies and checked the closet where the bank of batteries were kept. There were holes in three of the batteries and several of the connecting wires were singed.

"We're lucky this whole place didn't go up in flames," LB said.

"It's almost like someone is watching out for us," I said.

"Is there any way to salvage it?" Cat asked.

"I don't think so," Allie said. "If there's power left in any of the remaining batteries, I'm pretty sure I can get the shelter door open, but there won't be power to run the lights, or the freezer."

"So, we're screwed," Cat said.

"Let's see what we can salvage, then we'll decide what to do next," LB suggested.

Several of the batteries had shorted out. Their connection

points were burned, the wires melted onto the leads. But the bottom two batteries seemed to be okay. We unhooked one and lugged it out to the barn.

"I think we should move the Bronco and the trailer to the barn," I said. "I've got a feeling we may need to hit the road quickly."

"You've got a feeling?" Cat asked.

"A feeling, or something more significant?" Allie asked. "Maybe a prompting by the man upstairs?"

"Whatever it is, Cat and I are going to get the Bronco," I said. "Good luck with the shelter door."

"Don't need luck," LB said. "I got me a top-notch wrench spinner right here."

"Hey, I'm more than just a handywoman you know," Allie teased.

It was fun to see the two of them being jovial. Before escaping Camp Abilene, I didn't think Allie was capable of mirth. Knowing she lost two children in the Rapture, I can see why she was hurting. But since getting away and spending almost all her time with LB, she was coming around. He had the ability to sooth a person's raw nerves. When he put a hand on my shoulder after the firefight in the middle of the night, I know I felt better. And, from the way they were flirting, I'm pretty sure they were more than just pals.

Cat and I made our way out the back of the barn and started across the open field. I was carrying my pistol in my hand. I didn't want to fight anyone, and I certainly didn't want to shoot at anyone, but I wanted to be ready if I had to.

"Are you okay?" Cat asked.

"Me?"

"Don't pretend with me, Hank. I know you," she shrugged. "I don't know how you endure so much and keep going. If I had done what you had to do in the house last night, I'd be a basket case. I mean, I'm practically a basket case now."

"Why's that?" I asked.

"You want the whole list?"

"Nope, just what really matters," I told her.

It was easier to focus on her issues than examine my own. And she didn't seem to mind that I wasn't talking about how I was feeling. The truth was my own emotions were so raw that I feared I might break down sobbing if I didn't stuff them down hard deep inside. You're probably thinking that by doing that I was just prolonging the inevitable. And you'd be right, but I thought I would have time to work through everything later, when our lives weren't on the line.

"Here's what matters the most," she said. "Everything has changed, and not for the better. There's a big part of me that's wondering why I'm not headed for the mountains right this very minute."

"Alone?" I asked her.

"I've always been alone, Hank. Until I met you, I thought I'd always be alone. I can handle being around people for a short while... a weekend... maybe a couple of weeks at best. I've never had a regular boyfriend," she admitted. "I haven't lived in a proper house until the war started. I don't know if being with you is keeping me alive or making me weak. I just know something isn't right and I have no idea how to fix it."

"Maybe the Holy Spirit is knocking on the door to your heart?"

"No!" Cat said. "Religion isn't the answer for everything, Hank."

"What's happened?" I asked. "You didn't used to be so anti-God."

"LB told me what happened at Camp Abilene, just before the raid. You weren't going to tell me, but he did."

"What?" I asked, even though I knew exactly what she meant.

"Oh, is that how you're going to play this? Since when did you become mister tough guy who isn't honest with me?"

"What can I say, you married a bad boy."

She chuckled, but the joke wasn't enough to get me out of the doghouse.

"You talk about God all the time, Hank. And that's fine for you. But you were almost executed. Your friend nearly had to shoot you in the head because of all this God business. Enough is enough. We have to start thinking about how we're going to survive."

"Surviving isn't the main thing," I told her.

"And what is?"

"Telling people what's really going on."

"Who cares about other people?" she asked, suddenly turning and getting close. "Why can't it be me and you. That's all I want. Just me and you, someplace safe, till all of this is over."

"It can't be. Because there is no place like that," I told her. "There's no safe place, not anymore. And the truth is much too important to horde it. We have to get the word out."

"Even if it gets you killed?"

"Yes, even if it gets me killed."

She slapped me. I didn't see it coming and her hand lashed across my face so hard my ear started ringing.

"What...what'd you do that for?" I asked.

She was already stomping away.

"Because..."

She didn't finish and I didn't force her too. Part of me was angry, really angry. There was a voice in my head telling me to let her have it, that she didn't know who she was messing with. But another part of me was heartbroken. There was more in the slap than just frustration. It was the end of something special, something I cared about. And it seemed to me like we had passed the point of no return.

We didn't speak again. When we got to the Bronco, I got behind the wheel and she climbed into the passenger seat. The old vehicle's engine whirred for two seconds before it caught and rumbled to life. I eased it out of the shed. Driving a stick shift wasn't something I was used to. We bumped and rumbled our way across the field and into the barn. By that time Allie and LB had the shelter door open.

"Good news," LB said. "The freezer had a backup generator. It's a portable one and should keep the food cold another day or so. We don't have to get in a hurry."

"That's great," I said, thankful for the deep shadows inside the barn. I could still feel the red mark on the side of my face where Cat had slapped me, and I didn't want LB asking about it.

I left to get the trailer, which was left haphazardly out in the field with some old hay spread across it. LB and Allie had done a good job of making it look like it had been there for decades just like everything else on the farm. It was a simple, two-wheeled trailer with a long tongue. Pulling it back to the barn by myself wasn't easy, but I didn't mind the struggle. Or the time it took to complete the task. I broke down a little at one point. Tugging on the heavy trailer felt good. It was a physical release to some of the pent-up emotions I was feeling. By the time I got to the barn I was sweating but feeling a bit better.

LB helped me connect the trailer to the Bronco. If he noticed my face, he didn't say anything. By that point I was red-faced from pulling the trailer, but my eyes were puffy and blood shot from crying. Part of me felt like such a baby, and I couldn't help but wonder how I was supposed to help anyone. I had recorded over a dozen short videos that I planned to upload to various sites once we were on the road again. It wouldn't be safe to upload them from here, since they would almost certainly draw attention from the government watch dog groups that hated God and wanted to see all Christians beheaded. The last thing we needed was for a group from the government tracking us down out here.

There was an old smoker in the barn. Like everything else it looked ancient. But it was big, the kind used for social events. LB wanted to smoke as much of the meat from the freezer as possible. He set out all the cuts he thought he could use, along with various spices from the food supplies down in the shelter. Then we pulled the smoker into the noonday sunlight and inspected it.

"She's got some rust," he said. "But I think we can use it."

"We need wood to burn," I said.

"There's plenty around the farm. It's almost all mesquite, and that's got a good flavor to it."

Everyone was exhausted. While LB prepped for his overnight smoke, the rest of us napped inside the shelter. By nightfall he had enough meat thawed, cut, and seasoned that he was ready to start his fire. Cat and I still hadn't talked. She was asleep and there was no need in waking her up.

"What if someone smells the smoke?" Allie asked. "We could be asking for trouble."

"It's a cold night," LB said. "Who wouldn't want to build a fire if they could?"

"Well, they might also smell the food," she pointed out.

"Nah, they'd have to be a hundred feet from the barn for that. Anyone who gets that close will have the jump on us already. Besides, some fresh jerky will be great once we hit the road."

"If you say so," Allie said. "I never liked it."

"You don't like that nasty stuff they sell in gas stations and supermarkets. You ain't never had the delicacies I smoke up, baby. Trust me, you're gonna love it."

Once he had the fire going in the little smoke box built into the side of the big barrel smoker, he started laying out the meat on the long, metal rack. He and Allie were at the rear of the barn and went to the other end to keep watch. The hours crept by, but I had no trouble seeing. The light in the sky was bright enough that I could see to the farmhouse and nearly to the road beyond. I didn't think anyone could sneak up on me, but Cat managed to sometime after midnight.

"I just came to say goodbye," she said softly.

I turned, expecting another fight, but instead I found her in a long coat she had found on the farm with her go bag in hand and a larger backpack filled so tight it was straining the seams she had sewn it together with.

"What?" I asked.

"I'm leaving, Hank," she said, her voice barely more than a whisper. "I'm sorry I hit you, but you broke my heart. You can't make someone love you, Hank and then just throw your life away. It isn't fair, and if you really loved me, you wouldn't do that. Do you have any idea how cruel it is to be so careless with your life? It's painful to watch, and I just can't do it anymore. I have to go. I have to protect myself."

"No," I said, "don't leave."

"It's the right thing for me," she said.

"You don't know what's out there," I told her. "It's dangerous."

"I'm used to dangerous," she replied.

"Cat, please. I'm sorry."

"I know," she said. "You're a good guy, Hank. And I thought maybe we could work. You saved my life, after all. But it's no good. I'm miserable, and things are only getting worse. I have to go."

She didn't wait for my reply. She just turned and ran off into the darkness.

# CHAPTER 9

I KNOW what you're thinking, it's the end of the world and I'm worried about a lover's spat. It's absolutely true. That's what I was concerned with, and all I cared about. But what could I do? Chase her down? Keep her on the farm against her will? I wanted to shout for LB and Allie. I wanted them to help me get her back, but even though my heart was splintering like ice beneath my feet, I knew I had to let her go. Holding on to her would only make her more miserable, and I didn't want to do that. Still, I ran out of the barn and caught up with her.

"Wait, Cat. Please, just wait," I said.

"I've made up my mind, Hank," she said, swiping at the tears rolling down her cheek.

"I love you," I said, taking her in my arms and holding her tightly. "I won't stop you, but I needed to tell you that."

"I know," she said. "I love you too, but I can't stay and watch you die."

"Okay, I get that," I told her. "I really do. I just need to make sure you have everything you need. Did you get food?"

"I got food, Hank. I got blankets and medicine. Not a lot, I don't need much, but I took what I needed."

"Did you take a Bible?" She sighed but I pressed on, desperate for her to see how important it was. "Look, I know you're sick of it all, but the truth is in there. Please, tell me you took one. Or let me go get you one."

"I have it, okay," she said. "I took a dumb Bible, and I won't use it to start a fire, I promise."

"Okay," I said, feeling a sense of relief that quickly morphed into sadness. "I'm sorry I let you down, Cat."

"I'm sorry I couldn't be what you wanted," she replied. "Maybe, if things weren't so crazy..."

"Maybe," I said. "Be careful out there."

"I will be," she said. "Good-bye Hank."

We hugged again. I was crying but didn't care. She was too, but there was determination in her eyes. Standing aside, I watched her until she disappeared in the darkness. Then I cried some more.

It took me a long time to return to the barn. At dawn I found LB pulling little strips of meat out of the smoker. He was whistling happily. Allie was asleep on a pile of hay nearby, wrapped up tight in a wool blanket that I'm sure the two of them had shared during the coldest part of the night.

"Hey man, you gotta try..." his voice faltered for a second. "Hank? You okay there, man?"

"I will be," I said. "Cat left."

"Left for where?"

"Left to find her own path," I said.

"What? Is she crazy? She just left?"

"She didn't want to stick around and see me get killed," I said. "Can't blame her for that, I guess."

"Man, what are you talking about?"

"You told her what happened at Camp Abilene," I said. "She knows Christians are being persecuted. The truth is, it's only a matter of time for me. And she didn't want to stick around and see me die."

"So... she left you?"

"She did," I said. "Your jerky smells great."

"That's because it is great," he replied. "What are you going to do now, Hank?"

"Keep doing what I'm supposed to do. Sharing the good news, man. Telling the world what's really going on."

"That's a high calling," LB said. "Don't get me wrong, I appreciate you so much. It was your example that set me on the right path, you know? I would still be looking out just for myself if not for you, Hank. Or dead, probably, who knows. But damn, man, she just left?"

"It was a while coming," I said. "She's happiest on her own. I took her out of the mountains, and she gave it her best shot. I can't blame her for liking what she likes, you know?"

It was the only time I had ever seen LB lost for words. He looked genuinely sorry for me, and I really did appreciate him for that.

"I think I'm gonna get some sleep. You good here?"

"Yeah. Where you going?"

"Down in the shelter. That couch is calling my name."

"Cool man. I get that. As long as you're okay, I'm okay."

"I'm not okay, but I will be," I said. "And you will be too.

Cherish what you've got man. There's nothing more important than family."

What I didn't say was that I never could hang onto mine. My parents died when I was eight. Lorenzo was taken in the Rapture. Apparently, no woman could stay with me. It was a difficult situation to deal with. The tears returned as I trudged down to the library in the shelter. Fortunately, I was so exhausted that I fell asleep before I could dwell on my loss for too long.

The weather changed while I was sleeping. A wind kicked up. I can't say for certain, but I think maybe it was supernatural. I've heard people from all over talk about it. Those of us in North America had been living under a nuclear winter for months, practically since the war began. Ash, dust, and debris clouded the air. It hung in a heavy looking gray smog over the sky, diffusing the sunlight, and creating the ghostly glow at night. But what I had thought was a full moon was something entirely different.

The wind blew and before long the smog receded. The air cleared, and when it did, even though it was broad daylight in north Texas, the comet was clear to see. LB woke me just a few hours into my nap.

"Sorry, Hank, I hate to wake you up, man, but you gotta see this," he said.

He was on his way back out of the shelter before I had even sat up. My mind was foggy, and my heart was heavy. In that moment I couldn't even remember why I felt so bad. My face was puffy from sleep and from the tears that I couldn't hold back. But I managed to get to my feet and follow LB.

I staggered out into the sunlight, which made me squint. It

was brighter outside than it had been in a long time. And it took me a few minutes to adjust. Looking up at the sky, I could see the glowing object, but I couldn't look at it for long because it was so close to the sun.

"They're saying it's a comet," Allie said. "The air is clearing up all over the world. People are seeing it everywhere."

"Is this in the Bible?" LB asked. "I know there's some people who think that a comet might hit earth or something."

"How close it is?"

"Close," Allie said. "It's not on any of the charts though. The authorities are saying it won't hit us, but..."

"But what?" I asked.

"What if they're lying?" Allie asked.

"Wouldn't be the first time," LB said.

"LB told me about Cat. She can't be far. We could get the Bronco and go get her."

"No," I told her. "She knows where we are. She knows what's coming. The next judgment is an earthquake. I don't see how a comet has anything to do with that."

My mind was spinning, and even before I prayed for wisdom, the truth hit me like a sledgehammer. The Bible said that the sun would turn black, and the moon would be like blood. A blood moon was caused by the earth blocking the sunlight, but something else could do the same thing. And the Bible also said that the stars fell to the earth, like a fig tree that is shaken, shedding its winter fruit. But most frightening of all, what I hadn't thought of until that very moment, was that an object passing so close to earth would affect our gravitational field. It would put pressure on the tectonic plates, and literally cause the shift.

I didn't know if we should run to the barn and hide in the shelter, or if we should get out onto open ground. No place seemed safe. The sixth seal judgment was about to be opened, and there was nothing we could do to stop it.

"Guys, listen to me," I said. "That comet is going to cause the sixth seal judgment. There's going to be debris burning through the atmosphere. It might be dangerous, I don't know, but I think we should get in the Bronco and move it out into a field somewhere."

"The earthquake is gonna be caused by a comet?" LB asked.

"It's going to tweak our gravity. There's no time to waste."

We ran back into the barn. Allie climbed into the driver's seat. LB and I unhooked the trailer, then climbed inside with her. She drove out of the barn and turned toward the open fields behind the farmhouse. LB and I had our hands up, blocking the glare from the sun as we looked into the sky. We spotted the rain of debris immediately. There were hundreds of bright streaks racing across the sky. Some left dark trails of smoke, others just flashed for a second and disappeared.

"Are they going to hit us?" LB asked.

"Maybe we should have stayed in the barn," Allie said.

"No, it won't survive the quake," I said. "This is the best place to be."

She stopped the Bronco and we waited. But we didn't have to wait long.

# CHAPTER 10

IF YOU'VE EVER BEEN in an earthquake before, the strange rumbling sound probably tipped you off right away. I had never heard anything like it. Some people say it's the earth roaring, and that's a pretty good way to describe it. At first the quake was just a tremor. The ground vibrated. We could feel it through the seats of the old Bronco.

"I can't believe it," Allie said, her hands griping the steering wheel with both hands.

"It's too bad they didn't install seat belts in this ride," LB said.

He had both hands extended onto the dashboard. The old Bronco had no roof and no doors. It was an open cab. I thought in that moment that we should have installed a roll cage. Not that we had the time or the resources to do such a thing. And then the first waves came rolling across the plain.

North Texas is pretty flat country. It's pretty dry, the vegetation is scarce, and the trees are stunted and gnarly. Still, seeing the ground rolling like the wave of an ocean was terrifying. They were little waves at first, only a couple of feet high. But that was enough to make the Bronco bounce up and down. The powerful waves actually tossed the vehicle into the air like a toy. But somehow, I believe it was a miracle, she didn't flip. We rocked back and forth, bouncing from side to side. I had both hands on the front seats, my feet were locked under them, just trying to hold on and not be tossed out. The waves grew bigger. Four feet, then six, then ten. We were tossed from the Bronco. Everything was shuttering, rocks breaking, trees toppling, everything being tossed around like we were dice in a Yahtzee cup.

If you're reading this, you know the horror of it. I was completely out of control, being tossed around like a rag doll. Each time I hit the ground, it was like I was being smacked by a giant. And then, as if to prove it could become even more terrifying, the sun went dark. It must have been growing dimmer all the time, but all I knew was that one moment I could see, the next I couldn't. I didn't know if the Bronco was about to flip over and crush me, or where my friends were. Most of the time I couldn't even tell which way was up. It was like being tossed down a steep hill. I couldn't stop, couldn't get my bearings. I wanted to protect myself, but there was no way I could. It was the most horrific thing I have ever experienced, and somewhere in the midst of it all, I thought about Cat. I hated that she was experiencing the earthquake alone. Would she even survive it? I couldn't say. All I knew, was that my heart hurt more than my body, which was flipping, flying, dropping, and slapping hard onto the ground.

The ground had changed radically. It rolled like liquid,

but the sudden changes were having an effect on the ground too. It ripped and split apart in places. Rocks long buried were spit up into the air, only to fall back and smash onto the ground. At one point, I hit a tree and grabbed onto it for dear life, only to discover it wasn't in the ground. It was bouncing along, just like me.

The roaring sounds were loud, but at times I heard LB's gruff voice shouting, or Allie screaming. I was screaming too. In my mind I was begging God to stop the quake, to save me and my friends. But the quake didn't stop. As you know, the official estimate was twenty-two minutes. Buildings all over the world toppled. The entire topography of the Earth changed. North and South America were split. The fault line that bisects southern Mexico broke apart. Australia and New Zealand were rotated and pushed north. The Rock of Gibraltar crumbled into the Mediterranean ocean. The entire continent of Africa spun, tearing itself away from the Arabian Tectonic plate, it rotated nearly ninety degrees, so that South Africa faced east into the Indian Ocean.

There were more fault lines under the ocean. They smashed together, forming long mountain chains in just under twenty minutes. The oceans heaved, rushing inland in some places, and draining away in others. Some islands were swamped. Some were lifted high out of the sea and surrounded by stunning cliffs like those along the eastern edge of Great Britain.

Eastern Siberia was separated by a massive rift. Entire villages were lost, swallowed by the giant crack in the earth's crust. The western coast of North America was already a radioactive wasteland, but large chunks dropped away and were lost under the ocean waves. Volcanic mountains crumbled inward, collapsing upon themselves. It wasn't catastrophic, but rather cataclysmic. Entire cities all over the world were toppled. Millions died from being buried in the rubble, and hundreds of thousands of people were lost when the ground tore open beneath them, only to be smashed back together with the next wave.

Eventually the comet passed. The sun became visible again and filled the world with a hazy, weak illumination. Dust filled the air. I had to cover my face with my shirt just to breath without coughing. For a while I just laid still. My equilibrium was completely off. By some miracle no bones were broken, but I was cut by rocks and by the impact of my body on the ground. Bruises covered me, and my back spasmed. After a while I sat up, driven by my concern for my friends.

"LB!" I shouted. "Allie!"

Nothing looked the same. The farmhouse was gone, not just collapsed, but smashed to bits and scattered. The barn was the same. Somehow the Bronco had stayed upright. The big tires and oversized suspension had worked to keep the vehicle right side up. I was amazed that it seemed undamaged and in awe that it was nearly half a mile from where I lay. Getting to my feet wasn't easy. Like I said, everything hurt, and not just sore, but cramping muscle spasms racked my back. I had never hurt like that before. At times they cramped so hard I could barely inflate the lungs in my chest.

Blood was dripping into my left eye. I swiped at it with my fingers and felt a flap of loose skin on my forehead just above my eyebrow. Somehow my go bag had stayed on my back. I pulled it off and got some gauze out of the first-aid pouch. I pressed it against my forehead to stop the bleeding and went searching for my friends.

Allie was crumpled on her side nearly a hundred yards from where I lay. Her left leg was bent sideways at the knee, and she too had blood on her head and neck.

"Allie," I said, my voice gruff and dry.

She didn't respond. There was a tree on the ground nearby. Most of its branches were missing. Those that remained were nearly torn off. It didn't take much effort to break two free. I carried them to Allie and snapped the dry wood into pieces the right length for a splint.

"Allie, can you hear me?"

She was out cold, which in my mind was a blessing in disguise. I pulled out one of my wool blankets from my pack and my lock blade knife out of my pocket. The blanket cut easily into strips. I knelt down by Allie and lifted her broken leg. She groaned but didn't wake up.

"I'm sorry," I croaked, then I pulled her leg straight. It popped with a wet, grinding sound, that she quickly drowned out with a terrible scream.

"Hey, hey," I said, "It's over. The bad part is over now."

Her eyes were fluttering, and I thought she might speak to me. But her eyes rolled back in her head, and she passed out cold.

"Maybe that's for the best," I said.

Getting the crooked tree branches in place and tying them with the strips from my blanket wasn't easy, but I got it done. Allie moaned a few times. I got more gauze from my go bag and wiped off the blood from her face. She had a cut on one cheek and one across her nose.

"That's gonna leave a mark," I said. "But we're still breathing. Stay right here. I'm going to get the Bronco."

I doubt she could hear me, but it felt right to communicate with her. As I staggered over the uneven ground, being careful not to trip and fall, I searched for LB. The big man was nowhere in sight. I didn't know how that was possible, but there were a lot of things that didn't make sense in that moment.

I made it safely to the Bronco. The keys were still in the ignition, and to my delight it started right up.

"Dang, they don't make 'em like that anymore," I thought to myself as I slowly turned the SUV around and drove toward Allie. What had been flat pastureland before was now rough, buckled Earth. There were cracks and little up shoots that made the ride back to my friend rough. Fortunately, the Bronco had two bench seats. I got Allie's pack off and settled it in the rear seat. Then I picked her up. It hurt, but I managed despite my cramping muscles. The sudden shift in gravity on her broken leg made her groan. It was swelling too, but the splint I had fashioned was holding.

I put her on the back bench seat. There were no safety straps, so I used more strips cut from my blanket, tying her down onto the bench seat. The Bronco was made for utility, including the seats. The back and bench portion were two separate pieces, and there was nothing under the seats but the metal framework they attached to, so getting the straps around the bench seat wasn't difficult. I tied simple slip knots on top of her body just in case she woke up. With her head resting on her pack, and her body tied down with three straps, I set off in search for LB.

It was almost dark when I found him. He was conscious but laying down. I could tell he was hurt, just not how bad.

"Hey man," I said. "We found you!"

"How's... Allie?"

"She's got a broken leg, but I splinted it. She's sleeping it off in the back of the Bronco. What about you?"

"Been... better," he said, trying to smile, but his normally bright teeth were stained with blood.

"What's wrong."

"Busted... rib," he said. "Damn... thing's... stuck... in my... lung."

That was bad news, and I wasn't sure what to do. I couldn't leave him there and moving him would probably make things worse.

"You sure?"

"Pretty sure," he said. "Been coughing... up blood... since I woke... up."

"Well, this is as good a place as any to make camp for the night."

I went into survival mode. There was no sense in going back to the farm. It was gone, completely destroyed. And while we did have supplies there that I wanted to get, for the time being it was best to just get my friends as comfortable as possible.

I had one more blanket in my pack. I pulled it out and covered LB up.

"Thanks... man," he managed to say.

"Don't try to talk. I'm hoping that if the swelling goes down, it will stop pushing your rib into your lung."

He gave me shaky thumbs up. I found the anti-inflamma-

tory pain meds in my first-aid kit. He could have used something stronger, but we didn't have anything, and I wouldn't
have risked it anyway. A small bottle of water was all I had to
drink in my pack. That would have to change, but for the
moment it was enough. LB was already slightly propped up
on his pack and took the pills I gave him.

"Alright, there's a lot to do," I said. "I'm gonna hike back to
the barn and see what I can salvage. You hang tight, alright?
And if Allie wakes up, tell her I'll be back soon. It's best if she
doesn't try to get out of the Bronco though. Her leg is in pretty
bad shape."

I turned to go, but LB grabbed my leg. I turned around,
kneeling beside him, doing my best not to let my aching back
show too much. He took my hand, gripped it hard and looked
me in the eye.

"Thanks... Hank," he said in a wheezy voice.

"I'm gonna get you fixed up, brother. Just stay calm and
keep breathing easy, okay?"

He nodded. I got up, checked on Allie, and set off. It felt
like a futile errand, and I was praying hard with every step.
*God, show me what to do. Heal Allie. Heal LB. And show me
what to do, please. I need you now. They need you. We're in a
bad way here, Father. Please, show me what to do.*

# CHAPTER 11

I PRAYED ALL the way back to what was left of the barn. Along the way I saw one of the fuel barrels. It was upside down, but undamaged. The shed it had been in was completely destroyed and I didn't see the other barrel, but one was a great find. God was answering prayers.

At the barn, which was merely a heap of old wood, I found the steel door to the shelter on the ground. The concrete walls that led down into the shelter were cracked and broken. Some of the cinder blocks had fallen in on the stairs, but I could squeeze through them and get down into the shelter. The food and library were a mess, but the structural integrity was still in place. The rest of the shelter had fallen in on itself. Fortunately, as we divided up the supplies in the shelter, we moved the medical goods to the shelves where the food had been. I got a flat of water in disposable bottles and filled an old gym bag we had found in the farmhouse with all the medical supplies. I carried all that out and set it on the ground. Then I went back down for blankets, paracord, and tarps. These went into a blanket I unfolded and used like a sack. Finally, I carried out the crutches.

Back on the surface, I got my load together and trudged back out to where LB and Allie waited. It took a while. I had to stop four times to rest. Maybe it was the blood loss, or the muscle spasms, or just the trauma of the earthquake itself, but I had zero energy. I was breathing hard when I reached the Bronco. I pulled out a bottle of water, chugged half of it, and then put the rest in the passenger seat.

"Hey man, I made it," I said, returning to LB.

He had been asleep, and there was sweat on his forehead. When he opened his eyes, they looked weak, like holding the lids open was a chore.

"You're resting," I said. "That's good. I'm going to fix us up a little shelter here, man. Just sit tight."

I used the crutches like tent poles and stretched a tarp out from the broken windshield of the Bronco, pulled it back over the rear where I had the crutches tied to the back, and down to the ground. It covered Allie and LB. I tied the sides to large rocks, which were conveniently sticking up out of the ground after the earthquake. Once I had the tarp stretched out on all four sides, I pulled out the extra blankets. I got Allie covered up with a couple, then used the rest for LB. I didn't like him laying right on the ground, but I didn't want to move him either. The ground would leach up and drain away his heat, but there was little I could do about that. With the shelter up, I made LB drink some water. After a few swallows, he swooned. I didn't know if that was good or bad. He was clearly in shock, but perhaps his injuries were worse than I knew.

I knelt over him and prayed for healing. It was all that I could do.

After collecting an armful of broken limbs and whatever wood I could find, I started a fire as close to LB as I dare built it. I made a fire ring with stones, and even built up a little rock wall behind the fire to reflect the heat back toward him. Then I sat down beside my friend and settled in to wait. Night fell, the world around us was still, and I dozed. Every time I woke up, I prayed. Several times in the night LB woke me up coughing. I didn't know what to do for him, or if Allie not waking up all afternoon was good or bad.

At dawn, I was up and tending to my friends. Allie woke up an hour later. She was in a lot of pain, but I felt relieved that she was conscious.

"My leg is killing me," she said.

"It's a pretty bad break," I told her. "But the worst is behind you."

"Can't get worse," she panted.

I got her water and some pain killers. They were over the counter but better than nothing.

"Where's LB?" She asked.

"He's here."

"Where?"

"Laying down," I said, pointing behind the Bronco. "He's hurt too."

"What's wrong?" She asked, trying to sit up.

"Don't," I told her. "There's nothing you can do for him. And hurting your leg trying to get out of the Bronco will only make things worse."

"Tell me what's wrong with him, Hank!"

"He broke some ribs," I explained to her. "One's gouging his lung. We're waiting to see if the swelling will go down and relieve the pressure."

"What if it doesn't?"

"I don't know, Allie. I'm sorry. I could try to get him into the Bronco, but where would we take him?"

"To a hospital," she said, as if I had lost my mind.

"There are no hospitals," I told her. "There's nothing left of the barn or the farmhouse. They're just gone. I can't imagine there's anything else."

"So that's it? You're going to just let him die?"

"No," I said. "I'm praying for him. I don't know what else to do. If I move him, it could make things worse."

"You have to figure it out, Hank. You can't let him die. Please, Hank. I'm begging you. Do something."

She was getting tired. I felt bad for her and tried to reassure her, but the truth was I was losing hope. LB's breathing was ragged, and even though I was giving him water on a regular basis, there was fresh blood on his teeth.

The day dragged on and on. I felt powerless. While the others slept, I made trip after trip to the old barn. To my surprise, the trailer was still there, just buried in the shattered beams and mangled metal from that roof. I got it cleared off but moving it would be impossible without the Bronco. I did manage to get everything out of the shelter. One of the walls was leaning inward at a precarious angle, so I moved everything I could. The little fridge with antibiotics and insulin was somehow still working. It was plugged into the portable solar charger, which was down to about ten percent of its battery. I got them both out of the shelter, and even managed to find a pair of foldable solar panels still in the box they came in. I took everything back to the camp, but all the medicine in the world was worthless without the knowledge to use it.

I pulled up LB's shirt and saw the terrible bruising on one side. I broke open an emergency ice pack from the first aid supplies and held it against the broken ribs. His eyes fluttered open, but he couldn't speak. When he tried, his face twisted in pain, and a gurgle came out instead of words.

"Don't try to talk," I told him. "We've got to get the swelling down."

He pointed to the Bronco.

"She's okay. Her leg hurts, but she's not in danger of dying..."

I almost said, "like you." The slip up made me angry, and I had no way to vent that anger. My friend was in trouble, and I couldn't help him. Why God wouldn't heal him was a mystery to me. Didn't He know how much I depended on LB? Cat had left, and though I couldn't be sure, I was afraid that LB was dying. That thought filled me with dread and more than a little resentment.

LB gave me a knowing look. He nodded.

"You know I will," I said. "But you're not going to..."

I couldn't finish. Tears ran down my face. We held one another's hands tightly. Tears were leaking from the corner of his eyes. Once our emotions had settled, he held one hand flat and mimicked writing.

"I'll see what I can find," I told him.

Getting up, I started rummaging through our supplies, most of which were stacked up in the open cargo bed of the Bronco. I had to bend over to get under the tarp, but I found an old notebook and pen. As I backed out from under the tarp and stood up to stretch my sore back, I saw someone walking toward me. I ducked back under and handed the notebook to LB.

"Don't die on me man," I whispered. "Someone's coming."

He tapped my pistol, which had survived the earthquake while the M-16 rifles had been lost.

"Yeah, it's good. Locked and loaded."

He nodded.

"It's just one person that I can see. Coming from the north. I'll be careful."

After giving him the pen, I crawled back out from under the tarp and stood up. The stranger was closer. He had on dark clothes. I couldn't say how I knew it was a man, maybe it was the way he walked, or some type of spiritual discernment. I've heard people argue that those of us who came to faith in Jesus after the Rapture don't have the Holy Spirit dwelling in us. I can't say for certain, but it seemed like God was leading me at times. He led us to the farm where we got the supplies that we so desperately needed, along with shelter and resources that were just about unheard of to most people. And when I saw the comet in the sky, somehow, I knew what it was going to do to the planet. I can't explain how I knew, the knowledge just popped into my head. And when I saw the dark figure approaching, somehow, I felt like the burden I was under got a little lighter.

"Shalom my friend," the stranger called out.

"Hello," I called back, my hand still resting on the hilt of my pistol.

"I am not a threat," he said. "You survived the earthquake, praise God. May I join you for the evening?"

"Sure," I said, although I had no idea why. Maybe it was his strange greeting, or maybe the fact that he was friendly. Mostly, I think I just wanted someone else to tell me what to do to help my friends.

"I am Jonathan," he said as he strolled toward the camp.

"Hank Downs," I told him. "Where are you coming from?"

"New York," he said with a grin, "by way of Amarillo. I was in the emergency medical department at Northwest Texas Healthcare. It's a teaching hospital. That's what I do, I teach emergency medicine. I got stuck down here when the Vanishings threw a wrench in the works, if you take my meaning."

"A doctor?" I asked. "You're really a doctor?"

"I really am."

"Oh, thank God. Thank you, Jesus! I've two friends that are hurt pretty badly. Please, will you take a look at them."

"Of course, of course," he said.

Since that day I've learned to control what I say and to who. But little did I know, I was safe with Jonathan. He was, in fact, an answer to prayer. But all that will be made clear in time. He checked out LB first. The only thing Jonathan carried was an old fashioned, black leather doctor's bag. He had no change of clothes, no food, no water, and no weapons. He was wearing casual pants, a button-up shirt, and around his neck was a blue and white scarf. Everything was dirty, as you might guess, but he seemed completely comfortable and at ease.

"You've got a broken rib, my friend," Jonathan told LB. "We're going to fix you right up, just wait and see."

Out of his doctor's bag he pulled out a big syringe.

"Does the sight of blood make you faint," he asked me.

"No," I said around a lump forming in my throat.

"Excellent. You can help me. Here, get on his other side. We're going to sit him up. That's it, nice and slow."

LB's face was twisted in a grimace of pain, but he didn't make a sound. I had his hand in mine, and my other hand on his back.

"Now," the strange little doctor said, "this is going to pinch a little, but then it's going to feel better, I promise you that, okay?"

Jonathan gently pressed the needle of the big syringe into LB's side. He squeezed my hand so hard I thought my knuckles might shatter, but then as Jonathan drew out the fluid he relaxed and even took a deep, shuttering breath.

"That's better, eh? I thought so, my friend. And I think maybe we could draw off some more. Hold on, here we go, just a little pinch."

When he finished LB was smiling and was able to talk again.

"Thank you," he said in a gravely whisper.

"You are welcome my friend. God sees you. Never stop believing that. God will never leave his children. Now that's real medicine. Let's get a nice tight wrap on these ribs and you'll be feeling better in no time."

He pulled out a roll of medical tape. It was five inches wide. After cutting off LB's shirt, we wrapped it around his body. I could tell that it really helped with his pain.

"Now, you want to avoid any kind of strenuous work for two weeks, at the least. At the very least, you know. Otherwise, you could cause more damage. So, take it easy."

"You got it... doc," LB whispered.

"Who's next?" Jonathan asked. "You? That's a nasty gash on your forehead."

"No, not me," I told him, leading him over to the Bronco.

"Well, hello, young lady. You've had a rough time I see," Jonathan said when he saw Allie.

"Who's this?" She asked.

"A friend," I told her. "He's a doctor."

"Who did the splint work?" Jonathan asked, pulling a small vial of clear liquid out of his medical bag.

"I did," I confessed.

"Excellent improvisation, my friend. I couldn't have done it better myself. Hold on dear, I know you're in a lot of pain. This is going to help."

He injected the medicine into her good thigh.

"Morphine," he said. "She'll be feeling alright very soon."

"That's great," I said.

"Indeed. I'll need to check her break. That will hurt, but she shouldn't feel much. Once the bone is set, we can maybe fashion a better splint, but I doubt it. You've done excellent work. Were you in the medical field before the Vanishing?"

"No sir, I worked for Lorenzo Maltza and before that I was— "

"Lorenzo Maltza! Are you serious? The Supernatural Podcast? That Lornezo Maltza?"

"Yes," I said, shocked that this man knew who Lorenzo was.

"My friend, this is a providential meeting. I must tell you how I came to faith in Yeshua as the Mashiach."

After checking Allie's leg, Jonathan used butterfly adhesive strips to close the gash on my forehead. Then we settled into the front seats of the Bronco. It was that or sit on the ground, and the bench seat of the old SUV was much more comfortable. I gave Jonathan a bottle of water, and we opened a jar of peanut butter which we both spread on crackers to eat.

"After the Vanishing," he said, "I saw the flying ships all over the world. I was not a believer at the time in the supernatural. In my mind, as a physician and a professor, how could I believe in such things? No, I would never, until I saw the UFOs with my own eyes. Still, I had my doubts and went in search of what I could learn. That is when I discovered that much of the latest information on UFOs is not in books or magazines, or even blogs, but podcasts. I listened to Arthur Doll of course, and Reggie Davidson, but I could find no record of the idea that the aliens would take the children of the world away. So, I began to look for a counter point of view. And before long, I came to Lorenzo Maltza. I can't tell you what it was about him that I found so appealing. I think perhaps it was the fact that someone was posting his interview and lectures that talked specifically about the Rapture."

I felt my face flush. It seemed impossible to me that I was actually meeting someone who came to faith in Jesus because of the interviews and lectures that I posted online.

"His point of view wasn't just different, it felt inspired. He was talking about the God of Israel, and yet I felt like I didn't know this God. So, I studied the Torah and the Tanach. I listened to his case that Yeshua from Nazareth filled the prophecies in our own holy scriptures. How had I missed this? Why did my brothers and sisters so quickly dismiss this man who claimed to be the Mashiach, who's life and death are... dare I say it... his resurrection confirmed that he is the son of Almighty God? And then, I was forced to make a decision. Head knowledge isn't enough, and so I threw myself on the mercy of Yeshua, and he accepted me! And it's all because of Lorenzo Maltza. Tell me how you knew him."

"I had just left the Air Force, and he offered me a job," I told him. "I was helping him archive his interviews and lectures. He became my best friend, although he was more like a father to me."

"And yet you are here," Jonathan said. "That is truly a mystery."

"Well, it isn't because Lorenzo didn't share the truth with me. He did, over and over again, but I was stubborn. I thought I had plenty of time. And then one day, he rescued me from a demon that was trying to possess me."

Jonathan's eyes grew round, and he grabbed my arm. "You are a believer now, are you not?"

"I am," I said with a nod. "I recognized what happened when Lorenzo disappeared. And I gave my life to Jesus right then and there. Since then, I've been trying to share as many of his videos to the internet as possible. But as you know, that's become very dangerous."

"Indeed, but you have a high calling my friend. You must not stop sharing the good news."

"I don't plan to," I told him. "And thanks to you, I won't have to."

We spent the day together, sharing stories, checking on

LB and Allie, and going through the medical supplies I had salvaged from the shelter. It was, in many ways, a really wonderful day. Was I afraid of what had happened to Cat? Of course. Part of me wanted to track her down just to be sure she was okay, but I knew that would an impossible task. Staying where we were was a much better option, because she knew where to find us if she wanted to return. I wished that she could hear Jonathan and see that my work wasn't just a vain pursuit. But she had made her decision, and all I could do was pray for her.

Jonathan wasn't just a physician. He was an inventor of sorts. He collected some of the wood planks that had survived the earthquake without being smashed to bits and made Allie a much better splint. A long plank ran down the outside of her leg, and a shorter one was put on the inside. We also wrapped it with strips of cloth from my blanket to pad the splint and create a makeshift cast.

By that evening, LB was able to get up and move around. It was an incredible change. He was stiff and in a lot of pain, but he was improving. The next day we broke down the camp I had put together, loaded everything into the Bronco, and began a very slow trek across the field to the remains of the old barn. Fortunately, the classic SUV with its off-road suspension had no trouble with the uneven terrain. It wasn't a smooth ride, but it didn't jolt the passengers enough to make their injuries worse.

Jonathan and I got the trailer attached to the Bronco, and from there we were able to load up the remaining barrel of gasoline. Of course, part of me wanted to stay at the farm just in case Cat returned, but there was no real shelter there any longer. A tarp might keep us dry in a rain shower, but I didn't want to risk getting caught out in a storm. So, we set out, moving south, toward the first of the hidden caches.

Everything looked different. There were hills where the land had been flat, entire forests of trees were gone, but in some places, things looked almost normal. None of the old farmhouses survived the quake, but with a little investigation, we managed to find all the caches LB and Allie had made. Slowly the trailer began to fill with food, medical supplies, and survival gear. By the time they got all four caches loaded, half the trailer was filled with supplies. In many ways, it made me nervous. Even covered with a tarp, the trailer looked like a giant target. And we were down to just one pistol for protection. But there are other ways to protect what you have, and God was about to provide for us in a way I didn't expect.

# CHAPTER 12

WE MADE camp the first day of our journey by a small spring. There were some standing trees nearby; short, gnarly mesquite trees that were perfect for a little camp area. We ran a paracord between two trees and hung a tarp over it to make an A-shaped tent. But as the sun began to sink into the horizon, a group of people were spotted.

"How you want to play this?" LB asked.

We were standing by the Bronco and watching the strangers approach.

"They look pretty haggard," I said.

"Desperate people do desperate things," LB said. "If this comes to a fight, I won't be much help."

"If it comes to a fight, we're in real trouble," I said. "I don't think Jonathan will be much help."

"It's all on you, bro."

I didn't disagree and decided that it would be best to meet the newcomers before they reached our camp. If they were hostile, I felt like it would be better to know that upfront and put some distance between myself and the others. Allie had already been moved to the shade of the tent. With her bone set and the splint in place, she wasn't in as much pain, but she couldn't move anywhere on her own. And even with help, she was very slow. LB could get around okay, but he was stiff and careful. Moving the wrong way sent stabbing pains through his chest and abdomen.

Jonathan was an interesting guy, and a very compassionate doctor, but he was not a fighter. I didn't really think of myself as one either, which meant we were extremely vulnerable to anyone with weapons or a few people looking to take what we had by force.

"I'm going to meet them," I told LB. "If anything happens, get Allie to the Bronco and get out of here as fast as you can."

"I don't like that plan," he said.

"We don't have a lot of options here. I'd rather they didn't get too close before we find out what they want."

"It's your decision, Hank, just be careful. We can't afford to lose you."

"Thanks," I said, knowing that in reality, I didn't bring a lot to the table. I was the spiritual mentor of the group, answering questions when I could, but I was still just a baby Christian myself. If not for Lorenzo's interviews and lectures, I wouldn't know anything. I had salvaged several books from the farm, which we all passed around. Jonathan was especially interested in anything to do with his faith in God, and the Judgments of the Tribulation. He was Jewish, and excited to see his people accept Jesus as the Messiah.

LB gave me a reassuring pat on the back, and I set off

walking quickly toward the strangers. As they came into focus, I realized that they weren't armed. At least none of them were carrying weapons out in the open. That didn't mean they weren't a threat, but I was hopeful we wouldn't be slaughtered for our supplies.

"Hello!" I called out as the group of strangers drew close.

"Howdy," a tall man with a cowboy hat said.

The strangers were sizing me up. I saw more than one taking note of my pistol which was still in the hip holster.

"My name's Hank," I said.

"Trey," the man in the cowboy hat said. "We met a friend of yours."

I was surprised and a little frightened. But then the group, about twelve in all, parted, and in the midst of them was Cat. I couldn't believe it. She had one arm in a sling fashioned from a few dirty rags, and both her eyes were black from a blow to the face. But I would have recognized her anywhere.

She moved slowly toward me. The rest of the group just watched. My entire body was buzzing with emotion.

"Cat," I said.

"It's me," she said. "You were right."

"I'm just so glad you're alive."

"Me too," she said. "Trey and his friends found me. I broke my arm in the earthquake."

"Are you okay?"

"I will be," she said. "Do you think you might..."

She didn't finish her question, and I couldn't stop myself. I went to her and threw my arms around her. For all I knew the group had tortured her for information and was there to steal everything we had, but I honestly didn't care. I had numbed my pain by staying busy, taking care of LB and Allie, getting everything together for our trip south. But in the quiet moments, my heart ached so bad I wanted to die. I didn't think I would ever see Cat again, yet there she was. I couldn't help but wrap my arms around her and hold her close.

To my surprise the group clapped and cheered. Cat even laughed a little.

"I didn't know if you would take me back," she said.

"I love you," I said over and over. "I love you."

After a few moments of blissful reunion, I stepped back and looked at Trey. "Thank you for taking care of her."

"Did what we could but that ain't much," he said. "We're just trying to make it another day, you know?"

"I do know," I said. "But we have food, water, medical supplies." I looked at Cat. "We even met a doctor after the quake."

"We don't want to impose, but we won't turn down a free meal and some rest," Trey said. "To be honest, that sounds like heaven right about now."

I looked at Cat, and she nodded. "They're good people, Hank." So, I led the group back to our camp. Introductions were made. Jonathan went to work helping the injured. Cat had fractured her humerus just a few inches above her elbow. Jonathan said it would heal in time if she didn't use it. She was all too happy to get some rest and have a few pain killers. She had shared all her medical supplies with Trey's group.

I spent the next hour building a fire and boiling water. We made spaghetti with canned sauce, simple and filling. Everyone was hungry. Trey's group didn't even have water filters or a way to make fire. Soon, the group was settled in the shade, eating the first meal they had enjoyed since the great earthquake. There were eight men in the group, including Trey and four women besides Cat. Most had been injured in the earthquake. Many had lost friends. They were all exhausted and frightened.

"I told them you know what's going on," Cat said. "I mean, I tried to explain it all, but still don't really understand everything."

"You don't have to understand," I told her. "Believing is what's important."

"I do," Cat said. "After the earthquake, I was hurt and dazed, but the one thing I realized is that you were right all along Hank. God is real. I promised he could do whatever he wanted with me, as long as I could see you again. Trey and his friends came along the next day. And now, here we are."

Trey ambled over to us. He was tall, very thin, and probably twice my age. He wore blue jeans and a tattered western shirt, the kind with snap buttons, and a southwest print. I could tell he had lost weight. His jeans were cinched up around the waste with a thick, leather belt that he had punched new holes in. On his feet were dusty, well worn, cowboy boots.

"Mind if I join you two?" He asked. "I hate to spoil the reunion, but Cat says you know what's going on. And that you predicted everything that's happened since the Vanishing."

"I didn't predict it," I said. "It's in the Bible."

When I looked up, the entire group of newcomers were looking at me. They weren't judging, they were eager to hear what I had to say. Glancing at LB, he gave me an approving nod, and Jonathan was grinning like he had just won the lottery.

"Tell us more," Trey said. "We're all ears."

"Okay," I said, and laid out the entire scenario, from the Rapture through the six seals of God's judgment on the earth that we had endured.

"So, what comes next?" One of the women in the group asked.

"The seventh seal judgment is the preparation for the next set of judgments, call the trumpet judgments," I explained. "It'll be marked by thunder, rumbling, and more earthquakes."

"Oh, no," an older man said. "Not again."

"These quakes won't be as bad as the last one," I said. "But there are more dangerous times ahead. The point of it all is to get your attention. God is at work to draw us back to him."

"So how do we get to him?" the woman asked.

"The Bible is clear on this point," I said. "Everyone who believes that Jesus is the son of God, that he died on a cross for your sins, and that he rose on the third day, will be saved. All you have to do is believe."

I spent the rest of the evening and late into the night answering questions. LB and Jonathan joined in. Eventually, fatigue got the best of us all. People were given blankets from the shelter. They wrapped up in them and slept around the fire that had been built. I stayed on watch as long as I could. An hour or two after midnight LB came over to relieve me.

"You should be sleeping," I told him.

"So should you," he said. "You're pushing it too hard. Get some rest."

"No, I'll be fine. You need to sleep more than me."

"And I will," he said. "I can sleep all day in the Bronco if I want to. You can't. Besides, I might not be much good in a fight, but I can make some noise if bad guys come prowling around."

"Are you sure?"

"Absolutely. It's impossible for me to get comfortable laying on the ground, man. These damn ribs hurt too much. I'll keep watch, you sleep."

"Alright," I said, drawing my pistol. "You know how to use this, right?"

"Yeah, I think I got it," he said, and we both chuckled, although laughing caused LB even more pain.

"Sorry," I said.

"Go on, get some rest. That's an order."

I found Cat curled up beside Allie, who to my surprise was awake. I dropped down beside Cat, pulling my own blanket from my go bag.

"She's back," Allie whispered.

"Thank God," I said. "Are you okay?"

"Yeah, it feels good to be out of the Bronco at first, but then the cold sets in and starts the break aching pretty bad. But don't worry about me. I'll doze off eventually."

I didn't have any problem falling asleep. My body was so tired that even laying on the ground felt good. I wrapped my blanket around me and laid down behind Cat. She woke up long enough to scoot back into me. I put an arm around her, and she sighed. The next thing I knew the sun was up, and Jonathan was giving me a gentle shake.

That's how it went for the next few weeks. By day, we

moved slowly south. The injured and exhausted rode on the flatbed trailer. Those who were healthier, myself included, walked. As we passed places that weren't destroyed by the earthquake, a house here, a store there, people from our group left us, and other people, mostly people all alone, joined our caravan. Somehow, the Bronco was getting fantastic gas mileage. And while everyone was anxious to hear about what the Bible taught concerning the seven years of Tribulation, not everyone believed. A few were even belligerent when I brought up the topic. They accused me of all sorts of vile things and swore that I would be executed when the authorities caught up to me. But for a long time, there were no authorities, only survivors looking to make it through one more day.

Trey and Cat both put their faith in Christ Jesus. Over the weeks, as we moved down toward the Mexico border, people grew in the faith and recovered from their injuries. It was a happy time. Probably the highlight of that period was the transformation that took place in Jonathan. The Bible says that after the sixth seal judgment, God calls for his servants to be sealed. 144,000 Jewish people were to be set apart as witnesses to their fellow Jews, and to the world, of God's love and soon return. Just before we reached the border, Jonathan got sealed.

Only a few of us saw it happen. LB, Allie, Cat, and Trey were sitting up with me one night, talking. Suddenly Jonathan got up. He looked startled.

"You okay, Doc?" LB asked.

"Did you hear that?" Jonathan asked. "Did you hear someone calling my name? In Hebrew?"

"Don't even know what your name is in Hebrew," Trey pointed out.

"Yonatan," the doctor said. "In Hebrew, it is Yonatan."

"We didn't hear anything," I told him.

"That is strange," he said.

And suddenly there was a bright light. I know that sounds odd, but there's no other way to describe it. It wasn't a beam of light, but a warm, golden light suddenly lit up our camp. The sleepers didn't notice it, but I was shocked. I felt my friends tense up beside me. Even Allie, who was using the crutches from the farmhouse shelter to get around by that point, took a few steps back.

"What is happening?" LB asked.

"I don't know," I told him.

"Hank?" Cat said, squeezing my arm.

The light seemed to settle onto Jonathan. It was so bright that we had trouble seeing him. And then, we could make out a couple of other people in the light with him. But not ordinary people. They were big, at least eight feet tall, and very muscular. I couldn't make out what they wore or their facial features. They were barely visible in the bright light. The phenomenon lasted a minute or so. Then the big visitors rose upward. I remember looking up, expecting to get a better view of them outside the golden light, but they weren't visible. It was like they just disappeared. The light faded quickly, but Jonathan didn't. He was glowing for several hours.

"What just happened?" LB said. "Someone explain it to me."

"I don't know," I said.

"Was it aliens?" Cat asked.

"There's no such thing," I told her.

"Angels then," Trey said. "Had to be."

"He's right," Jonathan said, his voice trembling with awe.

"What's that on your head?" Allie asked.

Jonathan was bald on top, although around his ears and the back of his head he had hair. But what had been clear, tanned skin before, there was now a subtle outline. It wasn't easy to make out, we could only catch glimpses of it no matter how hard we looked. It was as if the symbol on his head was made of the same golden light, but only reflected into the visible spectrum occasionally. All I could say about it for certain was that it was like nothing I had seen before. Not a symbol or writing that was of this world.

"I think I was just sealed," Jonathan said. "They were angels. Did you see them?"

"We saw something," Cat said.

"I didn't see no wings," LB said.

"Who says they have to have wings to be angels?" Allie teased.

"Well, that's what you think of," he explained. "No halos either."

"We saw the light," I said. "And two figures, but they were hard to make out."

"What's it mean?" Trey asked. "How come you got sealed, or whatever?"

"Adonai told me that I am his witness. I am to make my way to Israel, telling everyone I meet along the way of his goodness, and his judgment."

He left us to sit near the fire with his Bible. I'm pretty sure he was there all night. The next day there was no trace of his mark or seal, but our doctor was a changed man. There were always people in our group who didn't believe. Jonathan began to teach them, in fact, he taught us all. He showed us things in scripture none of us could have guessed were there, from what the meanings of Adam's descents' names say when put together, to the ancient Jewish custom of marking scrolls with instructions and seals as a way of authenticating what was inside. Suddenly, the seven seal judgments made sense. They weren't just a metaphor about what was taking place in Heaven, the seals were the instructions on the deed to earth. Only Jesus was worthy of opening them and taking possession of our world. It was fascinating, but the one drawback was knowing that Jonathan's time with us was limited.

The weeks following the great earthquake were wonderful and restorative. Cat and I were back together. As we traveled south, we saw more and more people on the move. Some we helped, others we avoided. We didn't have an arsenal of weapons, but our group was large enough to discourage most bad actors to stay away. Unfortunately, the peace wouldn't last. Nor would the freedom to proclaim the truth. As spring gave way to summer, and we moved into Northern Mexico, survival became exponentially more difficult.

# CHAPTER 13

"SIR, PULL OVER PLEASE," a man in a solid black uniform ordered.

I say man, but he was like no one I had ever seen before. We were two days into Mexico, still moving slowly. Still picking up people who needed help. Our supplies had taken a hit, but that was okay. The Bronco was still holding up. There were no roads anymore, although pontoon bridges had been set up across the Rio Grande to facilitate the mass migration to the Yucatan Peninsula which Paul Eon, the High Administrator, as he was being called, had ordered people to do. The Bronco, with its fancy suspension and off-road tires, made the need for roads obsolete. We moved slowly but surely, south, our fuel supplies being topped off by the occasional car or truck we passed that still had gas in their tanks.

Eventually we reached a government checkpoint. I'm not sure where. The towns were in shambles. Most were completely destroyed, and others were mere fractions of what they had once been. We came to a settlement with large government trucks. I wanted to avoid it, but we feared that going around them might be more suspicious than not.

Trey had made his living as a carpenter. He used some salvaged wood to make a hidden compartment under the flatbed trailer to keep our Bibles and books on the end times hidden. We took turns driving and kept the injured on the trailer, so they weren't exhausted by the daily hike. Allie was still riding in the Bronco, although she had moved to the front passenger seat. She sat close to me and kept her broken leg stretched out along the bench seat. Behind us, LB watched our backs, along with a couple of other people with injuries to their legs and feet. Nearly two dozen more were crowded onto the flatbed trailer.

Trey and Jonathan were walking when we reached the settlement, which was really a government checkpoint. The walkers were usually a short way behind the Bronco. I still had my pistol, although I was grateful that I hadn't needed to use it since before the earthquake. We stopped near one of the government trucks that were surrounded by officials in black uniforms. They all had tactical rifles slung over their shoulders and more weapons hanging from heavy belts.

When we got close, I could see that they wore some type of armor under their uniforms, but what really shocked me was the size of the officials. They were all over seven feet in height. Their shoulders were broad, and their facial features seemed exaggerated too: big eyes, big noses, and prominent brows and cheekbones. When they spoke, their voices were surprisingly deep.

I pulled the Bronco to a stop and shut off the engine. It

was difficult not to feel afraid. Not only were we officially outlaws because of our faith in Jesus, but the new government officials were huge. And there was no doubt they were security personnel. I felt incredibly self-conscious, and wished I could signal for Cat to stay away.

"What's this?" one of the security people asked, pointing at the Bronco and trailer with his rifle.

"We're heading south," I said. "Helping as many people as we can along the way."

The security people eyed us suspiciously.

"Do you have IDs?" one of them asked.

"Not all of us," I said. "We're lucky to have the clothes on our backs, to be perfectly honest."

"Alright, exit the vehicle. You'll be searched and registered in the NARA database. Please hand over your firearm."

Don't get me wrong, I didn't want to just hand over the only weapon I had. But I had serious doubts that it would be of much value against the superhuman guards. I took the Beretta M9 from the holster, ejected the clip, and pulled the slide back to eject the round in the chamber. It flashed in the air, flipping enough over end. The security man's hand shot out and snatched the bullet from the air. It happened so fast I had trouble believing it.

"What a relic," the guard said, taking the old pistol and ammo clip.

"Any other weapons?" one of the other security members asked.

"Just pocketknives," I said. "We've got some tools in the trailer."

"Come with me," another of the guards said.

We were taken into a large, white tent and separated by gender. LB stayed close by me. His ribs were healing well, but he was still stiff and weak.

"This one had a gun," one of the security members told a regular looking man in a white doctor's coat.

"Strip, please," the doctor said.

"Is that really necessary?" LB asked.

"You are entering NARA territory," the doctor said. "All citizens get free healthcare, food, access to oral hygiene facilities. It's a weapon-free zone. You absolutely need to strip down, get inspected, and approved before moving on."

"Sounds fair," I said, even though in truth I found it to be intrusive and unnecessary.

We did our best to stay clean, but most people only had a single set of clothes. And finding clean water was difficult. I had no doubt we were pretty ripe as we stripped down and waited for the doctor to clear us. Once no communicable diseases were spotted, we carried our dirty clothes into another tent where portable showers were set up. The water wasn't hot, but it wasn't cold either. We had moved far enough south that the days were pretty warm. The semi-cool showers were refreshing, and our clothes were put in bags until they could be properly sanitized. We were given flimsy scrubs to wear as we met with NARA representatives who took down our names. I was a little fearful that LB and I might be in trouble for skipping out after the fall of Camp Abilene. I had been told I was being recalled to active duty, but no official paperwork had been shared with me. And while I had served in the United States Air Force, it was abundantly clear that we were no longer in the United States.

We were photographed, our fingerprints were registered using electronic devices, and we were issued new ID's. Mine said NARA citizen, level three, and I was instructed to keep it on my person at all times. We were also given three thousand digital dollars, our universal income. The sum would be issued into our NARA account every month.

"Three thousand," LB said as we carried our bag of dirty clothes from the government center toward a group of buildings that looked to be businesses. "You think that's a little or a lot?"

"We'll find out soon," I said, pointing at what appeared to be a cafe."

The buildings were made of stone and plaster. None had survived the earthquake unscathed, but they were mostly intact. New plaster was visible in places, as were tarps to cover holes in the tile rooftops. We sat down at an empty table that faced the tents and trailers of the government checkpoint. I wanted to be sure that our friends could find us easily.

"Look at this," LB said. "They have beer. You think it's any good?"

"I wasn't much of a drinker before the rapt— Vanishings," I said, glancing around nervously.

LB did the same. There were still videos posted online of beheadings every single day. The persecution of Christians was still going strong in all the populated areas. We could tell from the videos that there were areas in the world that hadn't been as devastated by God's judgments as North America, much of which was still a radioactive wasteland. Canada hadn't been hit with nukes, but the fallout had created a severe winter that had yet to let up. Without power, and dealing with more snow than ever before, the survivors were moving south like everyone else. We would have to be very careful about what we said and who we said it too from that point forward.

"Ten bucks a glass for beer seems mighty high," LB said. "But I'll pay. What are you drinking my man?"

"I'll stick with lemonade," I told him.

He got up and went inside to order. A help wanted sign hung in the window. It was printed in English and Spanish. I could smell something being cooked in the cafe, or cantina. It smelled spicy, although I couldn't tell what it was.

LB came back to the table with two glasses and a basket of chips. A small cup of dark red salsa was nestled among the tortilla chips.

"The beer ain't half bad," LB said as he sat down his bounty. "Careful with the salsa though. The proprietor said it's pretty hot."

"It almost feels like the good old days," I said.

"Hell yeah. I hope Allie comes out soon. Makes me nervous the longer she's in there."

"It has to be difficult washing up with a broken leg," I said.

"That's what I'm talking about," LB said. "They should let me help her."

"You know, I'm glad you have each other," I told him, taking a sip of the lemonade.

It was more sour than sweet. I had no idea what they were using to make the drink, but not sugar. The drink had a chemical aftertaste that wasn't very pleasant, but it was the first drink I had tasted besides water in a long time, and at ten digital dollars a glass, I wasn't going to complain.

"Yeah," LB said with a big smile. "She's a good woman. Too young for me, really, but I don't reckon anyone is seriously expecting to survive long enough to die of old age."

"She makes you happy," I said. "And I can tell she's glad to be with you too."

"She's not the kind of woman to show weakness if she can help it," LB said, munching on a chip. "Losing her kids really hardened her heart. It's hard for her to be vulnerable now. Not that I'm really the sensitive type, but there are moments when we really connect."

I knew what he meant. In all the long months I had known LB, I had never heard him talk about anyone the way he was opening up about Allie.

Trey was the next member of our group to come through. He looked frustrated and a little embarrassed. His scrubs didn't look great with cowboy boots and his wide brimmed hat.

"You believe this non-sense," Trey said, pointing over his shoulder with his thumb. "They thought I was carrying a weapon up my keister. What a bunch of idiots."

"You might not want to be so vocal with criticism," I said in a low tone.

"Yeah," he said, sitting down. "You're probably right. What was with the size of those guards?"

"Super soldiers," LB said. "The military has been experimenting with them for decades."

"I thought that was just make believe," Trey grumbled.

"No, it's real. And it isn't just the military," I explained. "Lorenzo was pretty certain that genetic manipulation has been going on for thousands of years. Almost all alien abduction stories have an element of sexual abuse. Women who claim to have been abducted multiple times nearly always become pregnant. Then after carrying the child for a few months, are suddenly not pregnant anymore. There are even documented cases with ultrasounds, blood levels, the whole nine yards. Then suddenly, no baby in the womb. Most ufologists believe the visitors have been doing genetic experimentation for a long time."

"Man, this is giving me the creeps," Trey said. "How's the beer?"

"Sour," LB said. "But it beats the hell out of no beer."

"I hear that. How much was it?"

"Ten credits," LB told him.

"Ten! Good grief, that's robbery. My fifteen hundred monthly stipend won't last long, that's for sure."

"Fifteen hundred?" LB asked.

"Yeah, why?" Trey asked. "How much did you get?"

"Three thousand," I told him.

"Well dang! The hits just keep coming. How'd you end up with twice as much as me?"

"I don't know," I said. "Let me see your ID."

He handed the laminated card to me. His picture looked odd. I had rarely seen Trey without his cowboy hat on. It had his name on it, and his government level was five."

"He's level five," I told LB.

"I guess carpenters aren't as valued as soldiers," he replied.

"Which is total BS in my opinion," Trey complained. "I mean look around. They need builders now more than ever."

"Don't worry," LB said. "I was just about to get another round. I got you."

"I'm good," I told him.

"You sure?" LB asked me.

"Positive. I'll wait here."

It was a long wait before Cat and Allie came out. In fact, Cat was nearly half an hour behind our group going into the government checkpoint. But Allie had gotten x-rays and a full leg brace with Velcro straps after getting cleaned up. Cat had found her struggling in the shower and was able to help. They came out of the checkpoint together. Allie was still on crutches and looked tired. Cat walked beside her and carried their bags of clothes.

After a quick update, I found out that Allie was level three, and Cat was five. When Jonathan finally came out, he was a level one. His income was five thousand NARA digital dollars, and he was required to report to Mérida ASAP.

"It looks like this is goodbye," he said. "The soldiers are taking me straight to the new capital soon."

"That's too bad," I said. "I was hoping we would have more time."

"Yeshua has a plan," he whispered to me. "Be very careful my friend."

"And you," I said. "We'll be lifting you. All of us."

"That is more valuable than gold," he said with the smile I was so accustomed to seeing. "Or digital dollars, I suppose."

We all shared hugs and prayed for him, although no one bowed their head or closed their eyes. We had to be careful and adapt to the dangers of our new society, where adherence to anything other than Pax Davino was strictly forbidden. In time, certain words like Lord, Savior, and even Father would trigger AI watchdogs. But that day, we were able to send Jonathan off with as much support as we could give him.

My mind was on the books hidden under the flatbed trailer. Our Bibles and prophecy books were out of reach. I wasn't even sure what the government was going to do with the Bronco and trailer. But it seemed obvious that they weren't going to hand it back over any time soon.

"Until we meet again, my friends," Jonathan said with tears in his eyes, despite the smile on his face.

"Thank you for everything, Doc," LB told him, patting his ribcage.

"You really saved the day," Allie said.

"It was my honor. I have learned so much," he said. "And I treasure you all."

Cat stepped forward and kissed his cheek. She whispered something to him, but I didn't hear what she said.

"May our friend bless you and keep you," I said. "And make his face shine upon you."

"And be gracious to you," Jonathan said, completing the passage of scripture that was a traditional Jewish blessing. "May he lift up his countenance upon you and give you peace."

We all hugged again, and then Jonathan left us. I should have seen that everything was changing. We had left the freedom to be ourselves behind and entered what was certainly enemy territory. Part of me wondered if perhaps we would have been better off just hunkering down somewhere and trying to ride out the next five and half years. The Sotos, my foster parents, had always taught me not to go looking for trouble. But I couldn't deny that we had helped a lot of people. There were believers because we had the opportunity to share some food and medicine with people on our trek south, who might never have come to faith in Jesus otherwise.

Jonathan wasn't the only person that left us there at the checkpoint station. Trey was a level five citizen, but his skills were in high demand. The cafe owner gave him all the food and beer he wanted in exchange for fixing up the building and constructing a small apartment onto the back of the cafe. In addition to the cafe, there was a store with clothes and basic necessities and another renting tents for travelers to sleep in while they were there. Another business was washing clothes by hand, and a government sponsored vendor was selling smart phones that were NARA approved, which no doubt meant they were programmed to spy on everything a person said or did.

To leave the check point, citizens had two options. They could walk or they could wait for the monthly bus. LB and I went immediately after saying good-bye to Jonathan and spoke to the security team about our Bronco.

"Do you have proof of ownership?" A big woman with a wide jaw and bright red hair said.

"No," I said. "But we drove it all the way from North Texas. It's our vehicle."

"I understand your position," the woman said. "But the North American Regional Administration is seizing all vehicles. Citizens will be housed in areas with everything you need in just a fifteen-minute walk."

"That's crazy," LB declared. "My lady broke her leg in the earthquake. She needs special transportation."

"I don't make the rules," the woman said, sounding like

Darth Vader. Her massive cheekbones and wide lips were so exaggerated she looked like a cartoon character come to life.

I did my best not to stare as I argued. "So that's it? You're just stealing it?"

"You'll get a ten thousand credit advance. Once the vehicle is valued by a member of the transportation department, any discrepancy will be issued to your account."

"So, no one will have cars?" LB asked.

"Public transportation will be available," the woman said. "It's part of the Climate Crisis Remittance Plan."

"What about our trailer?" I asked. "We had some gear too."

"Look around," the woman said. "It's up to the government to provide for the greater good. You're getting a monthly payment, aren't you? You'll get housing in or near Mérida too."

"But we had food, survival gear," I argued.

"You can get whatever you need at the commissary," she said. "There's nothing more I can do. If you want to make a complaint to the government when you reach Mérida that's up to you."

She waved us away and I decided not to push it anymore. She scanned my ID, added the credits to my account, and told me everything was in the system. I would be notified if it was decided that I was due more.

"Thank you for your help," I said, trying not to sound as aggravated as I felt.

We walked back out of the government tents near the checkpoint and back to where Cat and Allie waited with Trey.

"No luck?" Cat asked.

"None," I said. "They're keeping the Bronco and the trailer."

"How are we supposed to go anywhere without it?" Allie said.

"There's public transportation," I told her. "We can wait on that."

"What about... you know," Cat said. "With the trailer?"

"All our stuff was appropriated," LB said.

"Even the stuff they don't know about?" Trey whispered.

"Yeah, we can't just hang around after they find that," Cat said.

"No, we can't," I told her. "And we can't leave it either. That trailer is associated with my name. If they find that stuff, I'm a dead man."

"So, what are we gonna do about it?" LB said.

"First, we're going to spend the ten thousand credits on supplies," I said. "We're not leaving this place empty handed."

"About that," Trey said. "I been talking to Senor Ramas over at the Cantina. He's pretty desperate for some help. I doubt I could do much better than he's offering anywhere else."

"So, you're staying here?" Cat asked.

"It's a good option for me," he said. "Everyone wants to head south, so I'll be in pretty high demand."

"Can't blame you for that," I said.

"We weren't ever supposed to all stay together," LB added. "We gotta spread the good news, right?"

"That's right," I jumped in. "Just be careful about it."

"Trey, I..." Cat was clearly emotional. She had bonded

with the older cowboy. He had saved her after the earthquake and been an eager and enthusiastic new believer. She felt a strong connection with him.

"Hey now, I'll be okay," he said, giving her a gentle side hug. "I'm doing what I was made to do. And you've gotta do what you were born to do."

"Which is what?" Cat asked.

"Take care of this man, for one thing," Trey said, slapping me on the back. "He can't do what he's supposed to do without you. That's for certain."

"God's going to use us all," I said gently, taking her hand.

"I just hate seeing people go," Cat said, wiping the tears that had rolled out onto her cheeks. "First Jonathan, now Trey."

"Who knows," I said. "Trey being up here on the border might be incredibly useful to us."

"And if the work dries up, I'll be headed south," Trey said. "Keep an eye out for me."

"We will," LB said. "No doubt about that."

"And our stuff?" Allie asked. "What's the plan there?"

"We'll have to go and get it," I said, as if it were as simple as stopping by the local library and getting a book.

"But first," LB said with enthusiasm. "We's got some shoppin' to do!"

# CHAPTER 14

THE COMMISSARY WAS A SMALL STORE. Most of the clothes were second hand. We got tarps that were used, but whole and clean. We got wide-brimmed straw hats and insulated metal water containers. The government agents at the checkpoint had taken everything from us, including my pistol and our pocketknives. Weapons were illegal, so we settled for a camp shovel and a hatchet. We got farrow rods to get fires going and grabbed some blankets.

At the tent hotel we got our clothes washed, including our go bags, which had been emptied by the guards at the checkpoint. Tents were ninety-credits a night and slept two people. We rented two, then got a meal from the cantina. It was some type of chicken enchiladas, but nothing tasted right.

"Senor Ramas told me it's meat grown in a vat," Trey said as we gathered for one last meal. "Not sure how they make the cheese, but it ain't from milk."

"Cows produce too much pollution," LB said with a

chuckle. "The climate warriors were always after the farmers."

"So, everything is fake now," Allie said. "Wonderful."

"The salsa's legit," Trey said. "It might be made from canned vegetables, but it's good."

"And hot enough to kill anything that might hurt us," Cat said. "I hope there's better food wherever we end up."

"Mérida," LB said. "I looked it up. It's right out on the peninsula, not far from the coast. We could maybe get a little shack on the beach, make the best of it."

"Sounds idyllic," I said. "But you might not want to be right on the coast."

"We might not have a choice," LB said.

"What are you thinking?" Allie asked.

"The second trumpet," I said quietly. "Something big hits the ocean. Kills a third of the fish and swamps a third of the seacraft."

"You think it'll be bad in the gulf?" Allie asked.

"I'm just thinking beachfront property might not be the best investment," I said.

Of course, we were still a long way from Mérida, and the seventh seal judgment had yet to be released. The truth was, I had my doubts we would survive much longer. I hadn't uploaded any videos to the internet, but I had several ready to go. Of course, I didn't have my phone. It was hidden in the flatbed trailer's hidden compartment with our Bibles and prophecy books.

After dinner we watched the sun go down, then climbed into our tents. Two hours later, LB and I got out and went for a walk. As we surveilled the checkpoint and the security around the flatbed trailer, we had a difficult conversation.

"I been thinking," LB said. "Allie would never admit it, but she can't walk out of here."

For some reason, I hadn't thought about it. Her leg was healing, but it wasn't strong enough that she could walk without crutches. And the last thing I wanted was to push her to the point that she damaged her leg beyond repair.

"So, what are you thinking of doing then?" I asked.

"We gotta wait for that government transportation," he said. "She can't walk, and I won't leave her."

"Maybe walking out is a bad idea for everyone," I said. "It's still a long way down to the new capital."

"We can all ride together," LB said. "There's safety in numbers."

"I'll talk to Cat about it," I said. "But we have to get our stuff back first. I'll go over the fence. You keep watch."

"That's a military fence, man. You don't go over it, you go under."

The trailer was parked with the Bronco and several other vehicles in a fenced off part of the government outpost. There was a maintenance pavilion set up right next to the vehicles, and beyond that were the oversized tents for the security personnel. The tent we had rented for the night was a simple camping tent, just something to get keep the rain off, not that there was any rain. But the NARA Security members had nine-foot-tall, framed tents, probably with cots and small camp tables inside. We could see that a few of the security people had lights of some kind in their tents.

"Okay, I go under," I said. "This is my first break in."

"Not mine, I'm sad to say. Back in the day I was known for getting in places: concerts, movies, even a few houses and cars."

"Well, you get me in," I said. "I'll get our stuff and get back out again."

"They're walking the perimeter," LB said. "Two sentries. They're only five minutes apart."

"That doesn't leave us much time," I said.

"No, only half of that before they'll be on the same side of their compound as you."

"So, what are you telling me?" I asked.

"I'm saying, you gotta get in quick, then hide. Wait for the guard to pass, about five minutes. Then get our stuff and hide again. Wait until you see the guard pass, then count off five minutes again."

"Piece of cake," I said, starting to feel nervous.

"Yeah, let's hope they can't see in the dark."

"Oh crap, I didn't think about that."

"I saw a report once, right before I hung-up my spurs the first time," LB said. "Money was being funneled into secret programs through the aid being supposedly sent to Ukraine during their war with Russia."

"I remember that," I said. "We gave them over a hundred billion in aid."

"Supposedly," LB said. "That money was used for all kinds of black ops. But from what I read, the super soldier program was to enhance strength and speed obviously, but they were gene editing too. Trying to glean special abilities from animals. All kinds of crazy shi... Sorry, I'm trying to watch my language these days."

"So, the guards might be able to see in the dark," I said.

"Night vision like a big cat and maybe even long-range vision like an eagle," LB said, shrugging his shoulders. "At the time I thought it was nonsense. You can't take DNA from an animal and add it to a human being. I mean that's some real comic book stuff. But then, along came Covid and suddenly we're using RNA to deliver gene editing vaccines. When that didn't kill us all, I figured they had what they needed to do all kinds of scary experiments."

"It's starting to sound like the United States was just as bad as the Nazis during World War Two."

"Not the country, man. Just the politicians and the people pulling strings behind closed doors."

"Not the least of which was Satan," I said. "Sometimes I forget how influential the enemy truly is."

"Yeah, we're talking about a spiritual army at work in the lives of powerbrokers all over the world. They hide their tracks, but they're cooking up something big and we never even saw it until it was too late."

"Well, the good news is they lose," I said softly. "Satan gets his way for the next few years, but it won't last more than seven from the signing of the peace treaty with Israel."

"Wish we had done a better job of keeping up with the dates," LB said.

"All we have to do is count the days from when Paul Eon declares himself to be God in the Jewish temple. That'll be big news. When that happens, all we have to do, is try to stay alive for twelve hundred and sixty days."

"That all?" LB said with a chuckle. "No problem."

"I think it's time," I said, looking at the fence.

LB had been right. The sections in between the supports weren't taut. A few were even bowed up some. If I could get to one, I could pull it up and roll under it.

"Let's do it then," LB said.

My heart was pounding from fear as we dashed to the fence. I had no idea what the security agents would do if they caught me. Would they shoot first and ask questions later? Would they arrest us? Could we possibly talk our way out of the situation? There was no time to ponder what might happen. As soon as we reached the fence, I dropped to my knees.

LB leaned over and yanked up the fence. To our surprise, it pulled up easily. I got down on my stomach and rolled under the chain-links. As soon as I was in the security area, LB lowered the fence and used his boot to make sure I hadn't left a mark on the rocky soil. There wasn't much vegetation in the area, and our tracks would be visible if the guards were studying the ground.

"I'll make a circuit," LB said. "Don't take any chances."

"Roger that," I said, before getting to my feet.

I duckwalked to the nearest vehicle and hid on the far side. Laying low, I could see under the old Humvee. I stayed by the tires to minimize my own exposure. Thankfully, either the guards couldn't see that well in the dark, or, like most people stuck standing watch for hours, they were too bored to be vigilant. I was afraid when I saw the guard's huge boots approaching the area of the fence where I had rolled under. But, he or she, I couldn't tell from where I lay, didn't stop. They didn't seem to notice anything out of the ordinary. As the guard strolled on by, I felt a huge sense of relief.

Waiting was difficult, too. I had to give the guard time to move far enough past my location before I crawled over to the flatbed trailer. When I felt like enough time had passed, I made my way to the trailer and crawled underneath. That wasn't necessary to get our stuff, but I didn't want to take the chance that I might be seen. From inside my coat, I pulled out my new backpack. The hidden compartment had not been found. Inside were five Bibles, including Lorenzo's. I carefully placed them in the backpack, then waited.

I couldn't see the guard from where I lay, but I heard the heavy boots on the sand and rocks. They made a unique, grinding crunch with each step. It seemed obvious to me that they were big, heavy people. Yet they didn't trudge like most people. Their steps were measured, deliberate, and precise. There was a rhythmic quality to their gait. I waited until the sounds faded and pulled out the books on Bible prophecy. They were all showing signs of wear and tear. The spines were wrinkled, and the pages tended to fan out. Some had been marked up by members of the group who read them as we traveled south. I stuffed them into the backpack. The last item was my old smart phone. It no longer served its primary function. There were no cell phone towers left to boost the signal up into space. But Wi-Fi was still good. In some places it was stronger than in others, but the plan was to upload videos of me teaching the end times prophecies found in the Bible, and comparing them with what was actually happening in the world. I slipped the phone into the interior pocket of my coat.

Another guard passed while I lay still as a statue, and then I shimmed out from under the flatbed trailer. I moved back to my original hiding place and waited. A few moments later the guard passed again. Every time they came close, I got scared. But each time, they didn't stop or seem concerned. When the guard passed, I breathed a little easier. A minute later LB was back at the fence. I hurried out, pushed the backpack under the fence ahead of me, and rolled out again.

LB dusted me off as I got to my feet, and we started walking.

"Did they notice anything?" I asked.

"Nah, you were like a ghost in there."

"God is with us," I said.

"You know it."

We were on our way back to the area of tents but hadn't gotten far when a light flashed on behind us. We stopped as if the beam of light had some sort of power over us.

"Hey, you, there," a deep, menacing voice said. "Wait just a minute."

I was trying to look casual, but my heart was pounding in my chest like a jackhammer. My entire body trembled like a leaf in the wind. I hadn't been scared when I was accused of being a Christian at Camp Abilene. I was mere seconds away from death, and I hadn't been afraid. So why did the guards make me so nervous? I couldn't say, but LB and I turned around and squinted into the light.

"What are you two doing out so late?" the guard asked.

"Couldn't sleep," LB said. "We decided to take a stroll."

"I've seen you walking around the duty station," the guard said. "There was only one of you then?"

"No," LB said. "It was always the two of us."

"I only saw one," the guard said.

"What can I say, man. It's dark out here. We just went for a walk, that's all."

"What's your names?" the guard asked.

"Barski and Downes," LB said.

"What's up with your friend? He doesn't talk?"

"I talk," I said, fearing that my voice was too shaky and might give away my fear.

"We didn't mean to break any rules," LB said.

"You need to stay in the settlement at night," the guard said. "If I see you around here again, I'll run you in."

"Yes sir," LB said.

"We won't," I assured the guard.

He clicked off his flashlight and started back for the government compound. LB and I turned around and walked in silence toward our tents. Despite the cold, I was sweating through my shirt, but we had gotten what we needed. There was nothing left to do but divide it all up and leave town. Only it wouldn't be the four of us as I had imagined. LB and Allie were staying behind. I felt a pang of sadness at the thought of that, but there was nothing I could do to change it. LB was doing the right thing by Allie, and I had to let them go.

"I talked to one of the workers after dinner," LB said. "The government is running a shuttle from various points on the northern border to a port at Tampico on the Gulf Coast. From there, we'll be taking a ship across to Mérida."

"Tampico," I said.

"Yeah, sounds like there's transport there," LB said. "You walk the entire way down it might take you a year. There's bound to be trouble too. All kind of outlaws and bandits just waiting to jump whoever comes around. Two people, alone, no weapons, that's a recipe for disaster, bro."

"We'll see what's what," I said. "You keep in mind that if you get caught with a Bible, or any of these books..."

"Yeah, I know," he said. "I don't want that. But I'm prepared, thanks to you."

"Thank God, not me," I said.

"You and Cat are gonna be alright," he assured me.

"It's been an honor, Major," I said.

"The honor is mine, all mine."

We huddled together with Cat and Allie back at the tents we had rented for the night and divided up the Bibles. LB promised to get Trey's to him. Allie and LB both took one of the Bible prophecy books. I kept the copy of *After the Rapture*, and Allie held onto a book called *The Non-Prophet's Guide to the End Times*. We tucked them deep into our backpacks. I felt better having Lorenzo's Bible. His notes and cross references were more valuable to me than ten million NARA digital dollars.

Once everything was divided and carefully hidden, I looked at LB and Allie. The big man had an arm around Allie's shoulders. She was leaning on him, and my eyes burned with tears. The thought of moving on without them was difficult. Cat held onto my arm with her good hand, but kept her broken arm in the sling Jonathan had made for her.

"I had no idea how this day would end," I said.

"I wish we could go with you," Allie said. "I'm so sorry."

"Don't be sorry," Cat said.

"It's not your fault," I added. "This is part of the master

plan. We are all members of the body of Christ and each of us has his work."

"I thought you said that was for the church, and the church age is over," LB pointed out.

"True," I said. "But I still think we've all got a role to play in what God is doing. We may be late to the game, but he's still the same."

"Yesterday, today, and forever," Allie said, wiping a tear from her cheek.

"Take care of each other," Cat said.

"You too," LB said.

"We will," I assured my friend. "We'll be looking for you in Mérida."

"And we'll be looking for you," he said. "Every day. But if something happens, we've got what? Five and half years left?"

"Something like that," I said.

He reached out a big hand, and I shook it. Then he pulled me in for a hug. Allie reached for Cat, and the four of us stood like that for a long time. I prayed, we all cried, and made promises that we would see each other again. But we also knew the odds weren't in our favor.

Finally, we said our goodbyes. Cat and I set off in the darkness. I like to think we were being led by the spirit. I just didn't know it was right into the valley of death.

# CHAPTER 15

I'D LOVE to tell you how wonderful things were once we left the checkpoint, but the truth is, we struggled. Northern Mexico was a desolate place. We spent our first night completely exhausted, in the ruins of an old adobe shack. It was just two walls, and the crumbling remains of a third. I stacked some old timber beams across the two good walls, and we fell asleep arm in arm.

Food was scarce, and the water made us ill. I won't bore you with the details. We walked every day, and I posted videos to the internet whenever possible. We had to be careful where we put up our messages. It was mostly in chat rooms and back-channel sites. The world may have been in tatters after the great earthquake, but the global government, under the direction of Paul Eon and his otherworldly friends, made sure that the internet was well-policed. Most of my videos were struck down within hours of going up. And I knew sooner or later the security forces would come for me.

We weren't the only people posting videos about the Bible or about the truth of the regional government. The videos of the beheadings continued, and news broke of other truth tellers being hunted down. While many people were executed publicly for their faith, those of us who were putting out videos were simply disappearing. Worse still, the government was using AI to make videos of prominent Christians recanting their faith. It was the same old story that had been told in various ways throughout history. Anyone who didn't fall in line with the new global government or one world religion, disappeared, only to reappear a single time to recant everything they had posted before. Maybe some of them actually did reject their faith to save their lives, but the new AI systems could make videos of people talking. It looked and sounded like the real thing, only the message was different.

It was a strange time. We went from being the people who had food, medicines, and survival gear to get along comfortably, to being the people in need. It was humbling to say the least. But always, as the last of our food and water ran out, someone came along to help us. We stayed with the desperately poor, in hovels and shacks. We both suffered from intestinal issues that left us weak and in pain. Yet somehow, we found a way to keep moving. The temperatures warmed during the day as we progressed south, but it was always bitterly cold in the evenings. Never, in all my life, had I been so desperate. And yet, there was a richness that came from living completely dependent upon God. Cat and I grew in our faith. Our prayers became richer, more personal, and much more frequent.

But the real trouble came in what used to be Monterrey.

The Acuña Cartel had taken control of the area. Of course, we didn't know that. We were only looking for food and a place to take refuge for the night. There were times when I wondered if we had been wrong to leave LB and Allie. They were probably traveling in comfort or already in Mérida settling into their homes. Meanwhile, it was becoming clear that I would never be able to live a normal life again. Cat could have resented me for that, but she was completely supportive. In fact, when my faith faltered, hers held strong.

We found an old dog kennel. The house it had belonged with was in ruins, but the rectangle cage was still standing. I stretched my tarp across the top and tied it down on three sides while Cat started a small fire for us. All we had to eat was a handful of dry rice. We used water from the insulated containers we had purchased at the checkpoint and boiled the rice in a small pot we had found on our travels. We were huddled on a blanket, waiting for the rice to cook enough that we could eat it as the night set in. Neither of us saw the gunmen until it was too late.

They barked orders at us in Spanish as the dark figures came toward us out of the darkness. At first, I thought it was a security team from the government. But as the figures moved closer, we could see they were normal looking people.

"English," I said, my voice pitched high with fear.

"Gringos!" one of the gunmen said.

"On your feet," another of them said. "Hands up!"

"We're just travelers," I said, climbing to my feet. We were both tired and sore. Our stomach issues had left us weak. "Don't hurt us."

"We decide who lives and who dies," the leader of the group said. "You're on our land now."

"We're sorry," Cat said. "We didn't know."

"Get their gear," the leader snapped. "It's getting cold out here."

One of the gunmen kicked over our pot of rice. I watched the contents splash out and land on the ground with a feeling of dismay. It would have been our only meal of the day, and it had been cruelly snatched away.

"We don't have money," I said.

"Shut up!" their leader screamed.

My tarp was left behind, but our packs were picked up by the gunmen, who herded us into a street littered with debris and riddled with cracks. It hadn't been repaired after the earthquake, just reused until ruts had been packed down on the old routes. The gunmen had an old pick-up truck. We were pushed into the bed of the truck and surrounded by the gunmen who sat on the edges while their leader drove.

It was difficult to see at night, but I could tell we were pushing in toward what had formerly been the city center. In the distance, a massive mountain rose up. Even in the darkness it loomed over the ruins of Monterrey. We stopped at what had once been a high-rise building. The top floors had broken off in the earthquake, but the bottom two were miraculously intact. The truck joined half a dozen more parked in front of the building on a rubble packed street.

We were ordered out of the vehicle and into the building. There was no denying the men who shoved us from behind. Inside the building, we were amazed at the lavish furnishings. Battery operated lights hung from the high ceiling. It looked like we were in the lobby of a bank. The floor was polished marble, and there were Corinthian style pillars holding up the roof. Along the left side of the lobby was what had once been the teller windows. Behind them I could see pallets of food, bottled water, and all sorts of goods that had obviously been looted from a large store of some kind. The right side of the lobby had been a row of offices, but they were serving as living spaces for the cartel members. Over thirty rough looking men, all armed with automatic weapons, loitered in the lobby. Many were drinking beer and smoking thick cigars. There were women too, some were busy waiting on the men, others were obviously there to entertain. They all looked at us as if we were filthy creatures who had shown up without an invitation, and for sure that's what we were.

At the end of the lobby was an actual throne. I had no idea where it came from. It was made of wood that had been painted gold and was padded with thick cushions. The man sitting on it was short, balding, and armed with a chrome plated pistol. He had a scantily clad woman on one of his knees, and another stood on either side of his chair.

The leader of the gunmen pushed us forward and said something in Spanish. Another stepped forward with our Bibles and books in hand. He showed them to the man on the throne, who cleared his throat and spit at the sight of the Bibles. He waved his hand, and barked an order I didn't understand. Two women came out and took Cat. Two of the gunmen grabbed me by the arms and dragged me down a side corridor. The women were behind me. I'll admit I was screaming for Cat. I was afraid they would kill me and abuse her. I didn't mind dying, but I couldn't stand the thought of leaving Cat all alone with such rough men.

But they didn't kill us. Under the lobby was a makeshift bath house. We were stripped and hosed down, then given new clothes. Cat was then taken to the kitchens to help the other women working for the cartel, and I was dragged back up to the man on the throne and left standing in front of him. The man patted the girl on his lap, and she sprang up. He made a gesture with his hand and the girls around him retreated.

"Have you eaten?" the man said in a heavily accented English.

"No sir," I said.

"We will feed you. No one should die on an empty stomach."

It wasn't what I was expecting. I was brought a bowl of beans and rice with shredded pork that had come from a can. It might not sound great, but to me it was the most delicious meal I had eaten since leaving LB and Allie. I could only hope that Cat was getting to eat as well.

While I scarfed down the food, the man on the throne asked me questions.

"Do you know who I am?"

"No," I admitted.

"Don Carlo, head of the Acuña Cartel. You are on our land and it's clear you have no way to pay for such a trespass."

"I didn't realize," I said.

"Who are you?" Carlo asked, clearly shocked that Cat and I had just wandered into their territory.

I had been warned about the dangers on the road. We had

seen bandits but had been lucky to avoid them. Still, I had no idea that a cartel had taken control of one of Mexico's biggest cities. Not that there was much left of the city, but the cartel seemed to have it better than most. Plenty of food and supplies, and even a stable of slaves to wait on them hand and foot.

"My name is Hank Downs," I told him. "I'm nobody."

"Nobody?" Carlo said, raising his eyebrows. "Have you come here, Nobody, to teach us about your illegal God?"

That got a laugh from the cartel members. I shook my head.

"I'm not here for you. I didn't even know about you before this evening."

"Who are you here for?" Carlo said, opening one of the prophecy books and thumbing through the pages.

"We're traveling to the coast," I said.

"Why not take the government transports?"

"That's the reason," I said, pointing at the book in his hands. "I'm trying to get the word out. To warn people about what's to come."

"You're a prophet?" Another laugh from his men. "Or maybe a fortune teller?"

"I'm just a man," I said. "But the Bible predicted the times we're living in. The wars, the hyperinflation, famine, and death."

"I could have predicted it," Carlo said with a snort of derision. "The idiot politicians have been warning us of all that for years."

"It predicted the earthquake," I said.

"Easy to say after the fact," Carlo said.

"It tells us what's coming next?" I told him.

"Which is?"

"Then the angel took the censer and filled it with fire from the altar and threw it on the earth, and there were peals of thunder, rumblings, flashes of lightning, and an earthquake," I said. "Revelation 8:5. It's the opening of the sixth seal, part of God's judgment on the people of the earth."

"Bah!" Carlo said. "A storm. There are storms all the time. I do not fear a little thunder or lightning."

"He's stalling," one of the gunmen shouted.

"Hang him by his feet," another suggested. "We'll play the piñata."

"You intrigue me, Nobody. I wonder, are you mad?"

"I'm sane, sir," I said.

"Why should I fear this storm?"

"It's not just a storm," I said. "It will be like nothing you've ever seen. The word translated rumblings really means voice. You'll hear things, sir. I don't know what, or who exactly, but it won't be people."

"The boogeyman!" someone shouted. The rest of the group, including Don Carlo laughed.

I felt a knot in my stomach around the food they had just given me. My bowl was empty, and there was no reason for them not to kill me. I was praying for God's help silently in my mind. Escape wasn't possible. Not that I could flee and leave Cat behind. I was searching desperately for some way to convince the cartel to let us go. But there was nothing.

"I do not believe you, Nobody," Carlo said with a shake of his head. "We shall use your books to roll our cigarettes, eh boys!"

The cartel members began to shout and wave their weapons around. Carlo gestured, and I suddenly felt the cold muzzle of a gun in my back.

"Time to die, Gringo," said a gruff voice behind me.

I felt his hot breath on the back of my neck. Lifting my hands to show that I wasn't a threat, I looked at Carlo.

"Sir, may I make one request before I die?"

The leader of the cartel raised his hands for silence and the gunmen quieted down.

"What is your request?" Carlo asked.

"The woman that came in here with me is innocent. Please, don't abuse her."

"He thinks we want white women," Carlo said with a sneer. "We would not lower ourselves, Nobody. Your friend will cook and clean, nothing more, nothing less. Take him away. He no longer amuses me."

Rough hands grabbed my arms and pulled me backward. I tripped and fell, cracking my head on the floor. Someone kicked me in the side hard enough to roll me over. I was yanked up again. Someone punched me in the kidney so hard that I nearly threw up. I was hit in the shoulder with the butt of a rifle. And someone punched me so hard, I felt something give way around my eye. I dropped to my knees, holding my face, which was already swelling from the blow. Even with my eyes closed I could see bright sparks dancing.

"Get up!" someone shouted.

Before I could respond I felt the sharp point of a knife on my backside. With a shove I was stood up, the knife penetrating into the muscle above my right thigh.

"Take him outside!" Don Carlo ordered. "Don't let him soil my floor."

The mob converged around me. They half carried, half dragged me to the doors, but when they flung them open what they saw brought them all to a stop. All I could do was thank God for his faithfulness. Across the sky lightning was flickering in wave after wave.

# CHAPTER 16

THE THUNDER HIT like a sonic weapon. The building shook as the loudest thunder I have ever heard boomed overhead. It was so loud the hardened assassins from the Acuña Cartel ducked and covered their heads.

"Who's attacking?" Don Carlo shouted from the far end of the room.

One of the gunmen turned and shouted to him in Spanish. The lightning didn't stop. Nor was it just one bolt. Waves of lightning rippled across the sky, which, to my astonishment, was cloud free. I could see the stars in between the bright flashes that lit not only the heavens, but the city. I could see the cartel vehicles and the ruins of the buildings up and down the street.

Don Carlo came puffing up behind the group. Even though my eye was swollen nearly shut, I could see the fear on his face. The man who had everything, who commanded a small army of assassins, who had survived wars with the other cartels, and the great earthquake, looked up at the sky in terror.

"It's the seventh seal Judgment," I said, making my split lips flare with pain.

"El Diablo," Don Carlo said in a tremulous voice.

I didn't know much Spanish, but I knew diablo meant devil.

"No," I said, still on my knees. "It is the judgment of God. He is showing you his power."

He glanced down at me, a look of defiance on his face. At that same moment the ground began to shake. It was nowhere near as powerful as the sixth seal earthquake, but the familiar roar was heard, even above the thunder.

"Terremoto!" Carlo shouted.

Dust wafted from the ceiling. Across the street a wall fell over. In the light from the rippling lightning, I could see the trucks bobbing. The ground wasn't rolling in waves. It was more of a powerful vibration. The gunmen moved to a doorway and pulled their boss to what they thought was safety. Fortunately, the earthquake wasn't enough to bring the building down on us, but it was frightening just the same.

And then the voices were heard. Above the thunder, and drowning out the roar of the earthquake, voices spoke. I couldn't understand what they said, but it was obviously voices. The Bible sometimes describes the voice of God as being like the sound of mighty rushing waters. I got to see Niagara Falls while on a two-month exercise at the Niagara Falls Air Reserve Station. The sound of the water was overwhelming, louder than a rock concert. The voices we heard were similar. And even though I couldn't understand what I was hearing, I no longer felt afraid. Something deep within me welled up, and it was like seeing someone I cared about after a long absence. It was, I imagined, how I would feel seeing my parents again. There was a musical quality to the voices. They weren't singing, but they were harmonious and almost rhythmic.

My attention was outside. The sky was so amazing I couldn't stop looking at it. So, I didn't see Don Carlo coming for me. He grabbed my shoulders and pulled me. The boss was surprisingly strong. I was on my feet and turned around before I realized what was happening.

"What is this?" he hissed. "Are we going to die?"

"No," I said calmly. "We won't die. Not from this judgment."

"I don't understand," he said. "Why is this happening?"

"God is making one last effort to convince the world of his love. You're either for him, or you're against him."

"No riddles, porfeta! Speak plain or lose your tongue."

"This," I said, holding up a hand to the sky. I had to shout to be heard over the roar of the voices from the spiritual realm. "is predicted in the Bible. I can show you."

"You will show me!" he shouted.

His men had lowered their weapons. The menacing looks on their faces had been replaced by fear. Across the wide lobby I saw the women in lingerie crossing themselves and making gestures to ward off evil as they huddled together in fear.

I couldn't blame them. It seemed as if the world was going crazy, and we were all exposed, like ants whose hill had been kicked over. The urge to run screaming in panic was strong.

"Stay calm," I said in a loud voice. "It will be over soon. And everything will be made clear."

Several of the gunmen looked at me with relief. Someone had answers, and they were genuinely happy about it. As if in response to my proclamation, the voices from heaven ceased, and the earthquake ended. Thunder continued to roll and echo off the nearby mountains, but the sky grew clear. The stars reappeared and only the occasional bolt of lightning flashed.

"Bring him in," Don Carlo said. "We will hear what he has to say."

They had been rough and abusive as they dragged me away from Don Carlo's throne. On the way back, they supported me. Several of the men barked orders in Spanish. The next thing I knew the serving women came into the lobby. Some had ice packs, others wet cloths. Cat was with them. She looked a little less frightened, but also relieved to see me. I was grateful to see her, but my wounds had flared to life. The pain in my head was so severe it was hard to think of anything else. I felt weak and extremely tired. It wasn't just my body's response to the injuries. I had been beaten up before. And I wasn't in shock, but something was happening to me.

"Cat," I managed to say as she moved close.

Someone put the icepack against my swollen eye, and another of the women wiped the blood from my nose. I closed my eye as Cat slipped under one arm and supported me. The pain was getting worse, nearly overwhelming.

"Need to sit," I managed to say.

A chair was brought over, and I sat down in the middle of

the room. Now the next part may be a little strange. Most of us have never gotten a glimpse into the spiritual realm. I've heard it described as another dimension. But that gets a bit tricky to explain, and I'm no scientist. I just know that when I opened my one good eye, I could see.

There were more than just the gunmen and their consorts in the lobby. More than the serving women, and the cartel boss. In fact, the humans were in the minority in that place. And I won't lie, I was terrified. All around us, packed in the room like attendees at a concert, some on the floor, others on the walls and ceiling, and still more hovering in the air, were hundreds of demons.

Lorenzo would have known what to do. I remember seeing him calmly face down people intent on harming him or thrown into wild fits. He was completely unflappable. But I was no Lorenzo. I was just Hank Downes. And the last time I had seen a demon, it took possession of my body and tried to kill Lorenzo with a kitchen knife.

"Pray," I managed to say through clenched teeth.

Cat nodded. I saw her bow her head, but as soon as she did, the demons began to howl in protest.

"Louder," I said. "They're trying to drown you out."

"What?" Cat said.

"Pray louder."

I had forgotten about Don Carlo and his men. They were all armed, although they were no longer brandishing their weapons at me. My focus was on the infernal mob that were all around the room.

I prayed too, although the pain in my head was radiating

through my body, setting my bruised ribs and sore arms on fire.

"Jesus," was all I managed to say. "Jesus."

I wasn't loud. Cat was calling for help, praying for strength and wisdom, protection, and power. My voice was barely a whisper as I called out to my savior.

"Jesus... Jesus..."

But each time I said his name the demons howled as if I had hit them with an invisible hammer. They recoiled a step further from me. And as they moved back, the pain in my head, face, and body, receded as well. It didn't go away. My eye was still throbbing, and my teeth didn't seem to fit together right. My side ached where one of the ruffians had kicked me, and the cut in my backside burned. But the overwhelming nature of the pain seemed to be easing.

"Jesus..." I said with more confidence. "King Jesus."

That made them scream with agony. I can't honestly say that I knew what I was doing. Words came to mind, and I spoke them out loud. They were things that I had heard in Lorenzo's teaching or read in the Bible. They came to mind, and I proclaimed them.

"Lion of Judah... Lord of Hosts... the One who was, who is, and who is to come."

"What's he talking about?" Don Carlo asked.

His men looked bewildered, but they made no move to stop me. The demons shrank back, crawling over one another, trying to hide. Looking away from them wasn't easy. They were hideous and captivating at the same time. Part of me wanted to look at them, to stare, to drink in the strange, otherworldliness of them. But another part of me knew they were dangerous. Religious scholars might debate if I was vulnerable to them. Those who believed in Jesus before the Rapture were filled and sealed with God's Holy Spirit. Those of us who came to faith after the Rapture, did not have that privilege, but I knew in that moment that the Holy Spirit was leading me, directing my words and thoughts, giving me discernment and the power to resist the grotesque beauty of the demons in the old bank lobby.

I looked at Don Carlo, who was staring at me. "We're not alone," I said. "You and your people have attracted a crowd."

"What's he talking about?" Carlo asked.

"Demons," I said calmly. "There are hundreds of them in this room right now. We've been given a moment so that I can explain what's happening. Then you'll need to make a choice, Don Carlo. You, and all your men, will have to decide if you believe what I'm telling you."

"We believe!" one of the frightened gunmen said.

"Can you all understand me?" I asked.

"Si, si!" they all replied.

I've read about people speaking in tongues. Not the strange utterances that some believers say that requires an interpretation but speaking in one language and being under-stood in another. The two witnesses in Jerusalem have that gift. I've heard them on video speaking in what was clearly Hebrew, but I heard it as English in my mind. That gift, or ability, had nothing to do with me. I was merely allowed to be the vessel through which God had chosen to speak to the Acuña Cartel. It was an honor but nothing of my own doing.

"All the events since the Vanishing are part of God's efforts to bring people back to belief in him, and in his son,

Jesus Christ," I said. "The Bible describes these events as judgments. The first was Paul Eon's peace treaty with Israel and the world. It revealed to us who he really is. The Bible calls him the man of lawlessness, or the anti-Christ. It predicted that he would usurp three of the ten regional leaders and the others would give their own power to him.

"Since then, the second judgment was war. The third judgment was hyper-inflation that led to famine. And the fourth was the Death Flu. The Bible rightly predicted that a quarter of the world's population would die from these first four judgments."

The men and women around me, including Don Carlo, were hanging on every word. Beside me, Cat held onto me, silently praying. Around us all, the demons howled, but I could see shimmering light between us and them. Figures moved in the light. Big, bright figures. I couldn't make out their features, or very much about them, but I knew they were there.

"The fifth seal judgment was the persecution of Christians," I continued. "Those of us who came to faith in Jesus Christ after the Vanishing, which was God collecting his faithful believers before this period of judgment against the world. I'm sure you've seen believers beheaded online?"

Several men and women nodded. Don Carlo looked down, embarrassed and ashamed. It didn't take a prophet to see that he had probably beheaded a few Christians and probably worse. I remember news stories of missionaries going missing in Mexico and Central America. Some were held for ransom, others just vanished without a trace. But I felt no judgment, just the gentle urge to continue.

"The sixth seal judgment was the great earthquake, and now you've seen the seventh. It's a warning that even more dire judgments are coming."

"What is a seal judgment?" Don Carlo asked.

"The Book of Revelation describes a scene in heaven when a scroll with seven seals is revealed. In ancient times, ownership deeds were written on scrolls and preserved in clay pots. Sometimes those scrolls had special instructions, like who had the right to open the scroll, and what procedure had to be followed in order to sell, or taken possession of the things written in it," I explained. "When Adam and Eve sinned, it's like they forfeited ownership of planet earth. It was snatched away from them by Satan. But Jesus, through his voluntary, sacrificial death on the cross, paid for all our sins, and reclaimed ownership of us, of planet earth, even of death and hell. He's the rightful owner. The scroll could only be opened by him, and with each seal he broke, a judgment came on the earth for our rebellion.

"The seventh seal judgment also ushers in the seven trumpet judgments. So, we know what is coming next."

"What?" Don Carlo wanted to know.

"I'll be glad to teach you," I said. "But I sense there is a much greater need than to know the future. All of you men and women here, like Cat and I, we have all sinned. We have done things that hurt people... selfish things, sometimes shameful things. I don't have to convince you that we're all sinners. You know it, deep in your heart. Maybe you've pushed that quiet voice away. Maybe you've thought that you're far past any hope that God would want you or save you. But here's the truth: we can all be forgiven. We can all be made right with God through his son, Jesus. All it takes is to believe that he died on the cross to pay the penalty for all your sins, and that through his resurrection we too can live forever with him. You do that, and you'll be saved. It's simple, and I'll help you do it. Is there anyone here who's ready to believe?"

At that moment the group was completely silent. My eyes were on Don Carlo and his men, most of whom were staring down at their shoes. But out of the corner of my eye I could see the bright figures. They were in a fierce struggle with the hordes of demons. I couldn't hear their shouts and screams any longer, and I didn't take my eyes off the people in front of me, but I knew there was a terrible battle raging around us at that moment. And I had no idea which side would win, and which would lose.

# CHAPTER 17

I'LL ADMIT, for a moment I feared that the cartel would turn against me. They had been about to kill me less than a half hour earlier. Who would ever imagine that drug dealers and murderers would put their faith in Jesus. I could feel the tension building around me. One wrong move was all it would take for the gunmen to fall on me and Cat and kill us both.

But instead, a big man looked up at me. He had a square jaw, a livid scar above one eye, and a crooked nose. He had tears in his eyes and said, "I am ready to believe," in very accented English.

That was the first domino. I'd love to tell you that everyone in the room accepted the free gift of eternal life that night and turned away from their life of sin. But that didn't happen. About half of the gunmen prayed with me and put their faith in Jesus. The rest were hesitant, including Don Carlo. Almost all the serving women prayed with me, and many of the scantily clad consorts, but again it wasn't all of them.

In fleeting glances, I saw the bright figures winning a great victory over the demons in the room. And when I opened my eyes after leading the prayer, I could no longer see into the spiritual realm. But the mood among the cartel members shifted from fearful, to festive. Cat and I were the guests of honor. More food and drinks were brought out. Wine, beer, and tequila were the beverages of choice, but there was also a wonderful fruit punch. Everyone wanted to talk to us. The women gravitated to Cat, and I couldn't blame them. When I finally got a chance to look at myself in the mirror, I felt shocked. There was a lump the size of a small egg just above my left temple. My right eye was swollen shut and black all the way down to my upper lip.

But the men who had prayed with me came forward, one by one, confessing their sins. I don't know why, and I certainly didn't ask them too. Maybe it came from their Catholic upbringing, but I listened. And after each one told me how many men they had killed, how many women they had raped, and how many children they had abandoned, I encouraged them to pray. It wasn't easy. I've seen some bad stuff in my life. Foster care can be brutal, but the truth was, I struggled to see past the sins and crimes that the gunmen confessed to me. Their contrition was evident and obviously real, but still, I couldn't help but feel a little shocked at the crimes they were confessing to me. Of course, all I could do was tell them that they no longer needed to confess to me or anyone else. God knew all their sins and had paid the penalty when Jesus died on the cross. More than one of those tough, former criminals, left feeling so light and relieved that they literally danced.

It was late when people finally started falling asleep. We were given blankets and pillows in one of the rooms that had been a banking office. Cat and I were exhausted, yet also thrilled to see God at work. Up until that night I had questioned why I didn't just stay with LB and Allie at the checkpoint and wait for government transportation to Mérida. But it was clear to me after that night that God had a plan. And all I really wanted from that point on was to be useful to him the way I was that night.

The next day I met with Don Carlo and several of his lieutenants. A few had believed in Jesus the night before, but they all wanted to know what was coming. Cat and I were given food and whatever we needed. Our belongings were returned to us, including our own clothes which had been cleaned. I opened Lorenzo's Bible and did my best to help the cartel members see and understand what was coming.

"The first trumpet judgment," I explained, "will be blood and fire mixed with hail."

"Fire and ice?" one of the Lieutenants asked. "How is that possible?"

"I don't know," I confessed. "But here's what the Bible says. 'The first angel blew his trumpet, and there followed hail and fire, mixed with blood, and these were thrown upon the earth. And a third of the Earth was burned up, and a third of the trees were burned up, and all green grass was burned up.'"

"So," Don Carlo said. "Fire, we need to get everything inside."

"Including crops," another of the lieutenants said. "If a

third of the trees are going to burn up, we'll lose a lot of food if it isn't harvested."

"How much time does it say we have?" Don Carlo asked.

"The Bible doesn't say when the judgments will occur," I explained. "But most people who have studied all this believe the trumpet judgments will all come to pass within the next two years."

"How many judgments are we talking about?" another of the Lieutenants asked.

"Seven trumpet judgments, and seven seal judgments in the last half of the seven year tribulation period," I said. "We're about a year and half into this, so there's approximately five and half years left."

"Till what?" Don Carlo asked. "The end of the world?"

"No, not the end of the world," I said. "People call it the end times, but that's not accurate. Following these seven years of judgment on the Earth, Jesus will return. He will take control of the entire world, and rule for a thousand years from Jerusalem."

"I have to admit," Don Carlo said. "This is hard to believe."

"You don't have to believe it," I said. "But so far, every prophecy in the Bible had been one hundred percent accurate."

"We must believe, jefe," another of the lieutenants said.

"We'll do what we must," Don Carlo said. "And our first priority is to prepare for the fire and hailstorm."

The cartel boss glanced at me with something between appreciation and suspicion. I spent the rest of the day in my room. Cat surprised even herself by leading the women in

Bible study. She wasn't really comfortable being the leader, but she knew more than the others about the Bible. I was shocked when the big man with the scar above his eye came back to the bank lobby with a crate full of Bibles. He presented them to Don Carlo, who took one, and waved at him to distribute the books to whoever wanted one.

He came to me next, carrying his heavy box full of Bibles. I looked inside and saw Bibles of all kinds. Where he had found them was a mystery to me, but I couldn't help but be glad. I was happy to teach the group as much as I could about God, but nothing compared to having one's own Bible and studying it personally.

"I found these," he said. "It is good, no?"

"It is very good," I told him.

"I am Hector," he said.

"I'm Hank. It's a pleasure to meet you, Hector."

He beamed at the praise and continued passing out the Bibles to whoever wanted them. After that, Don Carlo stayed busy preparing for what was to come. He brought in as much food and water as he could. Meanwhile, when I wasn't teaching about Bible prophecy, Hector took Cat and I around town. The Acuña Cartel weren't the only people in the ruins of Monterrey. There were plenty of peasants among the ruined buildings and houses. Some were hostile, others were eager to hear the good news.

For a few weeks we were able to rest and enjoy the fruit of our labor. We didn't worry about what we were going to eat or if we were in danger. The locals saw us as part of the cartel and we were accorded a certain amount of respect. Not everyone was changed, but a big portion of the cartel gave up their licentious behavior, and not because of anything I said or taught. Occasionally, someone asked me if something was wrong, or sinful. I was careful not to speak on my own, but only responded with what the Bible said about a subject. Drugs had been commonplace among the cartel members. Since the Rapture, and more specifically, the second seal judgment, war, there was no more demand for illicit drugs. The cartels that survived the wars with the other gangs focused on survival. But with plenty of drugs at their disposal, and the world becoming more and more dangerous every day, the temptation to use their own product grew strong.

I couldn't find any specific verses in the Bible about using drugs. There were cautionary verses about avoiding drunkenness and remaining sober. My go-to advice was to pray about it and let the Spirit of God lead you into what was right and wrong. It didn't take long before I became the defector judge among the cartel members. Don Carlo certainly didn't mind letting me settle disputes and deal with problems. He was on the fence when it came to believing the Bible. More and more of his time was taken up with the harem of women he kept, and in procuring as much loot as his men could find among the ruins of the city. His patience with me was thin. Every leader wants good intelligence to make decisions by. And while I could tell him in general terms what was coming, I couldn't be exact or say when it would happen.

Teaching wasn't my only pastime either. I volunteered to help the cartel catalogue what they had. The old bank building wasn't the only property they had converted. They had several other buildings around the town that they were in the process of using as warehousing or fixing up for shelter.

One was a GMC factory which was filled with trucks waiting to be shipped out to various dealerships across the United States. They had secured several gas stations and protected the limited fuel supplies with strict vigilance. I was given full access and created a simple inventory so that Don Carlo could know what he had and how much. That information allowed him to trade with other groups outside of the city for things he needed.

It was a special time, and I didn't really want it to end. I felt like I was accomplishing something. More and more people were believing in Jesus each day. Hector and I grew close. He was my constant companion whenever I was outside the bank lobby. And he was always armed. But nothing lasts forever, and I should have known that trouble was bound to show up sooner or later.

In fact, it was my fault that it happened at all. I got so comfortable in Monterrey, that I decided to make more teaching videos. I never posted them from downtown. Hector was happy to drive me into the outskirts where I could post a video and speak to the locals. Of course, those videos were found by the watchdog groups. I was labeled a domestic terrorist and traitor. I didn't mind the online hate, but I should have seen the obvious conclusion to my posts. Yes, they were spreading the good news, and helping people understand what was really going on in the world. But maybe it was arrogance that kept me posting them. I honestly can't say. We all make mistakes. Still, it can be hard to live with the consequences when you know what you did cost people their lives.

# CHAPTER 18

"JEFE, THE TALL ONES ARE HERE," a gunman named Javier told Don Carlo.

I was sitting with the cartel boss, doing my best to explain what would happen in the latter half of the seven-year time of judgment, the period known as the Great Tribulation. Our struggles had only just begun. There would be a time when the Devil took direct control of the anti-Christ, Paul Eon, and things on planet Earth would go from bad to worse.

"Where?" Carlo snapped as he jumped up from the table.

"It's just a small group, eight in total," Javier explained. "They're on the east side of town."

"Probably the scouts," Don Carlo said.

"Tall ones?" I asked. "You mean the security personnel from the NARA?"

"They are not human," Carlo hissed. "Before the Vanishing, and long before the visitors showed up, your government had secret labs."

"The United States?" I asked.

"The US, UK, Russia, China, everyone," Don Carlo said. "I had spies there too, ready to send us the formula once your people perfected it."

"Formula for what?"

"Super soldiers," he explained. "Bigger, faster, stronger, and harder to kill, that was the goal. Your government called me evil and said my product was poison. Meanwhile, they were the ones with secret labs. They were the ones experimenting with gene modification. There are stories that would make your skin crawl. They didn't perfect anything. There were children from eastern countries, orphans you know, that died in secret laboratories. What do you think happened to the billions sent to the Ukraine war?"

"I suppose I thought the politicians were divvying it up."

"Oh, for certain they were, but think it through, Hank. Your government had one hundred senators, and four hundred and thirty-five representatives. If each of them was given ten million dollars of the Ukraine aid money, that would only be six billion. Your country sent well over fifty billion in cash, not counting the weapons sent. Think about those numbers. Billions of dollars, enough to buy ten of your American football teams, and more than enough to build an army of soldiers with special abilities. Javier, get everyone in place."

"Yes, Don Carlo," the gunman said.

"We've been preparing for this war," Carlo continued explaining to me. "NARA officials want complete control. I knew they would come, sooner or later."

"Can I help?" I asked.

"The preacher is a soldier, no?"

"I was Air Force," I said.

"We have no planes, my friend. But we have many guns. When your people left weapons in Afghanistan, we stocked up. When they sent anti-armor weapons to Ukraine, they were sold to my buyers. We are ready for whatever those inhuman soldiers bring."

The floors above the bank lobby weren't stable, but I followed Don Carlo up to the open area that had once been the fourth floor. We made our way through the rubble, along with Carlo's security guard, and Hector, who had become mine. I never talked to him about it, he just shadowed me wherever I went. From there, we could see most of the city, and the open, arid plains beyond. I couldn't see the security soldiers, but the armored troop carrier was easy to spot. They hadn't tried to hide it.

"I have people in place," Don Carlo said to me. "These gringos won't know what hit them. Give the signal."

His bodyguard was a large man with thick hair that hung to his shoulders. He wore a bulletproof vest and cargo pants. His massive arms were bare, each one thick with muscle and covered with tattoos. He pulled out a flare gun and fired it into the sky. It flew up like a bottle rocket and exploded. Almost immediately the streets below echoed with the reports of high-powered rifles. Don Carlo pulled out binoculars. After a few moments he growled, "They're splitting up."

I had a sinking feeling that the security force wasn't there to root out the Acuña Cartel, but to stop me from making videos. Elon Musk's Starlink had been instrumental in keeping the world up to date on what was happening across all seven continents. People didn't watch cat videos or make dance reels anymore. But every night we searched the endless stream of news and eyewitness videos from around the world. Paul Eon was tightening his grip on planet Earth. Millions of Christians had been murdered for their faith. Public executions had become common, as were drunken orgies. The alien visitors claimed they came to usher in an enlightened age, but in reality, the Earth had never been darker.

I used the near universal access to the world wide web to upload video teachings. First, had been Lorenzo Malta's interviews and lectures. But after losing his archive at Camp Abilene, I had begun to post my own teaching. I was no scholar, nor a pastor, despite what Don Carlo called me. I was just a man who had scoured the Bible and every book I could find on the end times. And it wasn't like the enemy was trying to hide what they were up to. Paul Eon, his alien counterpart, Shemi Hazah, and the officials of the global government were brazen in their actions. Who was left to stop them? No one.

The people like me, who dared offer a different narrative than the official one, were targeted for elimination. Once again, just like at Camp Abilene, I had settled into thinking that things would just go on and on the way they were. When danger and deprivation seemed like a thing of the past, it was hard to remember that hard times were coming. I had taught so many people about the judgments of God that were still ahead, and yet I had been lulled to sleep by the food, shelter, and comfort the Cartel provided me. Many of them had put their faith in Christ, but they were still loyal to Don Carlo. They were spread through the ruins of Monterrey, fighting the security forces who had come looking for me.

"It's time to go," I said softly to Hector.

"You don't want to see our victory, Hank Downes?" Carlo asked.

I was surprised that he heard me. "I think I'll go downstairs and pray," I said.

Hector led the way. We reached the stairwell just as the first explosion echoed up to us from the fighting below. I felt my heart sink. Maybe I was being too hard on myself, but I felt such intense guilt at that moment that I considered flinging myself off the building. I didn't want people to die in my place. And yet it was too late to stop them.

"Come on," Hector said. "It is not safe up here."

I followed him into the stairwell and down to the lobby. There was fear on the faces of the women gathered there, including Cat's.

"The security forces are in town," I said solemnly.

"What should we do?" Cat asked.

"I don't know," I said honestly.

"Come with me," Hector said. "I have supplies ready for you."

"What supplies?" I asked.

"Come and see," Hector said.

He was a man of few words, but his loyalty and commitment to God was inspiring. Violence had been as natural to him as breathing was to me. I couldn't imagine the horrors he had endured growing up that led him to join the cartel, which he did at age thirteen. He had been a runner, a guard, and eventually a hit man for Don Carlo. His name was Hector, but he was known as El Asesino, *The Assassin*. But all those traits had given way to a kindness and sensitivity that at times were almost shocking. On our trips around the ruins of

Monterrey he showed compassion for people. Nothing was off limits to Hector. He even gave the shirt he was wearing to an older woman whose own clothes were soaked in a rain shower.

He watched over me with such vigilance that I felt comfortable wherever I was. There were plenty of the cartel gunmen who hadn't accepted my message. They clung to their old ways and would have gladly put a bullet in my head, except that none of them wanted to tangle with Hector. His presence not only opened doors for me but protected me from dangers I didn't even know were there. And while I had been focusing only on spreading the gospel, he had been preparing for the inevitable.

Cat followed me and we both followed Hector. The first stop was our small room. Hector had procured me a leather satchel from somewhere in Monterrey. I kept my Bible and the books on prophecy in it. Cat had put together go bags for us, and I'm ashamed to admit I didn't even realize it. Each one had some food, our metal water containers, and a change of clothes. She got her Bible and put it in the satchel. We each carried our go bags and followed Hector downstairs.

One level down below the bank lobby was the maintenance spaces: the bathing areas, vats for washing clothes and bedding, storage for food, and even sleeping areas for the workers. It was a bit of a maze for me and Cat, who didn't spend much time below the lobby, but Hector led us through with confidence. We came to a room that was locked. Hector pulled out a key. Inside, he pulled the string on a light that turned on a bare bulb that hung from the ceiling. The room had been a maintenance closet. There were still some old cleaning supplies in one corner. But the shelves had been cleared and restocked with weapons.

"Put these on," Hector told us.

He handed me a bullet proof vest. It was heavy, but I was thankful to have it. The vest slipped over my head and fastened around my abdomen with a Velcro strap. He gave one to Cat too. Hector had on a military-style shirt and vest. His was covered with loops for ammunition and gear. Normally, he carried a large pistol and a bowie knife. But in the maintenance closet he added an M-4 automatic rifle, a dozen ammunition clips, and even some grenades.

"Are we going to war?" Cat asked, as he handed her a rifle with a scope attached.

"It is not safe here," Hector said. "Not anymore."

"So where are you taking us?" I asked as he handed me an ammo belt with several magazines already slung in the loops.

"Wherever you want," Hector said.

He picked up a sub-machine gun. It was a small, B&T APC9K, which I knew was used by personal protection details in the Air Force. It had a see-through magazine loaded with 30 9mm rounds. Hector checked the safety, then handed it to me.

"I'm sorry I wasn't more prepared for this," I said.

"What are you talking about?" Cat asked me.

"I should have known I'd bring trouble down on us when I posted those videos," I told her. "I guess I thought that since we were in Monterrey, that the NARA wouldn't try to stop us."

"You do God's work," Hector said. "Hector will protect you."

He picked up a heavy backpack and led us back out of the room. We went up a set of stairs that led to a side exit. As soon as Hector opened the metal door, we heard the shooting.

"How many security people are there?" Cat asked.

"Javier said eight," I told her.

"Don Carlo will slow them down," Hector said. "But we should leave before they breech the compound."

By compound he meant the area around the old bank building. Several of the stores and buildings in the old downtown area had been cleared of debris and rebuilt to house Don Carlo's men and their expanding horde of supplies. The rest of the city was officially under the cartel's control, but only the compound was off limits to other people. The city was in ruins, but it still had more food and supplies than anywhere else other than Mexico City. Survivors for miles around came into Monterrey looking for food, medicine, survival gear, even other people to partner with. There were spies from the rival cartels too, and the only law in Monterrey was that of the jungle. The strong took what they wanted, the weak tried to stay out of sight, and nothing was off limits. The tribulation had made some men into monsters. And it wasn't unusual to see victims of violent crime left to rot in the streets.

Hector led us to a 4x4 pick-up truck. The cartel had a seemingly endless supply from the GMC factory in town. Hector's was a short bed, with a roll cage, and quad cab. There were jerry cans full of fuel in the bed of the truck, along with a tool chest secured with a padlock.

Driving through the city was a slow, careful process. Hector turned south, toward the mountains. We were on the outskirts of town when a massive explosion rocked the entire city. We all turned and looked. The old bank building had been visible from just about anywhere since the great earthquake. But to our horror it was gone, replaced with a rising column of smoke.

"Eight security people did that?" Cat asked.

"They are not men," Hector said. "Not anymore."

"This is my fault," I complained.

"No one is pointing fingers," Cat said. "We did what we could to help them. There are souls in Heaven now because you had the courage to speak the truth."

"The super soldiers were always coming," Hector said. "Don Carlo knew, we all did."

"The government wants to control everything," Cat said.

Hector nodded. "The cartels are being put down, one at a time." His English had improved spending time with me and Cat, although he still spoke slowly. "Soon, nowhere will be safe."

I didn't disagree, but it was still a shock to realize how careless I had become. It was in that moment, as we drove out of the city on what looked like an animal trail, that I realized there would be no peace for us. Odds were high that I wouldn't live much longer. And while I was okay with that, I was afraid. Let's face it, no one wants to die. A person can be courageous in the face of death, but when we contemplate the danger we're in, it seeps deep down into our psyche and chills the soul. I did my best to focus on what the Bible says, "to be absent from the body is to be present with the Lord," but it was hard to get the images of the twisted, broken bodies that I had seen laying bloated in the streets out of my mind.

We were soon moving uphill, kicking up dust as we

bounced and shuttered up the foothills around the Sierra Madre mountains. It took an hour to reach the old cabin. It was made from an old metal shipping container and was mostly buried in the mountainside. A small camp was set up around it, including a camouflage net that was attached to the hillside. Hector drove under the net and stopped.

"What's this?" I asked.

"Home," Hector said.

Under the net was a five-hundred-gallon water cistern and more metal fuel cans. Near the entrance to the shipping container was an old camp stove.

We got out of the truck and Hector unfastened the big lock on the doors to the container. It swung open wide, and he propped it open with a rock. Before the Tribulation, Mexico was a warm country. After the nuclear blasts in the United States had kicked up enough dust and ash to put the western hemisphere into a cooling cycle. The days were warm, and the nights were cold. Hector had stashed blankets, boots, coats, and food in the old shipping container. There was also several folding cots and more weapons.

"This is incredible," Cat said.

"It will only be temporary," Hector said. "The enemy will come. When they do, Hank must take the eastern trail."

"You mean we will all take the eastern trail," I said.

Hector didn't argue with me, but he didn't agree either. Instead, he held out his hand.

"What?" I asked.

"The phone," he said. "They can track it."

Of course, in the old days the government tracked everything. But the phone had no service other than the WIFI signals from Starlink. I didn't think the government could track it without the cell phone tower network. Still, I felt pretty stupid to still have it.

"I didn't think about that," I said, handing him my phone.

He made sure it was on, then opened the tool chest in the back of the truck. Inside was a few buckets of survival food and a crate with a big rabbit inside. The rabbit had a harness around its chest. Hector took the rabbit from its crate, slipped the cell phone into the animal's harness, then set it free. The rabbit didn't hesitate. It scampered down the hill, headed west.

"You think that will fool them?" I asked Hector.

"As long as it remains on," he said. "But we can't hide forever."

"No, we can't," I said.

We watched the city. We were far enough that it seemed like a dirty spot on the horizon, but there was plenty of smoke rising from Monterrey into the sky. Hector waited for dark, then started a fire in the camp stove. There were lawn chairs in the shipping container, and cooking utensils. We made a pot of stew. It was mostly potatoes and peppers, spicy but filling. The night sky was brilliant. Thousands of stars were on display. We put on coats from the shipping container and huddled around the stove, wondering what to do next.

I did my best not to think of the people who had died fighting the security team. Maybe the new regional government would have sent them to retain Monterrey no matter what? Or maybe they died because the security team was after me. I thought of all the people I had met. Many were friends and new believers. What had happened to all of them? Waves of guilt washed over me. The food was like ashes in my mouth. I sat huddled next to the camp stove, trying to pray, but silently drowning in shame.

I can't say how long I sat that way. Sleep pulled at my eyelids, but I felt too guilty to rest. Cat retreated into the shipping container and wrapped herself in a blanket on one of the cots. Hector dozed in his chair, but I sat there brooding. When the sun came up, I felt sick.

From far away, the city seemed unchanged. But I knew the truth. It was filled with the destitute and the dead. Worse, still, was the knowledge that it was all my fault.

# CHAPTER 19

I SUPPOSE everyone has regrets at some point in time. I was busy feeling sorry for myself when the remnants of the security team found us in the mountains. Hector's hidden home didn't stay hidden for long. While I spent the morning sulking, Cat and Hector got busy when the sun came up. Hector took explosives from a crate that was marked United States Military in bold letters. How an assassin in Mexico got the crate, or the dangerous claymore mines it contained, was a mystery to me. If I hadn't been so lost in my pity party, I might have thought that God had directed even the mistakes of the United States government to protect his people during the Tribulation.

Hector took the mines and hid them along the trail to the west of the hillside. To the north, the terrain was steep and covered with loose rocks. The trail to the east was our escape route and to the south was the mountain itself. Hector rightly guessed that the security people would quickly overtake the cartel gunmen. Don Carlo's men were brave enough, but they didn't have the training and gear that the super soldiers had, not to mention their strength or stamina. A bullet would still wound them, but it took several to kill the security members, who also had state of the art battle armor that protected their vitals, their shoulders, hips, and thighs. They also had superior vision, weapons, and communications gear. While the cartel gunmen fought with savage ferocity, the security team fought with efficiency, speed, and superior tactics.

Hector also correctly guessed that the security team, down to just four individuals from the original eight, would come from the west. They must have searched through the mountain during the night, while my phone was still active and attached to the big rabbit. Finding it, they backtracked the animal to the hillside by late afternoon.

I'm ashamed to say I was still in the lawn chair by the camp stove when the attack began. Cat had spent the day preparing the truck. She refueled the vehicle, loaded the bed with the food, blankets, and medical supplies from the shipping crate, and made sure that everything was secured. Hector was checking his M4, when the first mine blew up. It sounded distant to me. I was so mired in my own thoughts I didn't even realize what was happening.

"They found us," Cat said.

"Get to the truck," Hector said.

"Come on, Hank," Cat said.

She pulled me up. I felt tired and weak. Instead of resting and preparing for battle, I had sulked like a child. It was one more mistake and one I'm glad didn't cost me my life.

We ran to the truck, just as another mine blew up. I had

the fleeting thought that maybe the mines would kill the security members, but a few seconds later another exploded.

"They're triggering the mines," Hector said grimly. "They'll be here soon. You must go."

"Not unless you're with us," I said.

Cat jumped into the driver's seat and started the vehicle.

"I will cover your escape," Hector said.

"No, I won't leave anyone else to die in my place," I insisted.

"We all die," Hector said. "And then the judgment."

"Hector!" I said loudly. "You are coming with us."

"Let's go!" Cat shouted through the open window on the driver's door.

Hector nodded and jogged over to the truck bed. He jumped in with more agility that I thought a man of his stature would have. I climbed into the passenger side and Cat had the vehicle moving before I got the door closed. My sub-machine gun was waiting for me on the console between the driver and passenger seats. I picked it up, just as Hector began to shoot from the open truck bed.

I turned around. There were three people moving up the hill. They all had large machine guns in hand. Hector pulled a device from his vest and activated it. A moment later the shipping container exploded. Rock and dirt flew out in every direction. At least one of the security members was hit in the blast and thrown off the hill. Debris rained down on the truck, which was bouncing down the eastern trail. And by trail, I mean an uneven ledge that ran in a long, steep curve around the mountain.

"That was close," Cat said.

"I should hav— "

"No!" Cat said. "Stop blaming yourself and get a grip, Hank. Before we all get killed."

It was a sobering command and I realized that she was right. I had dropped the ball and there simply wasn't the time to wallow in my guilt. There were still people depending on me. I checked the machine gun. It was ready to fire. I flicked off the safety and rolled down my window.

While Cat drove, I turned around in my seat and braced myself as I watched for any signs from the super soldiers. Part of me thought there was no way they could get past the land-mines and the explosion from the shipping container alive. But before we reached the bottom of the hill, I caught sight of the security team members moving on the trail above us.

"They're coming," I said, just as Hector began firing his rifle.

"How many?" Cat asked.

"Two is all I saw, and one looked injured."

It was true. One of the super soldiers was limping, but the pain of whatever injury he had sustained didn't seem to be slowing him down. The duo was moving at least as fast as the truck. Hector didn't stand much chance of hitting them. The bed of the truck was too unstable for the assassin to get a clean shot, but he did manage to slow them down.

I turned and looked ahead of us just as Cat got down to a level spot at the base of the mountain. Ahead of us, about a hundred yards away, was a boulder slightly bigger than the truck. Another fifteen yards beyond that was forest that had, for the most part, survived the earthquake judgment.

"Stop at the rock," I ordered.

Cat floored the accelerator. The truck raced forward, then slid to a stop just behind the boulder. I jumped out.

"What are you doing?" Cat screamed.

Hector stood up in the bed of the truck, his rifle popping in short bursts.

"We have to stop them," I shouted back, as I extended the telescoping stock on the submachine gun.

Raising it to my shoulder, I took aim. The weapon had red dot aiming system. The super soldiers were both charging downhill. I aimed low and fired. The weapon rocked against my shoulder and immediately started pulling upward. I yanked it down, firing short bursts. One squeeze of the trigger fired off three to four shots. My first burst was slow and wide. The second time I over-compensated and missed wide on the opposite side. The security member was bounding down the mountain, moving swiftly from side to side, completely unfazed by the fact that we were shooting at them.

The wounded individual had slowed, using cover higher up the hillside. But the other super soldier hit the open space and sprinted toward us. My third barrage was on target. The super soldier had armor over his thighs and knees, but his lower legs were vulnerable. I can't say how many bullets hit, but the security officer went down. For a moment he was vulnerable. I emptied my clip at him. Maybe one in five shots was on target, but enough to put some rounds into the man. Yet somehow, he rolled to a stop with his gun pointed in our direction. He was only twenty yards away. I ducked back behind the boulder a split second before a barrage of high caliber rounds chipped away at the big rock right where I had been. The enemy was not only hard to kill, he was a crack shot as well.

Hector had ducked down too. He pulled a grenade free, and threw it. I didn't wait to check the result. I leaped into the truck screaming for Hector to hold on. Cat didn't need any more encouragement than that. She stomped the accelerator and sent the truck racing into the woods just as the grenade exploded behind us.

At least one of the bad guys was still alive though. Bullets ripped through the trees to our right. Cat managed to turn away as she wove between the trees. The truck bounced and hopped, smashing into saplings, the wheels spinning over tree roots.

"I can't believe they're still alive," I said. "I shot one at least four times."

"They aren't human," Cat said.

I looked in the back. Hector was laying down, bracing himself with one foot and one hand, the other held his rifle secure. Somehow, he managed to see me looking and gave me a reassuring nod. We came out of the woods and onto a relatively smooth desert plain. Cat sped up and we drove until the truck had spent half a tank of gas. I expected the security agents to reappear at any moment, but the battle had slowed them. We stopped just as it grew dark. There was no place to take shelter, but there were plenty of scrub brushes. We cut enough to surround the truck and put some in the bed and on the roof. It wasn't perfect camouflage, but it was all we had.

That night, Hector stood watch. He had somehow managed to sleep in the back of the speeding pickup. I knew special operators from my days in the Air Force who said they could sleep anywhere. I never really believed them, but Hector proved me wrong. Cat curled up in the rear bench seat, while I reclined in the passenger seat. I, for one, was exhausted. Sleep came fast, but it was filled with nightmares. By four in the morning, I had slept enough. I relieved Hector, who started to argue with me, but I was already chugging a container of energy drink. While they slept, I spent the morning hours before dawn in prayer and reflection. The fight had shaken me out of my doldrums. I still felt guilty, but I focused on what lay ahead. People had died, and the security team was clearly in Monterrey for me, but that didn't mean I was directly responsible. In my mind I could hear Lorenzo's voice telling me that I hadn't sent the security team or ordered them to kill anyone. Nor had I encouraged Carlo to fight. Some people just saw no other choice, whether it was a rival cartel, or the police, or the United States government, Don Carlo and the Acuña Cartel would only see one option — to fight.

And like it or not, death was a constant in the tribulation. If I had been smart, I would have put my trust in Jesus before the Rapture. My failure to do so, and everyone else like me, meant we had to endure threats and death on an almost daily basis. We had survived, which meant it was time to stop looking back, and start looking ahead. The security team was still out there somewhere, and I had no doubt they would be coming back around soon. For all I knew, they could be targeting me as I emptied one of the fuel cans into the truck. All I could do was focus on the one hope that I had, that Jesus was waiting for me the second my ticket got punched.

At dawn we set out again, but we hadn't gone far when I

came to what looked like a utility station. There was a small fence around what looked like a concrete bunker. The fence had fallen down, probably during the earthquake. And there was no place to hide the truck, but I felt a quiet nudge to stop. Cat was still asleep in the backseat, and Hector was stretched out on blankets in the rear of the truck. The sun was up, and the sky above us was red. I didn't know if the Holy Spirit was speaking to me, or if I was just rattled from the fight the day before, but for some reason I wanted to get inside that concrete bunker.

I pulled the truck to a stop and got out. Getting over the fence wasn't difficult, but the bunker had a metal door with what looked to be a big lock. I got a grenade and some duct tape. I taped the grenade to the door, pulled the pin, and raced around the side of the small, concrete building. My improvised door opener worked, in fact it ruined the metal door and blew a chunk out of the concrete door jam. It also woke up Cat and Hector.

"What happened?" Cat asked.

"I think we need to get in here," I said.

"That's just a utility building," Hector said. "There's nothing we can use in there."

"Yeah, I understand," I replied. "But I still feel like we need to get inside."

Cat got out of the truck and stretched. Hector climbed out with a couple of flashlights he retrieved from the tool bin in the back of the pickup. I went around and looked inside the building. It was small, maybe only ten feet long, by eight feet wide. Inside was a service nodule for an underground gas pipeline. I'll be honest, it was kind of creepy inside. I heard the rattle from a snake, and there were spiderwebs in the corners.

"Maybe this isn't— "

Before I could change my mind, the hailstones began to fall. One hit the concrete building and another pinged on the roof of the truck. I wasn't sure what was happening. When I glanced up, I saw more hailstones. They were small, maybe marble sized, but they were trailing smoke.

"Get inside!" I shouted. "Quickly!"

Cat sprinted to me. We waited in the doorway for Hector, who came in with flashlights and guns. The hailstones were getting bigger. They had grown from marble to quarter sized. I could see the blood on them, and more blood was falling like rain. One smoking hailstone landed in the scrubby brush that had grown around the fence that surrounded the concrete utility building. Flames immediately sprang up among the dry leaves.

Hector went in first. The sound of his pistol was loud inside the concrete building. It made my ears ring. He shot four snakes, and my ears were ringing so loud that I wouldn't have heard it if another was inside. We huddled just inside the doorway, our back to the gas pipeline machinery. In another minute the hailstones were the size of golf balls and they were falling hard. Our visibility dropped to just a few yards. We heard the windows shatter on the truck as the hail grew larger and larger.

"This is weird," Cat said as the smoke from the burning brush wafted past us.

"Is the hail burning?" Hector said.

"Looks like it," I said.

He wasn't wrong. It was as if the hailstones were made of flammable liquid. As it melted, it burned, and so did almost everything it touched. The fat drops of blood hissed as it fell into the flames which covered nearly everything. The smell of smoke and charred blood filled the air. It actually made my stomach growl.

"Is this... a judgment?" Cat asked.

"Has to be," I said. "The first trumpet is blood and fire mixed with hail. It burns up a third of the trees and all the green grass."

"Ain't much out here to burn," Hector said.

"Thank goodness," I said.

The hail fell for a solid hour, then tapered off. The ground was covered with melting hail, much of it on fire. The bloody, misshapen ice balls were piled up higher than my ankles. All we could do was wait for the ground to clear. Hector spent the time skinning the rattlesnakes he had shot.

"What are you going to do with those?" I asked.

"Meat is meat," Hector said.

"Roasted rattlesnake," Cat said. "It takes like chicken... kind of."

"I'll take your word for it," I said.

Eventually the hail melted, the fires died down, and we ventured out of the utility building. I had hoped the truck would survive, but it was completely totaled. The cab was smashed nearly flat, and the tires were melted. We salvaged what we could. Most of the food was ruined, but we got our go bags, the leather satchel with our Bibles and books, and the weapons. Most of the blankets were burned to tatters, only what Cat and I had used in the cab survived. We set out walking east, but only went a few miles before we came to a tiny stream next to a flat sandy area. Everything was burned up, leaving no fuel for a fire. Hector cut the rattlesnake meat from the bones and seasoned it with salt from his pack then laid it out on the dry, flat rocks to dry in the sun.

From that day on fires were a luxury in northern Mexico. Likewise, shelter was hard to come by. I hoped that if the security super soldiers had survived the fire fight, that they were caught in the open during the rain of fire, blood, and hail. There didn't seem to be much that could survive outside. As we walked we saw coyote, wild dog, and even goat carcasses. Their bones were shattered, and their flesh burned in the fires. Only smaller animals that burrowed underground survived. We saw plenty of dead birds too and passed several smoking remains where small forests had burned up. Hector was smart enough to knock down the charred trunks, which were essentially charcoal. At night, when possible, we built fires using charcoal. Our food supplies ran out quickly, and I was happy to have the rattlesnake jerky. Proverbs 27:7 says, "A satisfied soul loathes the honeycomb, but to a hungry soul every bitter thing is sweet." And that's true, eventually even the rattlesnake jerky seemed like a delicacy.

And it wasn't just our little neck of the woods that burned. We saw dense smoke in the south. The rainforests that covered southern Mexico all the way down through South America burned. It was hard not to imagine how many people and animals died in the first trumpet judgment. How anyone at that point in time could choose not to believe in God was a mystery to me. You didn't need Bible prophecy to know that

God wasn't happy or to realize that judgments on the world were supernatural.

I had no way of knowing it then, since we had discarded my phone, which was our last connection to the internet, and thus, to the news of the wider world, but the global government was once more invoking the tried and true catch-all villain for the burning hail — climate change. A few climate scientists were trotted out, each one with similar theories of what caused the hail, and how man's abuse of the world's climate had led to the catastrophe. They also promised that the plagues should be over, but of course, they were wrong about that. It seemed, that any authorized explanation for the things going on in the world turned out to be wrong. The world by that point was firmly entrenched in two camps, the first distrusted anything the government said, and the other believed it completely and never, ever questioned the official narrative.

Please don't get lost in political ideologies here. The truth is politics weren't to blame for the ills that plagued planet Earth. Satan was in complete power, and I believed he relished in the death and destruction. Meanwhile, his viceroy, Paul Eon, continued to strengthen his grip over the global government.

Cat, Hector, and I took our time moving east. We were careful to avoid groups of people larger than two. It wasn't hard, since most people were alone, and they wanted nothing to do with us. Part of me felt like I should be going to everyone and preaching the good news, but I feared my days of speaking the truth to the world were over. The North American Regional Administration had labeled me a terrorist criminal. I didn't know it, but there were orders to kill me on sight. Fortunately, as my hair grew longer, and shaving wasn't practical, I didn't really look like the man they had photos and video of.

Eventually, we made it to Brownsville at the southern tip of Texas, just a few miles from the gulf. So much was destroyed it was like we were living in a post-apocalyptic movie. But I'll say this, there is an indomitable will to survive in humans. Everything flammable was burned up or charred. But that left stone, concrete, and metal. And on the outskirts of Brownsville we discovered a community of people living together in huts made from metal and stone, along with mud bricks. On land there wasn't much to eat, but the sea still provided its bounty. Fish, shrimp, and crab seemed to be thriving, and there was still seaweed. It was the only green thing left to eat, and people collected it daily along the coast. After weeks of trudging and starving, Brownsville seemed like an oasis of luxury. And most importantly of all, it had a thriving group of believers who took us in. That was a turning point in my mind. A short reprieve from the struggle, but it wasn't to last. The NARA was still searching for me, and their super soldiers didn't know the meaning of giving up.

# CHAPTER 20

"HOW'D you survive the trumpet judgment?" I asked.

Bobby Lane Dearman was a small guy, with the thickest glasses I had ever seen on a person. He perpetually wore an old Houston Astros baseball cap and was one of nearly two dozen believers in Brownsville.

"We were on the water," he replied casually. "It wasn't as bad out there."

He was not the type of person one thought of when imagining a professional fisherman. In fact, Bobby Lane was an aeronautical engineer, formerly of NASA, but had put his expertise into rigging up sails for many of the fishing boats that couldn't get the diesel fuel they needed to run the engines.

"We were hidden in a concrete utility building," Cat said. "If Hank hadn't had a feeling, we needed to get to shelter we might not have survived."

"We lost a few people here in Brownsville," Bobby Lane said. "It was tragic."

"The next judgment will be worse," I said. "A third of the seas."

"I'm praying that the gulf will be spared," he said. He was leading us out onto what looked like a cross between an old yacht and sailboat. A giant telephone pole seemed to have been mounted right in the center of the old ship with cross beams. There were ropes everywhere and I honestly didn't want to be near the water, but we knew we couldn't stay in Brownsville.

You're probably thinking that life couldn't get much harder, but I knew it would. The next two judgments would make life exponentially harder to survive. People were dying either from hardship or from public execution. It was so bad at that point that it seemed almost absurd. You're living through it, so you know what I mean.

We saw, via the ever-present internet signals, that not every part of the world was being hit as hard. South America and Australia were hit the hardest by the first trumpet judgment. The Amazon rainforest and nearly every tree in Australia were burned to ash. Eastern Europe was hit pretty hard as well. Grass fires swept across Africa and killed millions of animals. It was devastating. Yet the reports from other areas were being touted as good news.

The new Pax Davino temple outside the old town of Pisté, once known as Chichen Itza, had not only survived what the global government was calling a climate change event, it was reopened for pilgrimage. Worship of the feathered snake god KuKulkan was touted as a way to reach evolved personhood and prosperity, but the symbolism is pretty clear. The Bible calls Lucifer "that old serpent, the

Devil" and of course his most famous appearance was to Eve in the Garden of Eden. How people could see worship of a serpent by any name or appearance is a mystery to me. But each of the ten capitals was reopening nearby megalithic sites as new temples for pilgrimage and worship. Lorenzo would have known all about the old gods once worshiped throughout the world by different names to different people. All I really knew was that it was a false god and a false religion. But proclaiming that truth had made me a wanted man.

In Brownsville, many people had begun to live on the boats that provided their food from the sea. With no commercial fishing over the last eighteen months, the gulf was rich with sea life again. The locals took turns going out in their boats. One good haul could last weeks for the entire population of the little town, which had shrunk down to barely over a hundred people, and that was before the first trumpet judgment. Old techniques for preserving the seafood were being used, and there was still plenty of seaweed washing up on the beaches each day to keep the locals busy.

We had been in Brownsville for three days when word came in that a group of security super soldiers had landed in Tampico. The fishermen from Brownsville often met other ships as they worked the Gulf Coast. News was a valuable commodity. Everything from where the fish were schooling, to what news was coming out of Mérida, was traded for fishing gear. Nets, hooks, fishing line, poles, and even rope was hard to come by. And what angler doesn't know the joy of finding new tackle. A little news to replace a ripped net, or a snapped line, was the cost of business on the open sea, and everyone was desperate for an explanation as to what was happening in the world.

Of course, a person couldn't just come right out with the truth. Not since admitting that you believe in the God of the Bible could get you killed on the spot. It was a time of conspiracies and strategic conversations. A person couldn't give away too much, and theories were bandied about as people carefully tried to avoid saying anything that might get them into trouble. Piracy was also a problem. Just as there were bandits on the roads, there were pirates at sea. A good ship was valuable, fishing gear was even more so, and a fresh catch was in many circumstances, worth killing for.

When word reached us of a new team of super soldiers landing at Tampico, which was the hub for all the north Mexican NARA travel, I had no doubts about who they were coming for. The only question was how much time we had before they tracked us to Brownsville.

"This is it," Bobby Lane declared. "*The Show Stopper*, he declared proudly as he stepped on board. "I've been living on board a while now," he said. "You'll have to excuse the mess."

"You sure this is a good idea?" Cat asked me.

"No," I said. "But we can't outrun them."

"We were lucky last time," Hector said.

The three of us were pretty tight by that point, as you could probably guess. Running for one's life tends to bond people together.

"Sooner or later, they'll track us down," I said.

"But won't they do that in Mérida, too?" Cat asked.

It was a conversation we had gone over many times.

"Probably, but it's the last place they'll look," I argued.

"And we've got friends there who can probably help us hide or find a new place to go."

"What about the second trumpet judgment?" Cat asked.

"Statistically, the odds of it coming down anywhere near the Gulf of Mexico are pretty low," Bobby Lane interjected into our conversation. "The results will affect us no doubt, but the odds of us dying at sea are pretty small."

"But there's a chance," Cat said.

"There are no guarantees anywhere," I told her. "What do we have to lose?"

"I've never been fond of boats," she said. "I get seasick."

"I can help with that," Bobby Lane said. "I've got ear plugs in the cabin below. It's an old fisherman's trick to ward off sea sickness. You plug up one ear and trick your brain into thinking it's unreliable. So, your brain just trusts what your eyes see. Some people swear it works. I've never had that ailment, but I keep ear plugs on board, just in case."

Bobby Lane was a talker and was thrilled at the prospect of spending a few days sailing with a captive audience.

He led us down into one the two staterooms on board. He was living in the main quarters, but the second stateroom had four built-in bunks. There wasn't a lot of room, but there were only three of us. We stashed our go bags and weapons on the fourth bunk. Only Hector remained armed as we headed back up onto the main deck.

"Cindy Proctor is due back tomorrow, or the next day at the latest," Bobby went on. "She'll have the latest news, and a fresh catch too. We can prep for the journey until then."

We had been lucky to find the group of Bible believers. Most places were skeptical of strangers, but in Brownsville we were taken in and treated like family. It wasn't much of a stretch to see why they were so full of joy and hospitality, although I didn't ask if they were believers until I had seen a well-worn Bible conspicuously left out. The group were ravenous for any sort of information on the tribulation. They had a few Bibles among the group, but no commentaries or books specifically on Bible prophecy. We shared ours, and the group gave us rest, shelter, and plenty of food. I'll admit dried fish was a bit strange at first. Not as leathery as jerky, but not soft and flaky like cooked fish either. The locals in Brownsville didn't have a lot of spices, but there was plenty of sea salt. The fish were gutted, then cut into strips, and salted before being left to hang for days. The moisture was drawn out of the meat and left tasting a little like cooked fish that's left out for a while. Still, after subsisting on rattlesnake jerky and rodents for days, the dried fish was delightful.

We spent the rest of the day collecting seaweed. The beach was two hours walk from the pier. Driftwood was collected to use for cooking fires, but unfortunately wasn't good for smoking fish or building good structures. The sea salt made the wood brittle. It burned fast, too. But it was plentiful, and the nights were cold. Any kind of fuel for a fire was welcome.

Like the fish, the seaweed was cleaned, salted, then laid out in the sun to dry. By the end of the day, we had a basket full of dried seaweed, which would supplement the fish we would eat on the journey southeast, toward the tip of the Yucatán Peninsula.

"There's no heat," Bobby Lane said. "I've been toying with fixing up some wave generators or wind turbines to charge the batteries, but I haven't gotten to it yet. You'll need to bundle up."

When the sun set, we went down into the old yacht's main salon. It had once been a very ritzy common room. The bar was still in one corner, and there were sofas on each side, but right through the middle of the room was the new main mast. Bobby Lane had cut a hole in the roof to help support the towering beam. The teak flooring was covered with pits and stains from the sea water that got into the salon. And there were several metal poles at various angles bolted to the mast and the floor to give additional support. They had to duck under and climb over several of the support poles to reach the furniture.

"We should keep watch," Hector said.

"There's not much to see at night," Bobby Lane said.

"You do understand that the NARA security people are hunting for us," I reminded him.

"Oh, sure," he said, waving the explanation off. "They're miles and miles from here. We'll be long gone before they turn up... if they ever do."

"I wouldn't be so sure," Cat said. "I've seen them outrun a truck."

It was clear that Bobby Lane had his doubts. He was a man of science and had trouble dealing with reality when things weren't the way they were supposed to be. People weren't supposed to be able to outrun a motor vehicle, but the security team members weren't really normal people anymore. Bobby's need to understand things had led to a deep commitment to the scientific method. It had become his religion despite growing up in the Bible Belt. He preferred not to think about things he couldn't see or test in a lab. He knew about God but had no personal faith in him when the Rapture changed everything. Suddenly, all the things he had been told about by believers in his family and co-workers of faith, were undeniable. So, Bobby had surrendered his need to see and quantify God. He put his trust in Jesus, but some old habits were hard to break. Our stories about the genetic modifications of the NARA security teams were a bit of a stretch for Bobby.

"Well, be that as it may, you don't know for certain that they're after you," Bobby continued. "All we know, is that a group of them came ashore at Tampico. They could simply be replacements for those along the border manning the checkpoints."

Hector gave the engineer a sidelong look of pity, then turned his attention back to the window where he was keeping an eye out along the pier.

The motion of the boat rocking slightly wooed me to sleep. I would have preferred to sleep beside Cat, but we opted to take individual beds to get the best sleep possible. Hector roused me a few hours before dawn. When it came to the amount of effort going into our safety, he was carrying the lion's share. I tried to let him have a more equal role, but he wouldn't hear of it.

When I got to the deck, the cold air coming off the water was bracing. I can't tell you how much I missed caffeine. I could have used some that morning. It was hard to stay awake at first, and then when the sun rose, it was hard to keep my back to it so that I could watch the pier. If trouble was coming, it would be from land. There were no ships moving toward us, so I needed to stay focused, but the sunrise was incredible.

Later that day, Cindy Proctor came to shore. She was helming a shrimp boat whose net arms had been rigged with sails. It made the boat look like a frill-necked lizard with dirty white frills. We watched the ship approach the pier. While she was still a hundred yards out the sails were lowered. Several men in rowboats went out to her. Ropes were tossed to the men, who pulled the ship in close enough that she could be tugged into place on one of the many piers. Fortunately, the pier in the Brownsville harbor was made of concrete. Long, narrow walkways spread out into the water. Once Cindy's ship, *The Neptune IX*, was secured, her bounty was unloaded. Large crates on wheels were pushed out to the ship, loaded with fish, and brought back to where all the towns-people were waiting. I have never seen such coordinated effort. Some of the fish was cleaned and filleted. Others were gutted, scaled, and cut into strips before being salted and hung to dry. Still, other fish were chopped up and left in buckets as bait for the next fishing run.

Hand pumps were used to wash out the hold on *The Neptune IX* and on the docks once the fish had been processed. Just down the street, piles of driftwood had been collected and were set ablaze. The fresh fish were roasted on spits or grilled over hot coals. Some were wrapped in aluminum foil and cooked right in the fire itself. The entire town's atmosphere was festive. I counted eighty-two partici-pants and couldn't help but wonder if there were other small communities hanging on in other parts of the world.

We joined in. Processing the catch or cooking it wasn't in

our skill set. I mean, I could gut a fish and cut off some of the meat, but it wouldn't be pretty or efficient. The Sotos enjoyed sushi, but I was never a fan of raw fish. Could I eat it? Sure, but I didn't want to.

By evening most people had gone home. Staying up past dark was no longer appealing. The survivors in Brownsville preferred to rise early, work hard during the daylight hours, and rest when it got dark. We carried a basket of cooked fish back to *The Show Stopper*, ate our fill before bedtime, and got some sleep. At first light the next morning, as the wind shifted around and blew toward the open sea, we cast off our lines and lowered the top sail. Bobby Lane was a perfectionist. He kept his sails tied to the yard arms in such a way that he could pull certain lines to unfurl them without climbing up on the tall, timber pole. We moved out from Brownsville at a slow, steady pace. I'll admit, sailing a boat, even an improvised yacht, was exciting. There was something primal about harnessing the wind and heading out to sea.

An hour later, the harbor and the remains of Brownsville were nothing but a blurry line on the westward horizon. And for the first time since the security team was spotted heading into Monterrey, I felt my tensions ease a little. We each wore an ear plug, really, just a wad of soft wax, in one ear to ward off sea sickness. Cat still looked like she might succumb to the constant motion of the vessel. Hector seemed immune, but he opted out of lunch.

In the harbor the boat rocked and swayed. In the open sea, she rolled and pitched. The waves were slow, gradual lumps that flowed across the surface of the ocean. The modified yacht shuttered up, then slid down each one. It was repetitive, but the constant motion was difficult to adjust to. That afternoon, I slept nearly three hours. Hector slept six straight. As the sun went down, Bobby Lane turned over control of the ship to me. I stood at the steering wheel and held it steady as he shimmied up the mast and carefully folded up each sail, tying it in place with the same line he used to untie them that morning.

"How far do you think we got?" I asked him.

"The Cancun is about 750 nautical miles. With wind power alone, we'll get maybe ninety miles a day. But without GPS, it's impossible to know for sure."

"Will we be off course in the morning?"

"No," he said, coming back down and securing the lines he had just tied to the ship's wheel. "We'll sail due south until the coastline comes into view, then follow it."

"Why didn't we do that from the beginning?" I asked.

He looked at me through his thick glasses, making me wonder what he would do if something happened to them.

"The coast north of Tampico is filled with pirates," he explained. It's better to give them a wide berth."

"What do we have that pirates would want?" I asked.

"Food, weapons, a girl," he said. "Even the ship's sails are valuable these days."

A shutter ran down my back at the thought of people getting their hands on Cat. As soon as my shift at the steering wheel was done, I went down and checked on the submachine gun in my pack. It had a shoulder strap and, I decided it was best if I kept the weapon on my person until we reached our port. We weren't on a luxury cruise, as we were all about to find out.

# CHAPTER 21

HECTOR WOKE me shortly before dawn. We had cast a sea anchor and were waiting for Bobby Lane to wake up before setting sail again. But as the sun began to rise, I saw two other ships approaching. They were both smaller vessels, not quite rowboats, but only slightly larger. There was a large pair of sailing binoculars in a bin beside the ship's wheel. I pulled them out and focused on the nearer of the two ships. It was coming in from our bow, eight people rowing, and a ninth on a platform near the back. I also spotted what looked like a traditional outboard motor.

It was tempting to check out the boat moving in from our stern, but I had seen enough to know we were in trouble. Worse still, the wind seemed weak that morning. Even if we had the anchor lifted and the sails unfurled, I wasn't sure there was enough wind to outrun the approaching ships. It was barely dawn, the sky was still gray, and the sun hadn't breached the horizon, but its golden rays were starting to

lighten the sky. It felt more like twilight. I could see the silhouettes of the approaching ships, and the people working them,
but no real details. Dropping the binoculars back into their
case, I raced down to the primary stateroom.

"Bobby!" I called, knocking hard on his door. "Bobby,
we've got company."

"What?" he asked.

"Two ships. Headed this way," I shouted. "Hector, Cat,
there are pirates coming!"

It was a bold claim, but given the circumstances what else
could I assume. The ships weren't big enough to be plying the
open sea. And we were out of sight of land. They must have
seen us leaving and followed, rowing all night to reach us.
They must also have some way to see at night. I couldn't
imagine they could have reached by chance, or that they
would be able to get before and immediately behind us in the
dark.

I opened my state room and traded my life vest for the
bullet proof armor that Hector had given me. Next came the
belt, loaded with more ammunition for the B&T APC9k.
Hector was up, pulling on his own battle gear. Cat, who had
taken a turn on deck right at sundown and staying up later
than the rest of us, was slower to get up.

"Pirates?" she asked.

"Yeah," I said. "Has to be."

"What do we do?" she replied.

"Kill them," Hector said.

The line between murder and self-defense is sometimes
fuzzy. If a policeman shoots a suspect who is armed but
running away, is it justified? If a person breaks into your

home, but they are unarmed, would you really be protecting yourself and your family? I suppose one day Jesus will answer all those kinds of questions. But I will say that when you are on the open sea, with danger all around you, and people with bad intentions are approaching, the feeling of eminent danger is heightened. I checked my submachine gun. It was loaded with the safety on. Hector beat me out the door, but not by much.

We were the first ones on the deck. By that time the sky had turned pink, and there was enough light to make out details about the approaching ships.

"Guns," Hector said.

The nearest boat was still over a hundred meters from our ship, but the rowers were storing their oars and pulling out guns. I snatched up the binoculars and looked at the ship coming up behind us. It was farther away, with only six rowers, but seemed no different from the other ship.

"Holy cow!" Bobby Lane said. "Don't just stand there, get the anchor up."

Hector and I hurried to the anchor station. It was a motorized wheel that would wind up and draw the heavy anchor from the bottom of the sea. Only, the yacht had no power, which meant Hector and I had to pull the anchor up by hand. It wasn't as difficult as it sounded. The winch had a lever which we took turns spinning. The chain rattled, and the locking mechanism that kept the chain from sliding back out popped as it flipped past each tooth on the winch. Sound carried on the open water. There was no doubt that they knew what we were up to, a fact confirmed by the grumble of their outboard motors.

"If we get all the sails down," Bobby Lane declared. "We might be able to outrun them."

The first shot went over our heads. The boat was far enough out that we heard the bullet pass just before the report from the rifle reached us.

"They're shooting!" Bobby said, covering his head.

"Leave the sails up," I told him, before turning to Hector. "What do we do?"

"Keep your weapon down," he said. "Let them get close."

Cat was just starting up from the cabins below.

"Better stay there," I told her, gesturing with one hand.

"You don't need me?" she asked.

"Not yet," I said. "Bobby, you go down too. Get the first-aid supplies ready, just in case."

"Ahoy there!" a gruff voice from across the water shouted. "Put down your weapons and get everyone on deck."

"Who are you?" I shouted, as I moved to the rear of the boat so that I was facing the smaller of the two craft.

It was rushing toward us, creating a wide wake in the otherwise still water. The crew, seven in all, had put away their oars and were checking their weapons. Most appeared to be hunting rifles, but there were a couple that seemed to military grade. I held my submachine gun down beside my thigh, the stock was retracted. I flicked the safety catch off.

As I write this it sounds like I wasn't terrified, but I really was. My heart was pounding like a drummer on steroids. My stomach felt like someone had tied it into a knot. There was bile in my throat and my legs were trembling. I even had sweat on my forehead despite the cold.

"We're coming aboard," the gruff voice from the front of the ship shouted. "You resist, and we'll kill you all."

The boat approaching from the rear slowed. It was drifting toward us, the outboard motor lifted from the water. I saw one of the pirates bend down, grab a coil of rope, and toss it toward me. It unfurled as it sailed through the air, then slapped over the stern rail of our yacht. Bending down, I picked up the rope and started wrapping it around one of the cleats. At that same moment, from behind me I heard Hector's M4. It chugged out death in a deep, booming report. The pirates at the rear of our ship were only twenty yards away and getting closer every second. I saw them react to the shooting, but I did too. Their sudden effort to direct their weapons at me made their small ship rock. I wasn't smooth or fast as I dropped their line and brought the submachine gun up at my hip. When I pulled the trigger the weapon jerked in my hands, like a wild animal desperate to escape my grip. But I held it as steady as I could and poured fifteen rounds into the boat of pirates.

Not every bullet hit a person. The first four hit their bow. The leader of the group, the man in the back, even got a shot off in return. But he missed. I'm pretty sure most of the pirates had unloaded weapons. It's impossible to know if an assailant with a weapon has ammunition in their gun. But only one of them shot back at me, and my bullets knocked him into the water while he was working the bolt to load another shot.

The entire battle lasted four seconds at most. I fired off half the thirty-round clip on my first barrage, and followed it up with two more five-round bursts. Twenty-five bullets killed or seriously wounded the seven pirates, and compromised the thin, metallic hull of their boat. I turned, hitting the release for my magazine, and pulling a fresh one from my belt. It slid smoothly into place. As I hurried to where Hector was on one knee, emptying his own weapon into the other pirate boat, I pulled the charging lever. It popped back into place just as one of Hector's bullets hit the metal housing of the outboard motor. A spark flew over a puddle of fuel that was leaking from another bullet hole. The motor exploded, shredding the boat and the pirates inside that were still alive. Wood and bits of metal flew in all directions. I stumbled backward and fell on my rear. When I got up there was no sign of the bad guys.

"Hector," I said. "Hey man, are you okay?"

"I don't think so," he replied.

He was on his feet with his back to me. When he turned, I saw a shard of metal in his neck. Blood was pumping out from around the shard and soaking the front of his armor.

"Cat!" I screamed, rushing to the former cartel gunman. "Help me! Cat! Hector's hurt!"

To her credit, Cat bolted from the cabin with first-aid supplies, but there was nothing we could do. The shard of metal had severed Hector's carotid artery. I caught him as he sank to his knees. His M4 automatic rifle clattered to the deck. Hector leaned back into my arms as Cat appeared with a small first-aid kit. It seemed almost ridiculous in her hands as Hector's life blood pumped from his neck.

"Hank," the dying gunman said.

"I'm here," I said. "I got you, Hector."

"Thank you, Hank," he said.

I'm not sure he could see me. His eyes were clear, but he was looking past me.

"You're gonna be okay," I said, my own eyes flooding with tears.

"Hank," he said, his voice barely a whisper. "It's so beautiful."

Those were his last words. I'm pretty sure he was seeing Heaven, or maybe Jesus himself. His body suddenly went limp in my arms.

"No!" I screamed. "Hector!"

Cat dropped the first-aid supplies and instead, she wrapped her arms around my head. I'm not sure how long we stayed like that. I couldn't stop crying. Hector was like my shadow. I couldn't stand losing him. In many ways it was as bad as losing Lorenzo. Hector wasn't a talkative person. When Cat and I talked about world events and end time prophecies, he mostly just listened. Even when we asked him a question, his answers were always short and sweet. He was a man with a very nefarious past, but Jesus had forgiven him. The change in Hector was immediate and obvious. He was still a hard man, but he reveled in the second chance God had given him. And he was dedicated to me and Cat. Over the weeks we traveled together, a bond had formed. Having it severed was heart wrenching.

Eventually I put Hector down. We removed his body armor, cleaned him up as best we could, then let his body slip down beneath the waves. I won't lie. That day I questioned everything in my life, every choice, every decision. I felt as though someone had reached inside me and ripped out my heart. And to his credit, Bobby Lane never said a word.

# CHAPTER 22

WE SAW NO MORE PIRATES. Cat and Bobby sailed the ship. Looking back, I can say that I truly felt as though anyone who was close to me died. It wasn't the case, but I wallowed in that lie for days. When most people think of spiritual warfare, they imagine exorcisms or carnal temptations. In my experience it's much more insidious than that. A single lie told over and over can feel like reality. For three days, I was useless to the people who needed me. And it wasn't just self-pity, it was a debilitating lie. I feared that I was cursed. Would I get Cat killed next? We were hoping to find LB and Allie. But what would come of that?

I decided that I would turn myself in. If the government had me, they wouldn't go nosing around my friends. No one else needed to die to keep me alive. No one else needed to suffer loss because of the heat I was bringing. Of course, I didn't tell Cat. She would have vetoed the entire idea. But with the decision made, I snapped out of the grief stupor.

Bobby Lane and Cat both seemed relieved to see me back to my old self. But I wasn't being honest.

If not for the second trumpet judgment, I might have gone through with it. We were in sight of land by that point, following the coast. And when the Judgment hit, we were in the dark, literally.

I've seen videos of the object. It wasn't a comet or a meteor. The Bible says it was a mountain, and that's what it looked like: a giant-sized, rocky object. Where it came from no one can say. One minute there was blue sky and calm water, and the next minute the object fell. It hit somewhere in the North Atlantic. The impact didn't just cause a massive wave. According to the scientists, it passed through the water to the ocean floor and left a huge crater. Essentially, it broke open a hole in the ocean floor, so when the water rushed back, it funneled into the hole, creating a whirlpool.

I'm not an oceanographer. I can't tell you how the giant hole, and subsequent whirlpool, effected the Atlantic's currents, but I can tell you what happened to us. We had lowered the sails and were cruising along with hopes of finding a secluded beach to come ashore on. I had my books and weapons, extra clothes, and some food in a waterproof sack. Bobby called it a seabag, with two inflatables to keep it from sinking as we swam ashore. The plan was to sail as close to the beach as Bobby dared, somewhere before we reached Progreso, the little coastal town due north of Mérida. From there, Cat and I would swim in. I had even put on my life-jacket and was only wearing my boxer shorts and a t-shirt. The water was clear and not freezing, although it was much colder than it ever got before the Rapture. But a short swim wouldn't kill us, and Bobby couldn't risk running his ship aground.

But before we found a place that looked inviting, something strange happened. Despite the wind, we found ourselves moving away from land.

"Hey Bobby," I said, "what's happening?"

"Are we moving backward?" Cat asked, looking over the edge of the boat.

"I don't know," Bobby Lane said. "It doesn't make any sense."

I glanced up. The land, which had been clear enough that I could see rocks along the coastline, and trees, was losing focus as we moved away. The telephone pole mast was groaning, the dozens of ropes that held the sails in places creaked. The yacht shuttered under the pressure.

"We are!" Cat said. "We're being pulled out to sea."

"What's got us?"

"Nothing," Bobby said. "It's impossible."

That's when I knew exactly what was happening, even if I couldn't explain it. The second trumpet judgment killed a third of the life in the sea and a third of the sea fairing ships. I knew deep down that we were part of that number.

"I think we shoul---"

The pop of the mast snapping in half was louder than a gun shot. We all ducked instinctively, then looked up as the towering pillar groaned. The ropes snapped. Bobby was knocked off his feet, his glasses flying from his face and sliding across the deck. I bent over Cat, who was hunched by the stairs going down into the yacht's staterooms. Everything happened so fast, yet the mast falling seemed to be in slow motion. Yards of dull colored sails twisted, the ropes pulled tight, then snapping. One whipped across my shoulder in a fiery snap that left a nasty welt in its wake.

Then, the mast toppled over. The yacht's fiberglass railing was no match for the mast's weight. The heavy wooden beam smashed through the railing, hit the deck, buckling the wooden floor, then slid into the sea. The entire yacht tilted under the weight as the remaining ropes held the heavy mast and sails to the ship.

"Cut the lines!" Bobby screamed. "Cut the lines!"

In those types of circumstances, you don't think. It was what basic military training was for, to teach the body to react in moments of intense stress. When people have guns pointed at you, leaping up to attack is incredibly dangerous, but less so than cowering in fear. Something in Bobby's command triggered my own training. I was upright, moving to the nearest rope with Hector's ten-inch Bowie knife in hand. For some reason I had kept the knife out of the seabag. It was a custom-forged blade, made from many layers of steel that were heated and twisted before being pounded into shape. The guard matched the Damascus blade and the handle was bone. Hector kept it well honed, and I felt close to him when I held it. Maybe it was God's prompting that led me to keep the weapon tucked into a little loop on my lifejacket. It saved us from capsizing. That much is certain.

The first line was pulled so tightly, I barely touched it with the razor sharp blade, and it parted. The next rope wasn't as easy. I hacked and sawed at the line, cutting it strand by strand, or so it seemed to me. The third line shifted the heavy weight, and the ship settled a little. Bobby was scrambling around on his hands and knees on the slanted deck, searching for his glasses. Cat stayed by the stairs going down into the ship, as I scrambled to cut the lines. There were thirteen ropes holding the mast to the yacht. When I cut the last one, it seemed like we leaped away. The yacht rocked hard, and when I finally felt secure enough, I looked toward the shore. It was barely visible.

"What do we do now?" Cat asked.

"There's nothing we can do," Bobby asked. He had found his glasses and was putting them on with trembling hands. "We're in trouble."

The thought of diving overboard crossed my mind, but the sea was running almost like a river. In the distance where the shore had been, I could see a dark stripe.

"What is that?" I asked, pointing.

"Can't be," Bobby said.

We had joined Cat by the stairs going down below deck. I had one hand on Cat, the other on Bobby, as if I could hold onto them.

"Can't be what?" Cat asked.

"It looks like the water is receding," he said.

"What's that mean?" I asked him.

"I think it's going be a Tsunami," he said gravely.

That got me moving. "Stay here!" I shouted.

Nearby, under one of the built-in beach seats that lined the rear part of the deck, were more life vests. I grabbed them and returned to my friends.

"Odds are, at some point this ship is going down," I said.

"There's already water down below," Cat pointed out. "I can hear it sloshing."

"The mast must have cracked the hull," Bobby pointed out.

"So, we have to be ready to go into the water," I told them.

Cat and I already had life vests on and fastened over our chests. We put on a second, then wrapped a third around our waists. I tied the seabag to me, and the three of us braced ourselves. In the open water it's hard to gauge how much you are actually moving. The shore had disappeared, and soon the dark strip that Bobby said was sea floor, vanished as well. Bobby retrieved two life preservers, and we tied ourselves together with one of the last remaining ropes that hadn't been severed when the mast broke.

Eventually the sea began to grow rough. Across the surface I could see whitecaps forming and breaking. It wasn't the gradual roll of waves like before, but a choppy, uneven, shuttering motion. The ship groaned and shook, vibrations rattled through the hull. I knew instinctively if the ship went down before the big wave came, we wouldn't make it. Nor did I think we would survive long at sea. The water wasn't freezing, but if we were stuck for hours in the cold, it would zap our body heat, and we would perish from hypothermia.

There wasn't a lot of conversation either. The ship was pulled out, and before long, we saw the wave. A towering wall of dark blue was forming, and the yacht was headed straight for it. By that point we could see water on the teak flooring of the lower level. The bilge had flooded, and the water was rising. It wouldn't be long before the ship sank, and we were forced into the water.

"What is that?" Cat asked, pointing at the huge wave.

"The tsunami," Bobby said.

He looked miserable. His thinning hair was sticking out at odd directions, and the thickness of his two life vests made the skin around his face bulge up toward his thick spectacles.

"You should secure your glasses," I told him.

"Oh, yeah," he said. "I forget I'm wearing them."

He pulled off his glasses and tucked them into a zippered pouch on his life jacket. It was clear to me that he couldn't see anything without them. He kept his eyes closed, his mouth moving in silent prayer.

We were all praying by that point, begging God for help, for protection. But when the ship started up the huge wave, things became incredibly intense. Loose items on the deck, from spare bits of rope to shattered wood and fiberglass, slid to the stern. Pretty soon the three of us were holding onto a bar mounted on the roof of the salon, which normally came to mid-thigh on me. Eventually the wave was so steep that we were practically dangling. I thought the ship would flip over backward, but instead, *The Show Stopper* made it to the crest. The wave wasn't a massive curl yet. It was still building as it rushed toward shore that was miles away and was more like a huge mountain. While on the crest, which only lasted a few incredible moments, the ship righted itself and became almost motionless. We felt the sun on our faces and heard the squawk of sea birds. They were the only birds that survived the fiery hailstorm. Looking out across the vast expanse of ocean, I could see a haze in the distance that I was certain was land, although by that point, I was so turned around I didn't know what I was looking at.

Then, we plunged down the back side of the massive wave. It was like the most frightening roller coaster ever designed. Spray flew high into the air as we raced downward. Cat and I instinctively dropped down to our knees and used the side of the salon to brace ourselves. Bobby almost tumbled over the roof of the yacht's staterooms, but I managed to grab onto him and pull him back. When we hit the trough behind the wave, water rushed over the railing. I thought the yacht was finished, but she managed to reemerge, shaking off the excess water and wallowing a bit before we started up the next wave.

Subsequent waves weren't as big as the first, but they were still substantial. The yacht made it over four of them before sinking out from below us. The three of us were held aloft by our life vests and safety gear. When the yacht went down, we bobbed up, and then the current swept us away. I didn't think things could get worse than riding on the sinking ship. I was wrong.

# CHAPTER 23

THE COLD SALTWATER was a shock to the system. Fortunately, the three of us managed to stay together. I had the only knife between us, so our rope was tied to me, with each end wrapped around my companions and tied with a simple slip knot in case it became necessary to separate from the others quickly.

Being on the yacht surrounded by towering waves was terrifying. But things were much worse in the water. We could only see a few yards in any direction. The three of us clung to the pair of life preservers, linking our arms through the foam rings. Our multiple life jackets kept us above the surface of the water in an almost effortless manner, but we were completely helpless to the swirling currents.

Occasionally, strong rip tides sucked us down, but the life jackets and preservers pulled us back to the surface. If there were sea creatures around us, we didn't know it. The water was dark and cold. We were soon shivering, our teeth chattering. Fear gripped my mind like a vice, squeezing it until no rational thoughts were left. My prayers were barely cohesive and all about survival. *God help! Father please, get us through this. Don't let us die.*

At some point I was hit with a vague memory of reading about the apostle Paul being shipwrecked. All I really remembered was that he survived. We couldn't carry on a conversation as you might imagine. The best we managed were tremulous admonishments to hang on and not to give up.

When the waves lifted us high, we could hear the tsunami crashing on the shore, flooding inland. None of us saw it, but the sound was the world breaking. Somehow, we had been pulled out to sea, only to have our ship sink and then be flung back toward shore by the rushing waves. The surf roared, and I knew things were going to get worse. We were still a long way out from the shore when a wave picked us up. Near the crest, the wave began to curl. We barely made it through before the wave crashed down on itself.

"We won't make it through the next one!" I shouted.

"What should we do?" Cat asked.

"Hold on to the life preservers," I said. "If the ropes get tangled, pull yourself free."

The words were barely out of my mouth before the next wave rose over us. We held onto the life preservers as tightly as we could. But the wave broke, and we were suddenly twenty yards deep and tumbling end over end. I had no idea which way was up, but fortunately my life jacket was pulling me back to the surface. I had no idea by the time I reached the top what had happened to Cat or Bobby Lane. I had lost my grip on the life preservers, and before I could look around, the next wave crashed.

Once more I was pounded down, and to my surprise, I hit the sandy bottom of the ocean floor. The currents were vicious. After being pushed inland and down, the riptide sucked me back away from the shore. I managed to get to the surface, suck in a breath of air, and the cycle repeated. The fourth time I went down, the waves rolled me into the shallows. That's not to say I could just find my feet and stand up, or that the water wasn't over my head, but I could feel the seafloor angling up, and the currents were strong.

Sand was washed over my body, stinging my skin. I got another breath, was crushed by a crashing wave, then rolled higher up the shore. The riptide started to suck me back out, but my feet found the ground and I managed to push off, rising up quickly and getting caught in a rushing wall of water that hadn't curled yet. To my surprise I saw land ahead of me, or at least evidence of land. A huge boulder to my right, and trees ahead of me sticking out of the water. We were in the tidal wave that had rushed ashore. Somehow, I caught onto a palm tree and held on.

Wave after wave crashed into me or sent water surging past. My companions were gone. I let a wave lift me near the top of the palm tree. Grabbing on, I flung one leg over, and the water dropped away. I was above it. The palm was leaning and bent from the pounding waves. Its branches weren't strong enough to hold me, but they gave me purchase on the swaying trunk. The tsunami lasted for hours. I can't say how long, but I was dehydrated from the saltwater and exhausted from holding onto the tree that was battered by the waves.

Eventually a surge of water uprooted the palm tree. I was washed inland by the wave of water, well past the shore, into what had been a tropical rain forest, but had burned.

The tsunami had pounded the remains and snapped off the charred trees. It reminded me of old pictures of loggers floating trees downriver. When I lived in Spokane and visited the surrounding areas, there were pictures on display of lakes that were covered with floating trees, with loggers walking across them. I couldn't do that. The charred trees were too brittle, but I managed to get atop a boulder. There I lay, exhausted and waterlogged, dying of thirst while the waters surged.

Eventually the water receded. I was desperate to find Cat, but I didn't know where to go. I didn't know which direction she had gone. I couldn't even remember if she had been to my right or to my left when the first big wave hit.

"Cat!" I shouted. "Cat!"

The only sounds were the crashing waves. The surf was loud. And I was in a daze. I still had the seabag. Inside, we had water in insulated cans, but it wasn't until hours after I was safely ashore that I remembered them. I opened the bag and pulled out my water can. The liquid inside was tepid, but I didn't care. I gulped it down eagerly, before realizing that it might be the only fresh water I would get for a while. The tsunami had washed inland for a long way. What it had tainted, I couldn't guess. All I knew for certain, was I needed to be careful with my resources, and I had to find my friends.

I found Bobby Lane first, but it wasn't a happy reunion. The poor man had been bashed into some rocks. I wasn't sure if he drowned or died from the impact. His head was split open, and I could see bone that was stained pink from blood and sea water through the gash. There were cuts and abrasions all over his body. His glasses were shattered inside the pocket of his life vest.

Fear that I might find Cat in the same state cut my grief for Bobby short. Nor did I dwell on the fact that another friend had died. Bobby was a good man, but he had been wrong about the second trumpet judgment. His ship had been in the one third lost at sea, and it was only by a miracle that I had survived.

Night fell, and so did the temperatures. My body was dehydrated from the saltwater, but my clothing and skin were soaked. Everything was too wet to even consider getting a fire started. Instead, I pulled off my boxers and t-shirt. There were dry clothes in the seabag. I put on pants, a shirt, and a coat, then huddled by a pile of smashed logs that blocked the wind. It was a long, miserable night, and I don't think I had felt so alone since losing Lorenzo in the Rapture.

As soon as the sun came up the next day, I set out in search of Cat again. Eventually, I found a pile of life jackets on a jumble of rocks. They were hers, there was no question about it. But Cat was nowhere to be found. I went around and around the jumble of rocks before I finally noticed some blackened marks on the landward sign. The markings were hard to make out. The charcoal residue had been mostly blown off the boulders, but I eventually read the word *inland*.

From there I moved through the debris from the tsunami, no longer following the coastline, but moving inland. I saw branches forming arrows, and small rocks stacked up as markers. It felt a bit like a treasure hunt, and took most of the day, but eventually I found Cat. And it was no surprise that she wasn't alone. What did surprise me, was that she was helping a ragtag crew of desperados who had been hurt in the tsunami.

"Cat!" I shouted when I saw her.

I tried to run but I was too weak. My legs were trembling, and my eyes stung, but no tears came. I was still dehydrated. My tongue felt like a wad of bubble gum I had chewed on for hours, and my eyelids were like dry husks. Rubbing them didn't help. I had sipped water throughout the day, but it wasn't enough. Somehow, Cat seemed fine despite *The Show Stopper* sinking and her having been washed ashore in a tsunami.

"Hank!" she called out.

We fell into each other's arms, and I felt so relieved. We stayed like that for a bit, just on our knees, holding one another. Eventually we looked one another over.

"You're dehydrated," she said.

"How are you okay?" I asked.

"You sound awful. Let me get you something to drink."

I didn't want her to leave me, but I was too exhausted to stop her. Not far away, six people sat staring at me. As horrible as I felt, they looked worse. Two had broken bones, and the other four all had blood-stained bandages on various parts of their bodies. They sat leaning back against an old boat with a hole in it. I hadn't even noticed the stream nearby. Cat brought me a cup of cool water in a dented metal cup. I slurped it down between my cracked and swollen lips. It was the sweetest thing I had ever tasted.

"You've got the seabag, Hank. Why didn't you drink your water?"

"Didn't know how long I might need it," I said, my voice hoarse. "Who are they?"

"Locals," Cat said. "They were hurt in the tsunami. Their companions left them behind."

"Harsh," I said. "Bobby didn't make it."

Cat reacted as if I had slapped her. The tears came, and we commiserated together. I must have drunk a gallon of water by nightfall, but I was feeling a lot better. The locals didn't speak English, but we helped them as best we could. The next day, a group of disaster relief officials from Mérida showed up. They didn't ask a lot of questions. Everyone was in shock. They gave us food, took the injured for medical care, and told us where we were.

Somehow, we had ended up on the tip of the Yucatan Peninsula just south of where a coastal village called Dzilam De Bravo had been destroyed. We were encouraged to head north to the rebuilt 176 Highway that would take us inland toward the new capital at Mérida, and the pilgrim road to Chechan Itza.

We did as we were instructed, keeping our weapons hidden inside the seabag. We ate the last of the salted fish, but once we reached the new highway, which was just a smoothed-out dirt road between sections of burned up forest, we found more volunteers handing out food, water, clothing, and medical supplies. We weren't the only ones who survived the tsunami. Thousands of people from Canada and the United States had gone south, following the mandate by Paul Eon for global citizens to move into to the new capitals of the ten regions. Central Americans came from the south, and while resources were utilized to turn Mérida into a worthy capital city for the North American Regional Administration, many of the newcomers had settled along the coast where food was plentiful. They built huts on or near the beach. Some used driftwood, and others found old strips of sheet metal. There were plenty of abandoned shacks in the coastal villages just waiting for new occupants. But then the tsunami hit, and those villages were wiped out. Tens of thousands died, even more were injured in the surging flood of water from the sea.

Cat and I joined the parade of homeless, shell-shocked refugees, never knowing how our luck was about to change.

# CHAPTER 24

SOME PEOPLE DON'T BELIEVE in luck. I'm one of them I suppose. I believe in God, and that he's at work in the world. He was with us as we traveled down the dirt highway. We had survived so much that my gratitude for being alive was stronger than my grief. In fact, I was more grateful that Cat had survived than even myself. Although there were moments when my grief overwhelmed me, it was usually in the quiet moments when I was trying to pray. I would see Hector's face, hear Bobby Lane's voice, remember Lorenzo's compassion as he met with people. I missed them all, and felt sorry they were gone, even though I believed with all my heart they were happy in the presence of God.

Still, it felt like a stroke of luck when I heard a familiar voice. It was calling out to the people walking. Most of the survivors of the tsunami were in a state of shock. Despite the volunteers handing out bottles of water, and free fruit to help sustain the people, most of the refugees trudged forward, their heads down, seemingly oblivious to the volunteers along the road.

"Fresh mangos!" a deep voice called out in English. "Ripe, juicy mangos. They're free all day long or until we run out."

Cat and I looked up at the same time. LB was standing in the back of a small pick-up truck with several crates of mangos. We both stopped walking. The other refugees flowed around us, unperturbed that we were standing still in the middle of the road.

"LB?" I said.

Hearing his name, my big friend glanced up. His response was not as dramatic as I felt at seeing him. He just nodded toward the side of the road and kept calling out, "Free mangos!"

Cat and I walked over to the pickup. There was a pavilion tent set up next to the truck. Allie was in the shade. Her light skin was tanned dark, and there were bright highlights in her otherwise dark brown hair. She no longer had a cast or brace on her leg, but there was a wooden cane hooked over the back of her lawn chair. In front of her was an older couple sipping water from paper cups.

"Have a mango," LB said in his booming voice. "Take a load off in the shade why don't you."

"Sure," I said, taking a couple of mangos.

Allie saw us, but reacted just the same as LB. There was recognition in her eyes, but a look on her face warned us to keep quiet. We sat down on the ground in the shade of the pavilion. It was a small, ten-foot by ten-foot pavilion with folding metal legs. The blue material on top was faded from hours in the sun and lined with white traces of salt. I took out

Hector's knife and cut up the mango. It was juicy and sweet. We hadn't had anything so sweet in a long time. I felt the sugar rush immediately as I swallowed the juice that filled my mouth with each delectable bite.

"What gives?" Cat whispered.

"I don't know," I said.

"They recognized us," Cat said. "I'm sure of it."

"Maybe that's the problem," I said.

I had hoped that by going to the capital that I might be able to hide in plain sight. But maybe I was wrong. Maybe going to Mérida was a huge mistake.

"Water?" Allie asked. "I can refill your bottles here."

She was sitting beside an orange cooler with a little white spigot. It was the cylinder type used at sporting events.

"Thank you," Cat told her, handing over our water bottles which were empty.

"Oh, it's my pleasure. We're happy to help," Allie continued. "Such a shame what happened. Have you seen the videos?"

"No," I told her.

She pulled a smart phone from her pocket and handed it to us. There was a video already on the screen waiting to be played.

"That was shot live from the North Atlantic," she said.

We tapped the icon on the screen and the video played. Someone, on what looked like a fishing vessel, was filming the sky. The camera work was unsteady, most likely from the motion of the ship. But the enormous rock falling from the sky was easy to see. It wasn't covered in flames or smoke. It wasn't even spinning the way you would expect. It looked like a massive, triangular boulder, and it was falling toward the ocean.

There was no sound on the video. I guessed maybe Allie had turned it off on purpose, and I didn't try to adjust it. Instead, I just watched. The object dropped into the sea. From a distance it looked exactly as you would imagine. There was a huge splash of water that flung up hundreds of feet high, only to fall back down like rain. But then, the wave hit the boat. The image was shaky to begin with, and only got worse, until it was lost. The video returned to the beginning.

"That's really something," I said.

"Climate crisis," Allie replied as she got water for another refugee who wandered to the pavilion. "The world has to equalize before things get better."

"Okay," I said, trying not to sound mystified but I was.

Cat bumped my leg with hers as a towering security official came striding past their little stand on the side of the road. It was a woman, or it once was I suppose. She was nearly nine feet tall, and her shoulders were twice as wide as mine. She had a big rifle strapped to her back and was carrying two large duffle bags. If she saw us, she made no sign of recognizing me. Of course, I looked pretty haggard. My beard was grown out, as was my hair. My clothes were worn out, and I was dirty from head to toe.

"We need to hide that stuff," Cat said, nodding toward the seabag.

Inside were our Bibles, books, a few items of clothing, and the rifles. Hector's M4 and Cat's sniper rifle were big weapons. We also had ammunition in the bag, including the belt with the spare mags for my submachine gun. Any of it would have been enough to get us in major trouble with the law.

"They're from SARA," Allie said casually. "Administrator Eon has an entire army of them to keep us safe."

"That's nice," Cat said.

"How long have you been out on the coast?" Allie continued.

"Not long," I said. "What about you?"

"Me and my husband," she said, glancing up at LB. "We have a mango farm on the pilgrim road."

"It survived the hailstorms?" I asked, almost slipping up and calling it the first trumpet judgment. I'm not sure what kind of reception that phrase would have gotten from the other refugees, but I didn't want to tip my hand when things were clearly tense.

"They say Kukulkan protected us," she said. I recognized the note of derision in her voice, but the jovial look on her face didn't change. The entire pilgrim road was spared, and Mérida too. The rainforest burned, but not our place. And the entire temple complex was miraculously spared."

"Oh," I said.

"Well," LB said, jumping out of the back of the truck. "That's the last mango."

"We should head back," Allie said. "If you're injured, we can give you a lift. Otherwise, you'll need to walk."

"Understood," I said. "Thank you for your hospitality."

"Think nothing of it, friend," LB said, scooping up our seabag and putting it behind the bench seat in the small pick-up's cab.

I acted as if it were his to do with as he pleased. Allie

slipped a note into Cat's hand, and we started walking again. As we trudged down the road, we eventually saw LB pass us in his pickup. Allie was in the passenger seat. The back was loaded with people, many of them with visible bandages.

Cat didn't look at the note from Allie until it was almost too dark to see. Refugees were being given reflective, mylar blankets. It was like being wrapped up in a deflated party balloon, but together with Cat, our body heat soon made us warm, despite the falling temperatures.

"It's a map," Cat told me after looking at the scrap of paper.

"It must have been something she already had drawn up," I said.

"Yeah, that's interesting. Looks like if we stay on the highway, we'll hit the pilgrim road. We turn south and eventually we'll pass by their place. It says look for the Mango Man sign."

"How far do you think it is?"

"I don't know," Cat said. "I wish we could have hitched a ride with them."

"Me too, but they're clearly being watched," I said. "We'll have to be careful."

"At least they're alive," she said.

We were laying down, one space blanket under us, one wrapped over our spooning bodies. Every move we made crinkled like we were wrapped in cellophane. It wasn't comfortable, but it wasn't completely miserable either. We were so tired that it didn't take long to fall asleep.

The next morning, we set out again, and just before noon, we hit the pilgrim road. The highway was a narrow dirt road that ran through the remains of the burned up tropical forest, but the pilgrim road was wide and lined with lush farms. Water flowed along one side of the road, and palm trees lined the bank. Most of the refugees were turning toward Mérida, which was visible in the distance. It was odd to see tall buildings again. There were cranes and clear signs of construction. We turned to the southeast, following the signs that declared Chichen Itza a world heritage site and one of the seven wonders of the world. I recognized the famous pyramid with its three hundred and sixty-five steps. Aztec history wasn't something I spent time reading, but I had seen enough movies to know the people who built the temple offered human sacrifices there. And it was not a surprise to realize it had become a center for worship again during Satan's reign in the tribulation period.

The journey took all day. We were completely wiped out by the time the Mango Man sign appeared. We turned off the pilgrim road, crossed over a stone bridge, and made our way to a small farmhouse. It was white with an unpainted, corrugated tin roof. There were barrels at all four corners of the house to catch rainwater. Beyond the small home, there was a metal building with big double doors. It looked more like a garage than a barn. The entire building was made of the same metal as the roof on the house. I could see a concrete floor inside and large bins full of mangos.

"House or barn?" I asked.

"I don't know," Cat said.

We headed for the house, but no one appeared to be home. I knocked on the door, but no one answered. Cat sat down on the steps to the wide porch, and I joined her. We didn't have to wait long before the sound of a cart was heard.

The wheels squeaked, and the cart rattled as LB pulled it. The entire thing was loaded with mangos.

"You gonna sit there, or can you help me with this?" LB said with a wide smile splitting his dark face.

"I doubt I'd be much help," I said getting to my feet.

He slapped me hard on the shoulder and gave Cat a side hug, before whispering. "Let's get indoors. You never know who might see us out here."

LB left the cart full of fruit and led us into the house. There was clean, wicker furniture in the living room, and a sturdy wooden table with chairs in the kitchen. The lights came on when LB flipped the switch. He opened the refrigerator and pulled out a pitcher of fruit juice.

"Ah, the modern conveniences," LB said, turning toward us. "You look like hell, Hank. Cat, you are as lovely as ever."

"Thank you, LB," Cat replied.

"It feels like we've been there and back," I said. "But I'm more interested in how you wrangled this place?"

LB got out four glasses and started pouring the juice. "Most people recognize my value, bro. I thought you would understand that by now."

"I'm just glad to see you again," I told him. "And Allie, where's she?"

"On the road," LB said. "She'll be home soon. She's working at a garage a few miles down the road."

"You have jobs?" Cat asked.

"Every citizen has a job," LB said, sipping his juice.

I picked up my glass. The drink was a mixture of fruit juices, mostly mango but I tasted orange and pineapple too. It was tart and sweet. After walking all day long, it felt amazing to be indoors, seated in a normal chair, drinking something that was delicious.

"We were at the checkpoint for a week before the government transport arrived. It took three days to reach Tampico... lots of stops along the way. We were riding in a covered trailer behind a big military transport that went maybe fifteen miles an hour."

"Sounds grand," Cat said.

"Better than walking," I replied.

"We were checked into a government facility in Tampico. Our military records had been noted at the checkpoint, and they were waiting for us. You must not have popped on their radar yet."

I groaned in dread.

"We took a nice boat ride up the coast," LB continued. "When we finally reached Mérida, they had a list of jobs available. For me, it was this, clerk at a grocery store, or public sanitation. Allie had more options. She took on at the government aid station down the road, does maintenance on government vehicles. They run transport from the capital to the Kukulkan temple out past Pisté."

"And everyone is expected to work?" I asked.

"It's not required," LB explained. "But it's sort of like volunteering for jobs in the service."

"Yeah, the kind of opportunity you can't refuse," I said with a sarcastic chuckle.

"Exactly," LB said. "We all got new IDs. The government is renewing their citizen registry database. Allie and I thought we would attract less attention by volunteering. Believe me, there's plenty who don't. Most people take their universal income and set up house on the beach."

"That was a great idea," Cat said.

"Yeah, we knew better," LB said. "You want to tell me how you ended up on the coast before a tsunami hit?"

"We weren't on the coast," I said.

"We rode the wave man," Cat said with a big grin.

"Oh, I gotta hear about this," LB said, looking through a window.

We heard a motor vehicle approach. The engine shut off and a door slammed.

"The Misses is home," LB said. "I better start dinner. We've only got one bathroom, but there's a shower with hot water."

"Yes please," Cat said.

"Go on, girl. Allie will bring you some clean clothes, too."

I looked at LB. "You mentioned something about me?"

"Oh, you're a popular guy around here," LB said. "I guess those little videos you made ruffled some feathers."

"I was afraid of that," I admitted.

"You went viral bro. At least one of your videos was downloaded over a thousand times before the watchdogs took it down. Other believers have been reposting them. All that stuff from your guy Maltza, too, and other Christian teachers. But you're the one that got away, so I suppose that makes the shot callers furious. Not long after we got settled here, a team of security personnel came by to ask us some questions."

"What'd you tell 'em?"

"Exactly what you'd want me to. Namely, that I had no idea you were a traitor. I told 'em we fell in with you up in

Texas cause you had wheels, and that I really didn't know much more. Told 'em you were a loner at Camp Abilene, just a logistics nerd, you know the drill."

"And they bought it?"

"Oh, hell no," LB said with a chuckle, opening a can of red beans and starting a pot of rice to boil on the little stove. "They've been watching our every move. They'll know you came here in a day or two... if they don't already. Not long after I started managing the farm, I got a helper from the city. He comes out most days, wanders around like he's doing something, but I think he's just here to keep tabs on us."

"I should go then," I said.

"Don't worry, we've got a place ready for you," LB said. "And you gotta see what's going on down the road, bro. You ain't seen nothing like it."

Allie came in. She wasn't exactly leaning hard on the wooden cane, but it was clear her leg hadn't healed properly.

"You made it," Allie said as she walked slowly into the living room.

I stood up and walked to her. "We did. It's so good to see you again."

"We were afraid they might spot you," Allie said.

"Doubt they would recognize him," LB said. "They had your service ID photo when they came asking about you."

"Maybe looking like a hobo will pay off," I said.

After Cat got out of the shower, I took one. The water wasn't hot, but it was warm enough. And there was real soap and even a bottle of shampoo. I scrubbed my head and beard with it, but I didn't try to comb anything afterward. LB had taken my filthy clothes out of the house. He was bigger than me. But with a belt and rolling the cuffs, his pants fit me okay. I put on a Mango Man t-shirt, and we settled in for dinner. LB made beans and rice, mango salsa, corn on the cob, and cornbread.

"Sorry, about the vegetarian food," LB said. "The only meat available is vat grown. It's nasty stuff."

"This looks fantastic," Cat said.

"We've been living on dried fish and seaweed. Before that, it was rattlesnake jerky and survival rations," I explained. "This is a welcome feast."

The food was good. The salsa had onions, jalapeños, and cilantro. The corn was juicy and sweet. It felt like comfort food. Maybe it was the company, but the meal made me feel better than I had in days. After we ate, Cat and I took turns telling our story. When we got to the part about running from the security force, their eyes widened.

"You fought them?" LB asked.

"Hector did the heavy lifting, but yeah," I said. "We didn't have a choice."

"Did you kill them?" Allie asked.

"Wounded for sure," I told her.

"With that tommy gun in your kit?"

"Yeah. I emptied the clip and only managed to slow one of them down," I said.

"Not surprising," LB said. "They're monsters. I don't even think they're human."

"What happened after that?" Allie asked.

"The first trumpet judgment," Cat said. "We rode out the storm in a concrete utility bunker."

"Was it bad?" Allie asked.

"It destroyed our four-by-four pickup," I said. "Crushed the cab, melted the tires."

"We saw video," LB said. "But it's all been scrubbed from the internet now."

"And it didn't fall here?"

"Nope," LB said. "I could see it in the distance. It looked like the air was on fire."

"The forest is all burned, but something stopped it from falling on us," Allie said.

"The Kukulcan high priest is a visitor," LB said. "Calls himself Melzee Cotas. He claims Kukulcan protected us. He's right out of an Indiana Jones movie."

"But what's going on at the temple isn't," Allie said.

"We can show them all that tomorrow," LB said. "For now, we better show them where they'll be sleeping."

"You don't have a guest room?" I asked.

"We do, but it's better that you don't use it," Allie said.

"I'll take 'em out, babe. You put your feet up and rest," LB insisted.

Allie didn't argue, and I could tell by the way she looked that not everything was okay with her leg. LB led the way from the cottage to the barn.

"We found this a couple of weeks after taking over," LB said.

"You took the farm from someone?" Cat asked.

"Nah, it was abandoned," he said. "But whoever owned this place had something to hide. Probably drugs, or maybe something worse, I don't know."

He had to move one of the big plastic bins. Fortunately, they had wheels and could be rolled out of the way. Beneath the cart was a wooden door that was covered with a thin layer of concrete. Even with an overhead light, the trap door was hard to see. LB pulled a screwdriver from his hip pocket, wedged it into the crack, then lifted the door up. It swung open on hidden spring hinges and revealed a set of stairs. The passageway was lined with rocks. I went down first. At the end of the staircase was a hidden room. The walls, floor, and ceiling were all cement, but there was a bed against one wall, and pipe going up into the roof. There were a couple of old sitting chairs, and a small table.

"Welcome to hotel Barski. The view ain't great, but you'll be safe in here," he told us.

"Wow, you just found this down here?"

"We found the room," LB said. "This furniture was piled up in a corner of the shed. Allie and I fixed it up thinking we might be able to help some believers. The fresh air intake goes up through the wall of the shed. You can't even see it unless you're standing on the roof."

"This is great," I told him. "But what about Allie. What's really going on with her leg."

"It healed," LB said. "But without an orthopedic specialist, x-rays, maybe surgery and all that, it just healed funny."

"I thought Jonathan got it set," I said.

"He did," LB said. "But there was a lot of damage. They checked her out at the hospital in Mérida. They can fix it, but they'll have to rebreak the leg, put in pins and screws. She wasn't up for that, and I got a real bad feeling in that place, bro. We opted out, and she's dealing with it. I give her leg a rub down every night man. That woman's tough. Course, she would have died, and so would I, if you hadn't been there to help us, Hank."

"I did what anyone would have done," I told him. "Jonathan is the real hero."

"And now he's a big wig at the hospital, at least..."

"At least what?" I asked.

"You know, it occurs to me that it might be best if you don't know everything that's gone on while you were galivanting around the countryside."

"LB?"

"I just got you back, man. The last thing I want is to have you go running off again."

"What's that mean?" Cat said. "Why would we leave?"

"Because Jonathan is no longer at the hospital in Mérida," I said. "What happened?"

LB shrugged. "I don't know, but the rumor mill is pretty wound up. He was running the entire medical establishment, bro. The hospital, the clinics, he even had a training program set up. Almost all the medics helping refugees were trained by him. There was talk that he might be the next Administrator. Then poof, he disappears. Some people say he got too powerful, or too popular. I suppose that's possible, but we know something about him that's not public knowledge."

"He's a believer," I said.

"Not just a believer," LB said. "He's one of the Jewish witnesses from Revelation seven. You saw the seal on his forehead, right?"

"Yes," I said.

It wasn't something that was strong in my memory. The bright light, followed by the glimmer of a symbol on his balding head. It wasn't the type of thing I would easily forget, and I was absolutely convinced it was what the Bible talked about.

*"Then I saw another angel ascending from the east, having the seal of the living God. And he cried with a loud voice to the four angels to whom it was granted to harm the earth and the sea, saying, "Do not harm the earth, the sea, or the trees till we have sealed the servants of our God on their foreheads." And I heard the number of those who were sealed. One hundred and forty-four thousand of all the tribes of the children of Israel were sealed."*

LB continued, "So, if the government had him..."

"They would have made a public spectacle of his execution," Cat finished the thought.

"So, what you think happened to him?" I asked.

"There are some rumors that he might be close by," LB said. "My guess is he's got a small flock hidden away somewhere. The trees out on the western fringe of the orchard seem to be missing a lot of mangos, if you catch my drift."

"Sounds like something we should look into," I said.

"That's exactly what I was afraid you'd say," he replied with a grin as he clapped a big hand onto my shoulder. "Damn, it's good to see you again, Hank. And you too, Cat. It does my heart good."

"You're a lifesaver, buddy," I told him.

The three of us embraced for a moment. Then LB stepped back.

"Your gear and books are stowed under the bed," he said. "Sleep well, my friends."

"We will," I told him.

And it was true. For the first time in a while, I felt safe. The underground room was cool, but not cold. Cat and I crawled under the covers of the bed. It was the first real bed we had shared since leaving Lorenzo's home in Spokane, Washington. I couldn't even remember how long ago that was. We snuggled together under comfy blankets, on a soft mattress, and fell asleep in each other's arms before we even knew what happened.

# CHAPTER 25

THE NEXT DAY, we set out early in the little truck that Allie used to travel to the waypoint on the pilgrim highway. Cat and I sat in the back while LB drove. Along the way, more travelers were picked up. I was shocked to see a woman with a baby in her arms. It hadn't really occurred to me that people could even get pregnant. We lived in a world with no young people, and the sight of a tiny baby was both shocking and exciting. I had never been the type to get emotional around babies, but I felt some pretty powerful emotions when the woman with the baby climbed into the back of the little truck.

The NARA government operated a rest stop along the pilgrim highway. It looked like a place that was made for travelers, but also included a small security post and a garage to service vehicles. The transportation department workers hadn't tried to lay down asphalt, but they operated a road grader and big wheel compacting machine. Clay was being spread with a modified tractor so that the road between

Mérida and the religious compound around Chichen Itza was well maintained and easy to traverse.

LB dropped Allie off. The truck was a luxury, one given to Allie to help her daily commute and also because she could maintain it. As she went to work in the transit department garage, we took the little truck on to Pisté. The little town had been hit hard by the earthquake, but the nearby religious site and constant flow of pilgrims, had given it a resurgence. Buildings were rebuilt, the streets cleared, and vendors lined the wide city square. LB parked the truck on the edge of town, and we walked into a community that was bright and busy.

"This is the new Pisté," he said. "Notice the rainbow flags."

"I saw that," I said.

"Does it mean?"

"Oh, yeah. Sodom and Gomorrah ain't got nothing on Pisté. Anything goes here, my friends."

We were speaking quietly so we wouldn't be overheard. It was soon apparent exactly what LB meant. There were a lot of people in the square. Some were dressed up in flamboyant costumes, and others were completely nude. Body paint, and exaggerated costumes mimicking sex organs, and rainbow-colored scarves, hats, and shawls were sold by vendors. Many of the local buildings were hotels and hostels, but people engaged in all types of lewd behavior right in the city streets.

"Kukulcan is a real piece of work," LB said quietly. "The high priest encourages all this. Most of the pilgrims are here on a sort of sexual holiday. People here do whatever they want in a sort of state sanctioned, religious right."

"It's part of their worship?" I asked.

"Depends on how you define that word," LB continued. "The priests don't even use it. The people aren't thinking about this deity while they defile themselves. It's more like a free zone. There are no consequences in Pisté."

"If they aren't here to worship," Cat asked, "what do they do at the temple?"

"Oh, you'll see," LB said.

We passed through the town square, then made the walk out to the ruins. At first everything was as I expected it to be, old stone walls half collapsed, piles of rubble, pits from archeological digs. But that was just the outskirts. The area around the grand temple was completely restored. Cobblestone paved the plaza. The pyramid looked brand new. The steps were restored. The angles perfect. I could smell the incense before we even arrived. And around the plaza we found small buildings with clay tile roofs. At one end of the plaza was a newly constructed building with a dome shaped roof, and opposite was a polished granite obelisk.

There were men gathered around the obelisk. They wore leather belts hung with rainbow-colored feathers and nothing else. They looked like bodybuilders complete with oiled skin to make their superhero physiques stand out. As I watched, a middle-aged woman went to the group, selected one of the men, and led him across the plaza to the domed building.

"What's going on?" I asked LB.

"Those men," he said, indicating the group around the obelisk, "are acolytes to Kukulcan. They represent him in what is called the high rite of mystical rebirth."

"I've got a bad feeling," Cat said.

"That's discernment," LB told her.

"What do they do in the dome?" I asked.

"They have sex," LB explained. "It's supposedly a way to bring back the good people from ages past. Sort of a perverted mockery of the resurrection. Supposedly, Kukulcan sacrificed himself for his people. The obelisk represents his manhood, the dome his fertility. Supposedly, the snake god was both male and female, somehow impregnating himself with his own reincarnation."

"That makes no sense," I said.

"Tell me about it. Around noon the visitor who is officially the high priest here, will come out of the pyramid, give a little speech, and then perform the sacrifices."

There were other people around the plaza with similar costumes as the men by the obelisks. A wide gamut of supposed genders was represented, and there were people with surgically altered bodies. Many were dressed like animals. They all took pilgrim lovers into the variety of buildings around the temple.

LB, Cat, and I stood watching for a while. Eventually, a bell rung. The sound was loud, echoing off the stone buildings.

"Here comes the worst thing you've ever seen," LB told me.

I've seen terrible things, both in real life and in dreams. I've seen demons who took me via dreams, into hades where the dead are tormented as they await judgment. I had seen the body of an actual giant. I had seen people dying, and people reveling all sorts of carnal acts. But I had never seen what Lorenzo Maltza would have called a reptilian. In the UFO groups, the aliens reported by those who claimed to have been abducted were typically small, hairless humanoids with big heads and big eyes called the Greys. I had seen one of those myself, although it was in the dark and the being's physical details weren't very clear. There were tall, blonde aliens that were supposed to be physically perfect. They were called Nordics. And finally, there were some aliens who supposedly looked like lizards of one stripe or another. Not animals crawling around on four legs, but bi-pedal, men-like, reptile creatures known in UFO circles as Reptilians.

The High Priest of Kukulcan, the feathered snake god of the Aztec people, was a hybrid being. He had the body of a man, including hands and feet, but from about the middle of his chest upward he resembled a snake. His neck was wide, like the hood of a cobra, his face angular and tapered. He came out of the temple completely naked. I saw no sex organs, which was pretty weird. His skin was dark brown, the scales were black, and the high priest even had a flickering, forked tongue. He communicated with a form of mental telepathy. I heard his voice in my head.

"The time of the daily sacrifices is nigh," the alien being said. "All ye who worship mighty Kukulcan behold his holiness as we make homage to his immutable power."

A man was brought out of the temple by two hulking acolytes. The man looked small, almost emaciated between them. And all the humans were overshadowed by the alien, who was several feet taller than his helpers. In the restored temple plaza, people began to chant, and as they did my vision began to change. For a moment everything looked wavy, like light refraction above a fire. And then, as things cleared, I saw to my horror a huge creature sitting on top of the pyramid. It was twice as big as the ancient temple and looked like a cross between a coiled serpent and a fat Buddha statue from a Chinese restaurant. The gargantuan creature seemed to be covered in black oil. It dripped from the coils which sat on the fat, bulging stomach and thighs of the creature. Its long neck moved, and the serpent head drew close as the high priest slashed a small blade over the captive's chest.

"Oh, no," Cat said, grabbing onto my arm.

I couldn't look away. The giant snake was hissing urgently, it's mouth open, the long tongue stuck out and trembling. The high priest reached a hand into the screaming captive's chest. I couldn't be sure, but it seemed like the hand was morphing from fingers to a scaly, clawed hand that somehow bypassed the ribcage and severed the captive's beating heart. The poor, emaciated man collapsed as the priest held up the heart. The crowd in the plaza screamed in ecstasy, but all together they weren't as loud as the huge serpent man on top of the pyramid. I tore my gaze from the high platform only to discover the entire plaza was crawling with demons. They clung to the acolytes, some even embodying the temple workers. Others were driving the people into acts of perversion. Some were yelling curses, others making lewd gestures, and still more calling for the captive's body so they could do abominable sexual acts with it.

The hulking guards complied with the cries and carried the man's body down the wide stone steps. Again, I looked away, feeling like I might be sick, which was when I noticed the bright figures beside us. Cat was between LB and myself but on either side of us were what appeared to be figures of pure light. They were behind us too, their radiance creating a kind of bubble around us.

"Who else brings a sacrifice to the mighty Kukulcan?" the high priest said, though the words just appeared in my mind.

I didn't see his mouth move, but he spread his bloody hands wide as if appealing to the crowd. To my horror I saw the woman who had ridden to Pisté with us, the woman with a baby. She climbed the steps holding out her tiny, naked infant in front of her.

"No," I said. "She can't."

"It's like this every day," LB said. "Pure evil."

The people in the plaza were in a frenzy. I saw many of them taking pills, or some type of drug. Many were disrobing, others danced in a gyrating movement that made them look as if their bones were as flexible as a blade of grass. On the temple, the woman dropped to her knees on the stone steps in front of the high priest. I wanted to look away, but I couldn't. The Reptilian reached out and snatched the baby from its mother by its feet. The woman screamed and fell on her face. The priest ignored her and lifted the squalling child up. The crowd in the plaza fell silent until only the baby's cries were heard.

I didn't think things could get any worse, but I was wrong. The huge serpent creature perched on top of the pyramid leaned down. It's black, forked tongue extended and coiled around the baby's neck. We could hear the gurgle as the baby tried to breathe, then a gagging sound as the snake's tongue squeezed. Even from a distance I could see the baby's face turning red, then purple.

"What's happening to it?" Cat asked, her voice a distressed whisper.

Another voice entered our minds at that moment, but it wasn't deep and somber like the high priests. It was bright and melodic. The best way I can think to describe it is the different between a flute and tuba. The new voice seemed to buoy my flagging emotions, even if what it said was disheartening.

"The prince of the Yucatan is killing her," the voice said. "But take courage, the days of the evil one and his followers are numbered."

The baby stopped crying and went limp. I knew it was dead, but I still flinched in horror when the high priest flung the baby into the air. It hit the stone steps of the pyramid with a bone crunching impact, then bounced head over heels down the long flight of steps.

"It is time that you left," the melodic voice in my head said.

I didn't disobey, or even want to. Cat, LB, and I turned at once and hurried from the plaza where the crowd of supposed worshipers went wild. It was louder than a pro sports game, almost a frenzy. I felt sick, and suddenly so tired that my feet dragged on the dirt path leading back to the village of Pisté.

There were more people in the square than before. I couldn't understand why more and more people were coming. Nothing seemed to make sense in my mind. Then a vendor shouted out to me.

"Hey, man!" the vendor called. "You can take Kukulcan with you."

He was holding out a wooden figure, practically right in

my face. I was horrified to see the dark wood carved into the same image as the fat, hybrid beast I had seen on top of the temple.

Another vendor shouted as I pushed past the first. "You need enlightenment? I've got it all, mushrooms, ololiuqui, peyote, DMT."

"No thanks," I said, pushing past him.

We made our way through the crowded town square. I started to feel like I couldn't breathe among all the people. Music was playing over loudspeakers, and everyone talking created a cacophony of sound that mixed with the close quarters to create a suffocating environment. I didn't want to touch anyone, but it was impossible not to. People were smoking pot... among other things I couldn't recognize. It made me lightheaded and dizzy. Finally, we got through the throng of people, back to where LB had parked the little pickup. He pulled out some plastic bottles of water from the inside of the truck.

"Here," he said, putting a bottle in my hand and Cat's. "It's warm, but it will help clear your head."

I took a gulp, then poured half the bottle over my head. We were in the sunshine, which seemed harsh there, but it wasn't excessively hot. The tepid water was somehow refreshing. We ate some dried mango and cornbread from the night before, then we squeezed into the cab of the truck and drove slowly back to the rest stop.

There was a communal building at the rest stop. LB bought us soda, chips, and candy bars from the vendor inside. Then we walked out to a grove of palm trees. Sitting in the shade, eating junk food, and feeling the breeze on my skin, I started to feel better.

"That was the most horrific thing I've ever experienced," Cat said.

"Now you know what we're up against," LB said. "I'm not even sure who's really in charge of NARA. I know the visitor has a lot of influence on the Administrator."

"Could you see the demons?" I asked.

"I heard the voices," Cat said.

"I got a glimpse the first time Allie and I went," LB said. "Couldn't sleep for three days. I never knew what I didn't know. Spent my whole life thinking religion was just a social gathering. It's kinda hard not to have regrets."

"Can't change the past," I told him. "The Bible says our sins are removed as far as the east is from the west."

"I can accept that about most things," he said, brushing a tear from his eye with a big hand. "We all done stupid stuff, and I done some really stupid stuff. I don't know if I ever told you I was married... twice. Blew it both times. But all the wrong I ever did don't compare with the fact that somehow, I was so self-absorbed that I missed the fact that God is real."

"So did I," Cat said. "I didn't really believe in anything."

"I was just a shell of a man," I confessed. "I did my best to stay off the radar."

"Ain't we a sad bunch," LB said, his jovial mood returning.

It was one of the things I liked best about my big friend. He was always in a good mood and did a lot to lift the spirits of the people around him.

"At least we know, now," I said. "And I'm so thankful for that."

"You know it," LB said.

"So, what now?" Cat said. "Tell me we never have to go back to that terrible place."

"Never say never," LB said.

"We aren't here to fight a religious war," I said. "But I'm glad we've got a lay of the land. We wrestle not against flesh and blood."

"Truer words were never spoken," LB said.

We waited there, just three old friends catching up, until Allie got off work at the end of the day. Then we rode back to the orchard together, taking as many people as we could a little way down the road in the old pickup. I didn't hold out hope for the people engaging in the carnal activities at Pisté and the old Chichen Itza complex. Several of the pilgrims we picked up had idols. Some were wooden, others were made with silver or even gold, but they all looked demonic. The forces of evil did nothing to hide themselves any longer. It was those of us with faith in one true God that were forced to hide. And the more I thought about Jonathan Weinblatt, the more convinced I was that I needed to find him.

# CHAPTER 26

THE DAYS FOLLOWING our visit to the Kukulcan temple were spent searching the forest. On either side of the pilgrim road, lay a wide section of land that had avoided being burned by the first trumpet judgment. Behind LB's orchard was natural rainforest for a couple of kilometers. In places along the road, it was thicker, and some of the properties, mostly farms, were larger than the orchard. But it was dense enough to hide in, which is exactly what Cat and I did.

Every morning, we woke before dawn, came out of the hidden room under the barn, and after a quick breakfast with LB and Allie, set out through the orchard. Our goal was to be gone before LB's helper, Danny Hagerty, arrived. The younger man drove an old, but well-maintained Mercedes Benz. That fact alone, made him suspect in LB's opinion. The government wasn't handing out vehicles to just anyone. Added to Danny's attitude, and his nonchalant schedule, the car was solid evidence that he was more of a spy than an agricultural worker.

The purpose of our trek through the jungle was twofold. My primary aim was to find where Jonathan was hiding. The more I thought about my Jewish friend, the more convinced I became that God had prompted his exodus from Mérida. A fact which was solidified when a team of security people showed up at the orchard. LB thought they were looking for me, but instead they asked if he had seen or heard of people in hiding. They wanted to know if his trees were being picked without his knowledge, or if he had seen people in the forest. They even showed him a picture of Dr. Jonathan Weinblatt, who they claimed was missing. LB didn't have to lie. He told them he hadn't seen anyone, and they quickly moved on.

Cat had a more practical purpose for our outings. She was a woman of the woods who felt right at home in the jungles. She could spot edibles and track wild game. Not that there was a lot of game animals left in the area, but one of her first tasks was to make herself a bow and some arrows. There were days when I left her sitting in the shade with her knife and several pieces of wood, which she used to make her gear. From braiding natural plant fibers into bowstring and snares, to collecting shed feathers for fletching on her arrows, Cat was right at home. Her first kill was a local variety of turkey, called an Ocellated Turkey. It was the perfect size bird for four people. She dug a pit, burned wood down to coals, and wrapped the turkey in banana leaves while covering the entire thing in dirt again. When we dug up the turkey several hours later, it was juicy and tender. Walking back to the farmhouse to share the bird with LB and Allie before we ate it, was the most difficult task of the day.

We collected fruit on our trek through the forest, mainly dragon fruit, and mamey sapote. It was important to both Cat and I that we contribute as much as we could. Money wasn't an option since it was digital and linked to our identity. And helping at the orchard wasn't possible either, since LB had a helper who was likely a spy. That left contributing food when we could, and with meat being a rarity, Cat's skills as a hunter were our best bet. Her snares captured small game, and her bow brought down the larger animals. You may not know this but there two types of small deer that live in the Yucatan forests. One could feed all four of us for several days as long as we could get the meat back to Allie's kitchen refrigerator in time.

We weren't the only people in the forest. It's not surprising that many of the people who had survived the Tribulation up to that point were outdoor enthusiasts. Beyond the forest, was a vast landscape of scorched earth and burned trees. In normal conditions, a forest would recover from a fire, but areas burned by the fiery hailstones were left barren. And the coast was ruined as the waters along the entire shoreline around the Yucatan Peninsula turned red. Almost all the aquatic life died. The coast was a nasty, disease-infested wasteland. We heard that some fishing vessels who put out into the deeper waters found fish, but the populations were decimated, and not just in the Gulf of Mexico, but all over the world.

For a little over two weeks, life settled into a sense of routine and normalcy. And then, after venturing out past the forest, into a rocky section of the land beyond, what was becoming known as the Blackened Desert, I found what I was looking for.

Cat was still in the rainforest, cleaning a collared peccary — a pig-like animal that ran in small herds through the forest. I was climbing between some pretty decent sized boulders when I noticed a wide grotto. It wasn't exactly a cave, more like a gap between the large rocks on the surface and the bedrock below. Inside were thirty or forty people. I was so surprised that I didn't even hear the man with a gun who came up behind me.

"Why don't you just stand easy there, pal," the guy with gun said as he pressed the muzzle into my back.

Cat and I didn't carry our firearms. Our knives stayed on our belts, the guns would draw attention, so we left them at the little room under the barn. I felt the stranger behind me reach out and pull Hector's bowie knife from the sheath.

"That's an important knife," I said. "It belonged to a good friend of mine."

"Sure," the guy with the gun said. "What's your name?"

"Who's asking?"

"The guy with the gun," he said. "Name!"

"I'm Hank," I said.

"What are you doing out here, Hank?"

"Looking for a friend of mine."

"Yeah? Who's that?"

I considered the fact that maybe I hadn't stumbled upon Jonathan's little village. Maybe they were outcasts, or another cartel group. But I took a chance and told the truth.

"Jonathan," I said. "Dr. Jonathan Weinblatt. Like I said, he's a friend of mine."

"Sure, he is," the guy said. "Turn around."

I did as I was told. The man with the gun was older, his hair completely gray, and his skin was darkened by the sun and peeling. He had an old double-barreled shotgun, but he lowered it as he looked at me.

"What'd you say your name was?" he asked.

"Hank."

"You're Hank Downs," he said, his whiskery face breaking into a grin. "You look really different from your videos."

"You've seen one?" I asked.

"I've seen all of them I think," he said. "Right after I got saved, I looked up everything I could. I learned so much, but well..."

"The security officers came looking for you," I suggested.

"That's about right," he said. "Fortunately, I found Rabbi Jonathan's tribe here."

"He's here?"

"Yeah," the gunman said. "My name is Ritchie Newman. I'll take you to him."

The camp wasn't as close as it looked. The grotto was much deeper than it appeared. The temperature inside was cool, and the people had spread out into little sections. No fires were burning, but I could see the smoke stains on the ceiling of the cavern, and there were stacks of blackened charcoal that had been gathered. Everyone seemed busy with one task or another, but they were all friendly. Ritchie didn't stay behind me. We walked side by side, and the other residents of the cavern smiled and waved.

"People are gonna flip when they find out who you are," Ritchie said quietly. "You're a bit of a celebrity around here. Rabbi Jonathan talks about you all the time."

"We spent some time together," I said.

"You planning to join us?"

"I'm here to catch up with Jonathan. We'll see what God has in store."

"Oh, man," was all Ritchie said.

At the end of the cavern was a small area that was curtained off with fabric made from natural fibers. Ritchie cleared his throat in an exaggerated fashion.

"Yes, what is it?" a familiar voice called.

"Not what, but who," I replied.

The curtain moved and Jonathan stepped out, his face pinched in confusion as he looked at me.

"Hank?"

"Yeah," I said. "It's me."

Jonathan threw his arms around me, laughing and crying out, "Praise God! Praise God!"

When he calmed down, he waved to the people in the grotto. "This is my very good friend," he said. "He will meet you all soon. But now, we must talk in private. Hank, come with me."

We stepped into his private space. It was simple, just a pallet on the floor for sleeping, a three-legged stool, and a table made from a slab of wood set on two large rocks.

"Welcome to my home," he said.

"You've got quite the set up here," I told him.

"It's not bad. We have to watch what we do. My people

get out mostly at night for water or food. Things are dangerous, as I'm sure you know."

"Yeah," I said, not wanting to get into what had happened
to me since we last saw each other.

"You, my friend, are an answer to prayer," he said. "You
know what's coming? The third trumpet, yes?"

"Yes," I replied.

"Then you know our time here is short," he replied. "And
God has plans for me. I've been praying for some time about
who to turn my flock over to. And, well, here you are."

"Wait," I said. "I'm not a leader, Jonathan. I'm certainly
no pastor."

"We are all what God wills us to be," he said. "The church
age has passed. We are refugees here, Hank. We are religious
criminals. If the security teams find us, they will kill us all."

"I understand that," I said. "I've seen what the security
teams can do."

"Then you know how to keep these precious ones safe," he
said. "Things will get even more dangerous once Wormwood
is upon us."

"Yeah, I suppose it will," I said. "So why are you talking
about leaving."

"God is calling me to carry the good news south,"
Jonathan said. "Time is running out. We must pray together,
then I will introduce you to the group. Where is your sweet
wife? Is she still with us?"

"Yes," I said. "Cat's in the forest. She harvested a
peccary."

"Excellent, they are delicious. God is so good. He provides

all our needs, according to his riches in glory. You still have his Word, yes?"

I nodded. "It's hidden with the rest of my belongings."

"Smart, we must be wise as serpents and as innocent as doves, my friend. These are precarious times, but God's will shall see through. Come, we shall pray."

I held up a hand to slow him down. "Jonathan, I'm thrilled to see you, but I don't know about all this," I said, waving my hand around at the grotto full of refugees. "Finding you was like scratching an itch. I was nearby, and thought you might be hidden out here, so I came looking. That's all. I'm not ready to leave LB and Allie."

"They will join you here," he insisted.

"Okay, well, they have jobs and stuff," I said. "They can't just leave everything and move out here to live in a cave."

He grabbed my arm and pulled me close. "Hank, you don't understand. This is not an invitation. I'm begging you to come for your own safety. Dark days lay ahead, my friend.

Reaching up, he pushed back the bushy thatch of hair off my forehead.

"You are not sealed as I am," he continued. "God will protect you, but there is danger on every side, Hank. You must come, and it must be quickly. Otherwise, you and your precious friends will not live to see the third trump."

# CHAPTER 27

IF YOU'RE LIKE ME, you get nervous at the idea of someone calling themselves a prophet or predicting the future. Jonathan didn't do that exactly, but his warning held weight. He wasn't just being cautious. The man was absolutely convinced that something bad was about to happen. Little did I know how careless I had been.

Two days earlier, as I left the secret room, the trap door didn't close completely. Maybe a hinge buckled, or a tiny pebble fell into the track, but it wasn't completely flush with the floor. My second mistake was being careless in pushing the mango cart back on top of the trap door. I left it slightly crooked, making it obvious that it had been moved.

Cat and I were long gone by the time Danny Hagerty showed up at the orchard. LB was busy pruning some of the trees, and Allie was gone to work at the garage. That left Danny free to do what he enjoyed, which was snooping. His suspicions had been up since finding the bones of a game animal we had eaten a few days earlier in the fire barrel where trash was normally disposed of. Danny had found himself in the middle of a rare moment of desire to actually accomplish something. His car was littered with trash from the city, so while being on the clock at the orchard, he decided to clean his car. His first trip to the fire barrel revealed the aforementioned animal bones.

It took Danny a while to decide something was wrong, and even longer to figure out what it was. Animal bones wouldn't just appear in the fire barrel. Even if LB had found a dead animal in the orchard, why dispose of it in the barrel instead of just leaving it out for the carrion birds and rodents? The strip of land along the pilgrim road was like an animal sanctuary, and there were plenty who would happily eat the carcass of any type of creature. So why bring it to the barrel and burn it?

Danny didn't know. Hunting was illegal by NARA law, and LB seemed like a straight-laced guy to Danny. Allie, who he thought of as a cripple, surely wasn't out in the woods tracking game. So that meant, either they were trading in illegal goods, or someone else was around the orchard. It was his suspicion that the latter was true that led him to tell his friend, an older woman who had used her position of influence to trap Danny in a romantic affair. Her name was Donna Sutton, and she was undersecretary of resources of NARA. She told him to keep tabs on LB and the orchard. If his suspicions were right, the discovery could be good for them both.

So, while nosing around in the barn a few days later, Danny discovered my carelessness. He saw the crate had been moved. This discovery prompted a closer investigation. Eventually, he found the trap door and the hidden room. Fortunately, LB returned before Danny could search the hidden room. But the following day, he returned and went through everything, the Bibles, the weapons, the clothes. And by the time I got back to the orchard that night with Cat, Danny lay in wait with a security detail on their way from Mérida.

"We have to go," I told LB and Allie.

"What?" the big man said.

"Cat's gathering our stuff," I explained. "I found Jonathan."

"I hope he's okay," Allie said.

"He is, but we aren't."

"How do you know that?" LB asked.

That was the rub. I knew because Jonathan had told me. It wasn't a "Thus saith the Lord," kind of prophecy, but after telling me we were in danger, the two of us had prayed together. I didn't hear an audible voice or have a vision. But something was nudging me to get moving, just as something had nudged me to stop when we were near the utility building before the hailstorm judgment.

"This may sound a bit crazy," I said. "But Jonathan had a premonition. He saw that we were in danger and that we need to get to where he is hiding."

Allie looked frightened, but LB just chuckled. "Well, that's one way to get you."

"He wasn't being facetious," I said. "It was prophetic."

"I don't know about all that," LB said. "But we're good right here. If you want to join Jonathan, that's fine. Although, I will miss that fresh meat your lady keeps bringing home."

"LB, you're in danger here, too," I said.

"What kind of danger?" Allie asked.

"I don't know."

"Look man, I know God is at work in your life, and you're a little stifled here. But there's no need to rush out. If the authorities were suspicious, we'd know."

"How?" Allie asked. "You know that Danny is up to no good. It is possible that we've been discovered."

"Baby, we're careful. We've been here long enough that don't nobody care about us as long as we keep doing our jobs."

Allie looked uncertain.

"So, pray about it," I said. "If you disagree, that's fine. But Cat and I are leaving. Tonight."

"You go out in the jungle at night, and you might never come back," LB said with a chuckle. "I don't like the idea of what all is out there waitin' in the dark. No sir."

"Please," I said. "We'll pray... together. It's important."

"Yes," Allie said. "We can pray."

LB put down the knife he was using to cut onions and bell peppers. He had just gotten a package of corn tortillas and a bag of ripe avocados. His plan for dinner was vegetable fajitas, unless we brought home meat. Cat had harvested a peccary, but upon hearing what Jonathan had told me, we sent the meat to the grotto via Ritchie, and hurried back to the orchard.

Allie got to her feet, and I left them in their little kitchen to pray. There have been times in my life when I was afraid. I remember when Cat came to me in Camp Abilene wanting to leave. I had been hesitant. The truth was, I didn't want to be destitute again, not when we had a sense of security and three good meals a day at the government aid camp. But my resistance had nearly gotten us killed. Cat was exposed to the death flu, and I was charged with traitorous beliefs. LB had been seconds away from executing me, when an even greater danger broke out as the gangs from the old city stormed the camp.

As I hurried to the barn to help Cat, I sensed the same hesitancy in LB. And who could blame him. He had a house. It still needed some repairs since the earthquake, but it was a home. Not many people had it that good. Electricity, gainful employment, even some privacy, or so it seemed. I never saw Danny, who had hidden his car down the road and snuck back onto the property to keep an eye on things. If he had been smart, he would have taken the contraband in our hidden room, especially the guns and ammunition. It would have tipped us off, but leaving it gave us an advantage over him, at least until the security team showed up. It wasn't like the old days where the police could be called and relied upon to show up in a timely fashion. The security teams didn't get into a hurry, especially when the target was unknown. Had Danny figured out who I was from searching our room, the entire incident might have gone down differently.

Instead, Cat and I gathered our things. We met LB and Allie on the porch of their little home. LB looked frustrated, but compassionate at the same time.

"We're going to help you get where you need to go," LB said. "That's the least we can do."

"But you're coming back?" I asked.

"Yeah, man, we gotta come back," LB said. "This is our home now. I can't just pull up roots again. If the bad guys are coming for me, well, at least I know what's waiting on the other side, you know?"

"Okay," I said, feeling a knot of dread in my stomach. "Come with us tonight. See Jonathan. If you feel the same after that, I won't try to stop you from coming back."

Flashlights would have been nice, but they would have been visible in the darkness. Fortunately, we didn't have to fight our way through the forest for long. From the orchard I made straight for the blackened desert. The moon was nearly full, so after we passed through the forest on a familiar trail that was pretty easy to navigate, we made our way to the grotto. Little did I know, Danny was creeping along behind us. We had no electronics, but Danny had a phone. And there was a squad of security members leaving Mérida that were tracking him through the wilderness.

We reached the grotto around midnight. Jonathan was waiting for us. The reunion was sweet. Cat, LB, and Allie were welcomed in with open arms, and we met many of the grotto's residents. The community had roasted the peccary, and there were leftovers which we were grateful for after our long trek through the darkness.

"I'm so glad you are all here," Jonathan told us. "I'm sure Hank explained that I must leave soon."

"He did, but why?" Allie asked.

"God is leading me. There are souls that need to hear the good news. That is why I was sealed. To be his witness here and beyond."

"Maybe Hank and Cat should go with you," LB said.

"You trying to get rid of us?" I jokingly asked.

"Nah, man, you know I love you. And I really love the food your lady brings home."

"How sweet," Cat said.

"But it sounds like a dangerous trip, Jonathan," LB continued. "Hank's packing some heavy heat. Might as well use it to keep you safe."

"God is my protector," Jonathan said. "He is my fortress and shield. Whom shall I fear? Indeed, it was for this very hour that I was saved, my friends. I have a calling that will not be denied. Now, let me bless you. At dawn, I will depart."

LB started to say something else, but Allie put her hand on his arm. Jonathan stood up, put his hands on each of us, and prayed out loud. He asked for wisdom, protection, unity, and guidance. He asked for the blessing of living until Christ's triumphant return but gave us into God's hands and his will. It was a wonderful, bittersweet time. I had just found my old friend and he was leaving, going where I could not follow. But having prayed with him that afternoon, I felt a sense of peace about everything. Little did I know, my faith was about to be tested like never before.

# CHAPTER 28

WHILE CAT and the others got a few hours of rest, I helped Jonathan get his belongings together. He had garnered a collection of contraband books during his time in Mérida.

"Did you know they had book burnings in the capital?" he asked me.

"No, I didn't."

"So much knowledge," he said. "So many great works written by great men of the faith, all lost when the world needs them like never before."

"Have you been to the pyramid?"

"Ah, Chichen Itza, Satan's throne. Yes, I have been there. I saw things I never dreamed of before in that wretched place."

"Then you know the enemy has free reign in this world, Jonathan. Going south alone is not a good idea."

"Many are the plans in the mind of a man, but it is the purpose of the Lord that will stand," He replied, quoting

Proverbs 19. "God is in control, Hank. Never forget that. Are you familiar with 2 Kings 6:13-17?"

"No," I told him.

"Never fear, those who are with us are greater than those who are with them," he said with a chuckle. "Read it, my friend. And I will pray for you."

We prayed together, and just before dawn, he stood up, looked me in the eye, and told me something I didn't understand at the time, but I'll never forget it.

"Jesus told Peter, before he was arrested and crucified, that Satan had requested to swift Peter like wheat. But Jesus prayed for him, that his faith might not fail. Things are not always what they seem, Hank. Keep the faith."

With that, he kissed me on the cheek and began saying his goodbyes to people he had gathered at the grotto. Shortly after the sun appeared, Jonathan set out. We watched him go. He was a doctor, and still wore a suit and tie, but also a broad-rimmed hat that made him look like an orthodox Jew.

"You reckon he'll be alright?" LB asked me.

"Only God knows," I said.

Shortly after Jonathan's departure, LB and Allie insisted on returning to their orchard.

"I still think it's a bad idea," I told him.

He shrugged. "Wouldn't be my first. Hope it's not my last."

"That isn't funny," I insisted.

"We'll be fine, Hank. Who knows, maybe you need someone between you and the bad guys."

"Take this then," I said, handing him the submachine gun and ammo belt.

"Nah, you all need it more than me," he said.

"I insist. I don't know why, LB, but I feel like you're in real trouble."

"I usually am," he said with his familiar grin.

Allie hugged me tight. "We'll miss you," she said.

"We're going to miss you, too. Please be careful."

"We will," she said, rubbing her bad leg.

"It won't hurt to stay a while and rest," I urged.

"If I don't show up at the garage, they'll get suspicious," she said. "I'll be okay. It's not my first all-nighter."

While the community got busy about their daily tasks, Cat and I watched our friends leave. The sight filled me with a sense of melancholy, but Cat got me busy. I meant to look up the passage of scripture that Jonathan had mentioned, but as people around me began asking questions, I completely forgot all about it. We were meeting with the various groups doing specific chores around the grotto. Some were in charge of getting water and washing clothes. Others made simple meals from the food stashed in the cave. Another group spent their days weaving henequen fibers to make thread, which would eventually be made into blankets and clothes.

Everyone was excited for me to teach them. They had seen my videos and poured over the Bible references I had shared. They had questions, so many questions. I felt inadequate, but in almost every circumstance, answers just sort of popped into my brain. I remembered Bible verses, or something from Lorenzo's teachings nearly every time I was asked about anything.

Meanwhile, as Cat and I were getting to know our new neighbors, the security team had reached Danny Hagerty. He had seen the community, although it was at night, and he couldn't make out many details. At dawn, he had fallen back to the edge of the forest, and was staying ahead of LB and Allie. The security team wasted no time. They rushed out of the forest straight toward LB. Allie couldn't run away, and before LB could even raise his weapon to fight, he saw half a dozen guns already trained on him. All he could do was drop the gun and raise his hands in surrender.

It was my worst fear. The security team was made up of eight super soldiers, each one towering over LB by at least two feet. They bound my friends' hands behind their backs with plastic straps. The leader of the group questioned LB and Allie. At first, they refused to answer, even when the leader drove his fist into LB's stomach. The blow was so hard it knocked the breath from LB's lungs and caused him to vomit at the same time. It took LB a few minutes to recover enough that he could answer a question. When he refused the security officer, a hulking man with a wide jaw and gaps between his teeth, threatened Allie. She cried as LB answered every question he could. When LB didn't know the answer to a question the security man stuffed a rag into her mouth, taped it over so she couldn't scream, and lifted Allie off the ground by her hair.

Another member of the security team squeezed Allie's bad leg when LB claimed he didn't know who was in the camp. Danny Hagerty had already told them Cat and I were living in the hidden room under the barn. As Allie groaned in agony, the gag muffling her screams, LB admitted that Cat and I were at the grotto. It must have been like a dagger to his heart to give me up, but they had no choice. For his trouble, the security team beat him for lying. Heavy fists pounded his face and ribs.

LB begged and swore he didn't know anyone else. They asked about Jonathan, but LB denied having seen the man. It was another mistake. They didn't know Danny Hagerty had been spying on them all night and had even taken a picture of the Jewish witness as he left the grotto. They turned their wrath on Allie to make their point to LB. He wept, swore, and promised to tell them whatever they wanted if only they would stop hurting her.

It was midday by the time the security team finished with LB and Allie. They were bloodied and bruised, but both were alive. The super soldiers weren't done with them though. Dragging LB and Allie back to the grotto, the security team fired their automatic weapons into the air. I was praying with a group when it happened. The terror on their faces at the sound of the gunfire was a reflection of my own.

"You in the camp!" the deep, gravelly voice of the security leader shouted. "Hank Downes. Come out with your hands in the air."

"You're surrounded," another member of the security team shouted. "You can't outrun us, even if you have a secret way out of that rat hole."

"What do we do?" Ritchie asked.

Cat was with him, along with a few other members of the security team. Between them, they had two shotguns and a couple of pistols. Cat and I had a sniper rifle and the M4 automatic carbine, but we held no illusions about the security teams. They were too fast and too strong to stop with what few weapons we had in the grotto.

"Stay here," I said.

Cat grabbed my arm. "You can't go out there."

"I just need to see what we're dealing with," I told her.

"They'll kill you on sight."

"I'm just going to glance out."

She shook her head, but before I could come up with a better argument, the leader of the security team shouted again.

"You're all going to be detained and transported back to Mérida to answer for your crimes," the gruff voice boomed through the grotto as if the security team had a bull horn. "We can do that the easy way, or the hard way. Makes no difference to us."

"This is bad," Ritchie said.

"What are we going to do?" an older man named Paul asked.

"We'll torture every last one of you to death," another voice said. I couldn't be certain, but I thought it was female. The super soldiers were so vastly changed that it was hard to tell.

"Or, if Hank Downes comes out with his hands up," the security team leader added. "We can let the rest of you go free."

"He's lying," Cat said.

"What difference is it going to make?" I asked. "You know we can't beat them in a fight."

"We can go down swinging," a woman named Patty said.

She had an athletic build and was a member of the security force. She had a revolver stuck in the waist band of her sweatpants. It was pretty small, and I guessed it was probably a .38 Special. Fighting the security force with small arms was like shooting BBs at a charging elephant.

"Better to die fighting, I suppose," Ritchie said.

"I don't mind dying," Paul argued. "But I don't think I could handle it if they started hurting people in front of us. Maybe surrender is the right thing to do."

"Hank Downs!" the security leader shouted. "I've got someone out here who wants to tell you something."

I froze, my heart dropping into my stomach. Not that I didn't instantly know that LB and Allie had been captured, but facing that reality was almost too much for me.

"S-sorry, Hank," LB said. He sounded funny, but it was definitely his voice. "Didn't have… a choice."

"Come say hi," the security team leader urged in a mocking tone. "Take a look at what we're capable of if you don't comply."

"Oh, God help us," Cat said, as tears flooded her eyes.

"We have to be strong," I said to her, then in a louder voice to the community of nearly forty believers hiding in the grotto. "We all knew this day might come."

There were more tears and people holding onto one another. A verse from the Bible popped into my mind. Something about being led away in chains to be slaughtered. I thought for a moment I might be sick.

"When they come, don't resist," I said. "Let Jesus be our example. He didn't fight, or even speak to the false charges of the chief priests or Roman authorities. But stay here and wait. Who knows what God might do."

The looks in their eyes made the gravity of the moment even heavier. I turned to Cat.

"You are the bravest man I've ever met," she said, before kissing me.

Our lips pressed hard together, and I could feel her tears hot on my cheeks. Then I left her there with the other people in the grotto and walked up the sloping rock toward the surface, toward the enemy, toward my demise.

# CHAPTER 29

IF YOU'VE READ my other books, you know two things about me. The first is, I've seen things that defy explanation. I call it the supernatural. From little green men to visions of hell. I've seen things that are not of this world. And secondly, you know that I can't explain why God has allowed me to see the things most people can't even wrap their minds around.

When I walked up out of the grotto, I didn't know what to expect. Tears flooded my eyes as I saw LB and Allie on their knees. Beside LB, who looked like had been in a fifteen-round fight with the heavyweight boxing champion, was the leader of the security team. The huge super soldier had a rifle in one hand, and the other held a massive knife under LB's chin.

Beside them were Allie, also on her knees with bruises and cuts all over her face, and a hulking female super soldier. The woman, whose face was overgrown to the point of being grotesque, had a sadistic grin on her face as she too held a knife under her prisoner's throat.

"I'm Hank," I said.

My voice was trembling. I was angry for being so stupid and angry for being weak. The other security team members were spread out between the blackened tree trunks. Each one held a big, automatic rifle, and every single weapon was pointed at me.

"Told you he would come," the leader of the security team said. "On your knees, Hank Downes."

I complied. The ground was solid rock, and it hurt my knees, but I did as I was told.

"He's the only one we need alive," the female holding Allie hostage said.

"You sure that's him," another member of the super soldier team asked.

"Well?" the leader asked.

That's when Danny Hagerty stepped into view. I didn't know him, but I had seen him from a distance. And when LB cursed, I knew who he was.

"You dirty, scumbag," LB shouted. "We treated you like family!"

"That's enough," the leader of the security team said. "Hank, I want you to watch this. I want you to see what we do to people like you. People who cling to bigotry and hate in the name of religion."

He raised his knife high, and I knew what was coming.

"It was an honor to serve with you, Major," I said. "I've never known a better man."

"The honor was all mine," LB said. "Keep the faith, Hank. No matter what."

I had to close my eyes. I couldn't watch my best friend get slaughtered right in front of me. We had seen hundreds, maybe thousands of executions, most of them Christians beheaded for their faith. I knew LB was going to be with Jesus, that his pain and suffering would be over in an instant. But I didn't want to see it.

"Look at me!" the security team leader said.

"No," I replied.

"Look or I'll slaughter everyone in that cave."

It took all my strength to open my eyes and look up at the brute holding my friend.

"Renounce your antiquated beliefs, and I'll let him live," the security man said.

At that moment my heart nearly stopped beating in my chest.

"Renounce your belief in God," the super soldier continued. "Swear that you'll never serve him again, and your friend will live. I'll even release him. He can go back to the orchard and live a normal life."

My knees were killing me, but I was pretty certain that they would have buckled at that moment if I hadn't already been kneeling.

"Don't do it, Hank," LB said.

"You'd let your friend die?" the security team leader asked.

It was more of an accusation than a legitimate question.

"They're all cowards," the female officer said.

"Just renounce your faith," the team leader urged. "Can you honestly say you don't have doubts? Is your friend's life worth your doubts? How can you live with yourself. You know

I have to kill him, but you could stop it. Just say the word. Say you don't believe, and I'll let him go right now."

I bowed my head and whispered, "Father, forgive me. Forgive my lack of faith. Forgive my fear."

"He dies then!" the super soldier screamed.

I closed my eyes. Time seemed to slow down. I heard the grunt of exertion as the super soldier swung the knife. It was a big as a machete and swished through the air. My breath caught in my chest. At that moment I wanted to say or do anything to save LB. It was as if I could hear the raucous shouts and jeers of ten thousand demons.

"I do believe," I whispered.

Instead of the sickening sound of blade cutting flesh, I heard the ring of steel against steel. My eyes popped open and what I saw astounded me. We were surrounded, but not just by the oversized security officers. There were eight of them, but there were thousands of demons with the super soldiers. Some were on the members of the security team, others surrounded the hybrid soldiers, and a few had fully subjugated them. It was a terrifying, overwhelming evil force, but they weren't alone. Or maybe I should say we weren't alone. Beside me, and facing the horde of demons, were hundreds of angels. I had seen them before, but only as dazzling silhouettes in pure light. This time I could really see them. They still glowed brightly, but I could see the beauty of their faces and the strength of their bodies. They were dressed in white robes with gold and silver sashes. Each one carried a massive sword that looked more like jewels than weapons. One of them, a towering figure with a long-bladed sword that looked as though it were aflame, had blocked the security team leader's killing stroke.

The man looked confused, as did LB. I felt hands on my arms lifting me, and then the entire scene became chaotic as the demons attacked. The angels were warriors of blinding speed and unrivaled skill. They cut through the demonic horde with an efficiency that took my breath away. And they sang as they fought, their voices pure and beautiful, despite their grisly task.

And it wasn't just the demons who were cut down. The security team were slain, their bodies cut to pieces. Some of the angels seemed overwhelmed by the enemy. Hundreds attacked a single angel, who looked to be knocked off its feet and covered with the dark creatures. But almost as soon as the angel fell, they rallied their strength, flinging the demons away. The two angels holding me up, used their swords whenever a demon rushed toward me. They were fast, working their blades as if they weighed nothing at all, cutting through the flesh and bone of the demons with ease.

The battle only lasted a few seconds, but in those seconds, I was astounded at all I saw. It was the most incredible thing I had ever seen.

Then the chief of the angel army turned to me. It was the same beautiful, glowing hero that had saved LB's life. When he spoke, the sound of his voice was loud, but pure, like the sound of a bell ringing.

"Yahweh has seen your faith, Hank Downes," the angel said. "Now behold the judgment of the Lion of Judah."

At that moment every angel looked up. A trumpet sounded. It was a long, clear note. And at almost the same time something that looked like a flaming meteor went racing across the sky. It was brighter than the sun, yet it didn't hurt my eyes. I could see thousands of smaller, flaming particles breaking off and flying to either side of the meteor.

"Is that?" I asked in a trembling voice.

"Wormwood," the angel said.

And as he said it, I could see a golden creature. It wasn't a meteor at all, but a living, breathing thing surrounded by living fire. I can't tell you what it was because there's nothing like it on earth, or even in our stories. But it was beautiful, fierce, and majestic. From its mouth spewed flaming debris that dropped through the air and covered the ground.

"You have been chosen," the angel said.

I was standing on the rounded mound of stone that led to the grotto. The angel drove his sword into the stone. Water gushed up around the blade.

"Drink," the angel commanded me.

I reached out with both hands and cupped the gushing water. Raising it to my mouth I sipped the cold, sweet water. And immediately I felt refreshed as the stress of the attack fell away, and my strength returned.

"This water is life," the angel said. "And you will bring the thirsty, the outcast, the weak, the shamed, and the desperate to drink of it, Hank Downes." The light seemed to grow brighter, or maybe my vision failed, and I couldn't look directly at the mighty, angelic warriors any longer. I stepped back, blinking fast, and before I knew it the angels and demons were gone. All that remained where LB, Allie, and the bodies of the slain security force.

# CHAPTER 30

JUST AS THE BIBLE SAID, Wormwood, the third trumpet judgment, turned a third of the waters of the Earth bitter, including the water in and around Mérida. In fact, all through the Yucatan, the waters were tainted except for the spring that flowed out of the rock. It ran down into the grotto and disappeared into a crevice.

All over the world, people got sick. Their bellies swelled, their temperatures rose quickly, and they soon fouled themselves. It was a rough way to die. People couldn't keep anything down, nor could they control their bowels. A day or two later, they died of dehydration. No medicines could help. No care could save them. It was a nightmare, and some people died simply because they were afraid to drink anything at all.

Bottled water became the most valuable substance on Earth. Not every water source was poisoned by Wormwood, only a third, but the entire world was terrified. And to make matters worse, the two witnesses in Jerusalem who wore rough clothing and could breathe fire on anyone trying to hurt them, declared a drought throughout the anti-Christ's three regions: Europe, North Africa, and South Asia. Many of the clean water sources dried up, but still people didn't repent of their sins. Most simply refused to acknowledge God at all, even though there were Jewish evangelists preaching in every country. We saw videos online of people proclaiming the gospel boldly, even though they were all flagged as disinformation and hate speech before being pulled down. Paul Eon, for all his talk of peace, waged a silent war on anyone who didn't share his view of the world.

After the angelic battle, I took LB and Allie into the grotto. They were both hurt pretty bad, and neither of them had seen what I saw. Likewise, the community in the grotto had missed the spiritual battle too, but the security team personnel were cut to pieces, and that was proof enough that I was telling the truth.

Danny Hagerty was spared. I shared the truth with him, but he was too frightened to accept it. Maybe God will bring forth fruit from the seed I planted with him, but there was nothing more I could do. I let him go, knowing he would return to Mérida. Maybe more security forces would come, but I wasn't afraid. I had seen God's armies fighting on my behalf, and nothing in the world seemed frightening in light of that. Danny would tell the people in Mérida about the spring, and they would come to see if what they had heard was true. And when they did, I would be ready. In fact, the entire community was excited about the opportunity to share their faith and help the lost, the hurting, the shamed, and the dying.

Later that night, around a little fire, my friends asked me

to tell the story again. I did so, gladly. It was an honor to have seen what I saw, and a privilege to tell others about it.

"So," LB said, panting a little because it hurt him to take a full breath, "you were just gonna let me die."

"Hey, at least I wasn't going to pull the trigger," I said. "Remember Camp Abilene?"

"Like you would let me forget it," he said.

We both laughed.

"What do you think happens next?" Cat asked.

"The Bible is pretty clear," I said. "The next several judgments are spiritual in nature."

"And terrifying," Allie said.

"But we'll be spared, right?" Cat asked.

"I can't say for sure," I said. "We aren't sealed with the Holy Spirit. It's possible we'll suffer too, but at least we'll be together."

"Here, here," LB said, holding up a cup of water from our new spring and taking a drink. "I feel better already."

"Good," I said. "Because just as soon as the two of you are well, we've got work to do."

"What work?" Cat asked.

"We're going into Mérida," I said. "We're going to take this fight to the capital. We're going to tell everyone we can the good news."

"Sounds exciting," Allie said.

"Yeah," I said. "And you won't want to miss it."

# AUTHOR'S NOTE

It's such a privilege to write these books. Don't get me wrong, its fiction, but it's based on true events that just haven't happened yet. That makes it a little like writing historical fiction, only I get to imagine what the judgments of God in the tribulation period will be like.

I'm taking a very narrow view of this future period of time. My goal is to tell about it as it happens to Hank. There are many parts of Bible Prophecy that I'm not getting into because our story isn't centered on the world stage. I hoping you're enjoying Hank's adventure, but I also hope you see that living during this seven year period of the future won't be fun or exciting. It will probably be much, much worse than I can describe it. It is my hope that it will inspire you to seek the truth for yourself.

Every day it seems something else from Bible Prophecy is proven true. It's all in the news, and it isn't being hidden. Instead, it's being touted as beneficial, from the UFO disclosures to the UN's 2030 agenda, the world is racing head long into exactly the kind of global government seen in the pages of scripture. But you might not see it, and certainly won't understand it, if you aren't checking things out for yourself. I encourage you to read your Bible. Nothing else can open your eyes the way scripture can. Take Jonathan's advice for instance. He told Hank to read 2 Kings 6:13-17. It's from a time in the history of Israel when the King of Syria was trying to wage war with the Jewish people. But God's prophet Elisha kept warning the king of Israel, so they never met in battle. The king of Syria was understandably frustrated, and so he sent his army after Elisha.

*"And he said, "Go and see where he (Elisha) is, that I may send and seize him." It was told him, "Behold, he (Elisha) is in Dothan." So he sent there horses and chariots and a great army, and they came by night and surrounded the city. When the servant of the man of God rose early in the morning and went out, behold, an army with horses and chariots was all around the city. And the servant said, "Alas, my master! What shall we do?" He said, "Do not be afraid, for those who are with us are more than those who are with them." Then Elisha prayed and said, "O Lord, please open his eyes that he may see." So the Lord opened the eyes of the young man, and he saw, and behold, the mountain was full of horses and chariots of fire all around Elisha."*

~ 2 Kings 6:13-17 ESV ~

Unlike in my story, the angelic army didn't slaughter Elisha's enemies. It's a great story detailing God's power and his grace. Elisha prayed that the army will be struck with blindness, and they were. Then Elisha lead them to the king of Israel, who thought maybe it would be best to slaughter the Syrians, but Elisha told him not to. He prayed that their sight will be restored, and the king threw a great feast for them, before sending them back home. As you can probably guess, the Syrians of that generation didn't attack Israel again.

There are a lot of people in the world who don't have eyes to see what is really happening. It's my hope that my stories might inspire people to look for themselves into what the Bible teaches. There is an enemy at war with God. There will be a day when God raptures his church and ushers in a period of judgment on the world. We have a supernatural guidebook, a message from outside of time, that uses world events to prove its authenticity. If you found such a book, wouldn't you want to know what it said? Wouldn't you want to really search for yourself and see if it was true. You can, you know. And I'm hoping you will.

Like always, I would love for you to leave a rating of *Surviving Wormwood* on Amazon or Goodreads. And maybe you could pass this book along to someone who might read it. That's all I ever want from my readers. And don't worry, there will be more to Hank's story, as long as God allows me the time to tell it. Until then, my friends, may you have many happy adventures.

~ Toby Neighbors, 7/03/23 ~